TOY OF THE GODS

SONJA DEWING

Copyright © 2019 Sonja Dewing

Cover art by Leslie Reilly

This book is a work of fiction. Names, characters, places, and incidents are the product of the author's imagination or are used fictitiously. Any resemblance to actual events, locales, or persons, living or dead, is purely coincidental. All rights reserved. No part of this book may be reproduced or transmitted in any form or by any means, electronic or mechanical, including photocopying, recording, or by any information storage and retrieval system, without the author's permission.

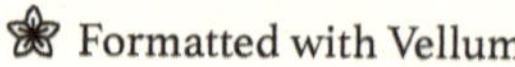 Formatted with Vellum

GET THE PREQUELS

Get the page turning adventure prequels to Toy of the Gods for free. Sign up for my email list at: http://eepurl.com/cAzV5v

ACKNOWLEDGMENTS

During the course of this book, there were so many individuals who helped me in writing this adventure: Rebecca McCain for coming with me to the Amazon and surviving my silliness, Ben Anderson for the many ways you inspired me to keep writing this, the original group of reviewers who had to see this story in its ugly NaNoWriMo form (Jim Schnedar, Maggie Hall, Victor Tackett, and Dr. Antoine Ho), and the new group of reviewers who helped make it even better (Elisabeth Loya, Trinity Tarrow, Micah Palmer, and Katy Hammel). I also want to give props to my editors: Jim of Daddy Wag's Editing, Crystal Chronis, and Shannon Kinsella Diener. And, some scenes wouldn't have been the same without knowing Charles White.

1

VIRACOCHA

The sun was setting in the Peruvian jungle. Trees stood more than two hundred feet tall and forty feet wide, their limbs crowded with orchids and other opportunistic plants fighting for sun and resources. On the ground, young trees struggled to reach the sun; vines and dense ferns vied for space among the fallen leaves and branches.

A flock of green macaws passed overhead as Sun Castel stepped out of the jungle into a clearing. His brother, Miguel, emerged from behind him and wiped the sweat from his forehead on his long-sleeved shirt.

"It looks like the Awa tribe has kept the area open," said Sun, lowering his machete.

Miguel nodded, pointing at the clearing with bright green grass, a towering pyramid, partly covered in the growth of the jungle, and remnants of smaller buildings. Behind the larger pyramid were smaller pyramids choked with dirt and jungle.

"They haven't touched the main pyramid, though," Miguel noted.

"They only use this open space for their camps. They don't need to bother with the pyramid. It works out for us."

The men set up their campsite near the ruins of the largest pyramid. It reminded Sun of the first time he and his brother had found the location, long since abandoned and visited only once by outsiders. An impressive sight for the tourists who would get to see it, if he and his brother agreed to bring them this deep into the rainforest. Miguel started the campfire and Sun cleaned the fish he had caught in the river. They didn't need to talk- something that Sun appreciated about traveling in the Amazon with his brother.

Although it was hot today, the light from the fire would be welcome, and the heat would help dry their clothes, wet from the extreme humidity. While the fire licked at the kindling, he looked around.

The place felt different. Sun knew there were millions of animals and bugs in the jungle; he could hear them pinging and chirping at every moment and could always spot something moving around him. But this was not the same. He could swear someone was watching them. His back tingled.

"Miguel."

Sun looked over at the main pyramid, a good six stories high. There was no opening, no door or window. The jungle around him was dark, as always, and getting darker.

"Yes?" Miguel looked up from the fire.

"Never mind," Sun replied. Maybe he had spent too much time in the jungle. He handed over the fish to Miguel and started pitching the tents. It cost them more weight to carry, but he preferred their separate tents with lined floors and zipped-tight doors. More than once, in their early days of exploring the Amazon, Sun had been bitten in the night by ants, the incessant mosquitoes, once by a snake, and many times by a dizzying variety of unknowns that had left welts. The bugs still got in somehow, but it was a lot less than before.

They watched the sunshine disappear as they shoveled down the fish. Sun wasn't looking forward to the trip back to the eco-resort. It would take a day to get back to the river, then several days in the canoe, having to get out and carry it when the river grew too shallow. However, they were about to be paid handsomely to bring tourists here in the high tech *Toy of the Gods*, and they had to come out to ensure they could find it again.

Sun set out the GPS and ensured it was working and connected. They hadn't used it to get here, but having backup wouldn't hurt.

In the distance, the flash of lightning accentuated that they were in the rainy season. It promised rain for the evening.

Sun pointed his fork at Miguel. "Now that we know we can find this place again, we'll need to leave first thing in the morning. It's going to take us days to get back with all the rain."

Miguel nodded and raised a hand in the air. "Okay. I know you're trying to tell me not to sleep in tomorrow. I get it."

"I'm glad you understand." Sun smiled. A clicking sound from the jungle made him jump. He scanned the darkness and the black outline of the pyramid.

"What's wrong?" Miguel asked, his face flashing in the light from the fire.

Sun laughed. "Nothing. Just spooked."

Miguel shrugged and disappeared into his tent. Minutes later, Sun heard Miguel's soft snoring. It always amazed him how his brother could nod off so quickly. Sun went through his standard routine of cleaning up from dinner and getting things ready for the morning.

Sun was down on his knees, moving his shirt closer to the

fire to dry it out when he realized that the sounds around him had stopped.

He stood up from the campfire and surveyed the silent darkness. His brow furrowed and he rested his hand on the machete strapped to his leg.

His wife always told him he worried too much. But he knew the jungle teemed with life at all hours. At a minimum, the cicadas should be filling the valley with staccato crooning. It was as if every wild animal and insect had disappeared from the area or been scared away. I must be crazy to even think of bringing tourists here, he thought.

Too many things could go wrong in the jungle. Not the least of which was this eerie, unnatural silence. Even the breeze that stirred the trees had stopped. He moved to call out to Miguel but realized he didn't want to call attention to himself if this was a tribe of unfriendly natives approaching. Although, he had never known the jungle to go silent for that.

He pulled the machete out of his scabbard and stepped out of the firelight. As soon as his eyes grew accustomed to the dark, he could make out the pyramid temple against the cloudless and moonless night sky.

The fire crackled, and the smell of burning cloth reached him.

Had he just seen a flash of red light? It was a pinpoint, perhaps the glint of the eye reflection of a jaguar approaching.

He stepped toward the ruins of the temple. The red light was weaving its way toward him on the ground. He could see it appear sporadically between the blades of thick grass.

It coalesced into a glowing, red boa constrictor. All thirteen feet of it.

"Shit!"

It was coming at him fast. Sun slammed down his machete. He felt it hit the ground but didn't hear the sound of it cutting through skin and bone. He leapt back, giving himself more space. He swung at it again, but the blade passed through it. He watched, open-mouthed, as the snake crawled through the solid machete as if nothing were in its way.

Too late he tried to move back again. The creeping, ghostly boa was wrapping itself around his feet. He was surprised to feel its substantial weight encircling his legs. He fell to his knees and grabbed at it with both hands. As quickly as it had come, the boa disappeared.

Sun looked around him warily, gulped deep breaths to calm his heart, and shook his head. There were no lights, red or otherwise.

He felt around his body for bite marks or other injuries. Other than his heart pounding and the sweat dripping off him, he seemed to be okay.

The sounds around him were reinserting themselves into the world.

Close by a grasshopper was beginning its violin act for a mate.

Sun had seen a shaman levitate, a small lizard that could spit poisonous tar five feet, and a giant, overly hairy caterpillar that could have doubled as a toupee, but this had to have been the strangest. Would his brother tell him he was crazy when he told him of the disappearing boa? He must be dreaming. If so, it seemed pretty damn real.

He pushed himself up from the ground and reached for his machete but instead brought his hand to his face. His hands were glowing a soft red. Then his bones glowed red heat through his skin.

Intense pain followed the burn spreading through his limbs. He screamed and fell to his knees. It didn't make sense to him that he saw the details of his bones, so bright through his skin.

As the pain and heat crept toward his face, he hoped that if this were death, it would come soon. Then a strange thought filtered through his mind, "Como lo quire."

He chokingly whispered the words back in his own language, "As you wish."

Viracocha opened his eyes. The first time in more than five hundred years that he had seen out of the eyes of a mortal body. A mortal was bending over him.

"Sun! Are you okay? What happened?" he asked.

Viracocha took a moment to absorb the memories from the man he inhabited. He considered killing the other, but if he was going to complete his new objective, he might need him.

2

——————

LESLIE KICKLIGHTER

Leslie awoke to the sheet clinging to her with humidity, a din of animal noise coming from the jungle and a smell of wet, warm earth. She didn't want to get up, but even at this early hour, it was too warm to stay in bed. She brushed aside the mosquito net.

The room had looked more menacing when she arrived in the dark with nothing but candlelight and lamps to show her the way. Now bathed in early-morning sunlight, the room appeared a bit cheerier. She was surprised by the beautiful cherry-colored wood of the floors and walls. In the corner hung a bright orange hammock and above her, the roof was a thick layer of palm fronds.

She had heard and read that the eco-resort was beautiful and that the rooms were built with an open veranda facing the thick jungle for privacy to give visitors a real sense of being in the tropical rainforest. The locals had put a lot of thought and funding into this place. It catered to adventurers and science enthusiasts who wanted to experience the jungle as close as possible.

However, she was not a fan of there being only three walls. The opening looked out to the jungle and allowed all that noise to wash into the room. It had also given the room a cave-like appearance at night.

Leslie stretched her jet-lagged muscles and swooped into a downward dog on the smooth floor. A gold-skinned grasshopper was ambling along near her. When she picked it up, it didn't try to escape but let her set it outside her door. She didn't want to step on it accidentally.

If she were home, she'd be going about her happiness-inducing morning trifecta: basset hounds, checking social media, and setting off her coffee pot. The basset hounds, Donald and Daisy, were staying at her friend's place in Albuquerque, probably sneaking onto her friend's couch when she wasn't looking. Leslie missed the troublemakers already. The internet wasn't available here in the Amazon basin, far removed from civilization. But at least she could do something about the coffee.

And she really needed the coffee. Between the creatures chirping and whirring and moving in the trees outside, there had been a lot of strange noises during the night. When she slept, her nightmares had haunted her. The memory of Carol's stricken face as the flashlight flickered and faded. Then, in the suffocating darkness, her friend's voice was slowly dwindling as her life left her. The sounds of the jungle and the unfortunate cave-like look of the room must have brought back the memories she had been avoiding. Leslie wasn't sure she was ready to face those memories yet-and certainly not right now.

She dressed in lightweight khaki pants, a green tank top, and tennis shoes. While she deftly braided her long brown hair and pinned it up and out of the way, she checked over everything she had crammed into her luggage. Her well-worn hiking boots, protective hiking pants and shirts, and wicking T-shirts next to fancy shoes, dresses, and her skimpy silk PJs. At least material-wise, she was prepared for the trip. She pulled out her journal and packet of pens and set them on the bed, partly to remind herself that she was here to write and investigate, not to just take in the scenery.

But now to take care of the reason she existed: coffee. She headed to the hotel's main building, connected to the bungalows by a series of wooden walkways. The walkways were suspended two feet above the muddy ground, and the wood was beaded with water from last night's rain.

The walk to the main house made her think of a botanical center. Here the jungle had been partially held back. Where trees had been cut down, now grew dense grass, flowering bushes, and in her short walk, she had already spied numerous and very different-looking mushrooms. All of which was surrounded by the dark, dense, and looming jungle of tall trees and small plants clinging to every available surface, even on the branches of the trees.

Entering the resort's restaurant, Leslie passed into the only place with a generator to run the cool curtain of air conditioning. Instead of the steady sound of jungle, groups and couples were hovering and talking around tables. Latin music was playing softly through a tiny speaker in the corner.

Not quite what one would think of as a restaurant, she thought. More like a high school cafeteria constructed of dark wood, big and open, with lines of long wooden tables and a small beverage bar in the center. A sign in English read, "Alcohol served at any time." Although she figured that would have been a pretty amazing high school cafeteria.

She grabbed a cup and helped herself to the coffee at the main table, then perused the handwritten menu. The place prided itself on fresh food and fresh ingredients. She could go for the American plate with steak and eggs or for the healthy plate with yogurt, cereal, and fruit. It was an easy choice.

"The American, please," she said when the server approached her. The woman then moved off to take the orders of a few others who had wandered in for breakfast.

Leslie didn't recognize anyone in the room, so she took a seat at an empty table. The coffee smelled so good, she quickly gulped it down, dashed up and got some more. Now she could slow down and savor it.

She had an urge to pull out a cell phone and check her social media. How she could use some internet right now. Instead, she scanned the room for entertainment. Two men were seated at the only small table; two Bloody Marys sitting in front of them. They appeared to be getting into a heated argument.

The one facing Leslie, strangely but impeccably dressed in a dark gray suit, moved his arms in wide sweeps, and his hand-some face was marred by his angry expression. Snippets of the conversation wafted to her like the occasional tantalizing scents of the restaurant's food.

"It's a simple enough request, Alejandro. I don't see why you ..."

The man with his back to her had a wide neck and short, graying hair. The light shade of gray formed a wave in his hair. He shook his head and stood up, shoving his chair back. He turned and stalked past Leslie.

The man still seated ran his hand through his short, blond hair and then leaned back and lifted his Bloody Mary to his lips. Even from across the room Leslie could see he had icy blue eyes that were now lasered in on her.

A small shock passed through her, but she made a point to smile. He smiled back.

She was relieved to hear a familiar, raspy voice coming from behind her.

"Leslie."

"Jessup!" She jumped up and gave the older man a hug. She couldn't help but look over his clothes, especially his garishly blue and orange shirt. "What's up with the jeans and Hawaiian shirt? What happened to your leather pants and jacket?"

He cleared his throat, his voice a product of his many years of smoking. "It's too damn hot for leather. For this vacation, I'm not the radio personality Jessup. I'm the mild-mannered version."

She laughed. Mild-mannered my ass, she thought. She shook her head and responded, "I've seen that video where you wrestle that guy half your age, and you were already in your seventies."

He smiled wide, the lines on his face drawn deep and long. "Well, I'm not getting any younger."

"Why don't you join me for breakfast?" Leslie offered, taking note that the blond man was now standing at the bar just behind Jessup, his back to them. Getting another Bloody Mary, she thought. Not a bad idea.

Jessup sat down next to her but shook his head. "Thank you for the invite, but I only have a few minutes. I already ate breakfast, and I have to find out who else is here."

"So, you're the one organizing everything?" Leslie asked.

He nodded. "It was a favor to the captain. I used my connections and people I knew from my work on the radio to find adventurous souls willing to take on the trip of a lifetime. And here we are."

"I'm glad you're coming."

"I would never miss out on a trip like this." His eyes lit up "We'll be the first, besides the archeologists from years ago, to see the ruins"–he pushed his index finger onto the table with each item–"and we'll be among the few people to move into the unexplored parts of the Amazon. Plus, we get to go back to the ship every night for a little rest and relaxation and sleep in a soft bed. Now that's my kind of vacation."

"You're not worried about problems with the tribes along the Amazon or that others have disappeared in some of those areas we're visiting?"

"That's old news." He waved his hand at her. "The last time anyone disappeared out there was over twenty years ago. Besides, we have experienced guides, and they've never had a problem." He leaned back and narrowed his eyes. "Are you trying to stir up trouble?"

She laughed. "Of course not. You know I'm writing about this for some magazines. I needed some backstory."

He looked serious for a moment, not something she saw him often do. "Look, I know you've been holed up in your apartment for over a year. Are you ready for this? Are you worried about the trip at all?"

She shook her head. "No. I'm fine. Really. It's about time I got out of my funk. And I have work to do for the magazines. I promised them a good story. Does the captain know I'm writing about this?"

"He not only knows, he asked for you specifically."

"What? Why?"

He shrugged and stood to go. "I don't know. I've known John a long time, and he doesn't always share information."

Leslie's food was delivered. Steaming steak and eggs made her stomach growl.

Jessup stood to go. "And with that, I will leave you to your repast. I have to go see if I can find Samantha Sorenson."

Leslie did a double take. "Samantha Sorenson? Please tell me this is not the self-prescribed celebrity. Spoiled and famous for nothing?"

Jessup nodded. "Well, she's not quite famous anymore. I'm guessing she agreed to come, hoping that some publicity might come from this trip. And John, he's fine having some big celebrity on board." He made a mock salute and then dashed away.

Leslie was taken aback. She might not be a movie or TV star, but she was well-known for her adventures, articles, and presentations. As well as for my latest failure, she thought.

When Jessup had asked her to come along, she figured this would be the perfect opportunity to move on and find a new direction. She did not need some spoiled woman making this trip difficult. The best she could hope for was that what she had seen on TV of Samantha Sorensen was just an act. Besides, if this trip were as easy as promised, it would be worth it.

From her purse, she pulled out the latest Entrepreneur magazine she had nabbed at the airport. The cover revealed a sun-drenched, brown-haired man dressed in workman's khakis and a black T-shirt. John Holbrook was grinning and standing next to a boat that with its strange gray facade and sharp angles resembled more of an airplane than a vessel. The subtitle on the magazine announced, "Entrepreneur engineers new way to travel. Will his first unorthodox test succeed?" The article mentioned there were a few setbacks- even a powerful financial backer, whose name wasn't mentioned, backed out at an inopportune time. But John had persevered and bootstrapped much of his company's progress.

Inside the magazine, she had secured a faded drawing, scanned from a book she had happened upon in her research, The Spafford Expeditions. The drawing was by Benedict Cecil Spafford, a swashbuckling British explorer of the early 1900s, who had persevered to discover the very same ruins she would see soon.

The image was of a pyramid in a state of overgrowth. In the

drawing, men were depicted like tiny ants, going through the motions of clearing away trees. Spafford had sent back reports to the Royal Geographic Society about the uncomfortable living conditions, although he noted he was glad there was a man to play viola at night, and he had reported that he thought he had found something amazing. At the bottom of the picture, Leslie had written a quote from his letters: *"The largest pyramid has no marked way to enter. Is it to protect something inside? We hope to find the entrance soon."* He and his men were never heard from again.

Rumors were that hostile natives had captured them. The ruins, far into the jungle, had not been revisited until almost a hundred years later by one Sun Castel and his brother, Miguel. A reluctant but interesting man, Sun told National Geographic that the site was challenging to get to but that the natives who moved through that area were no longer hostile. Now it was within reach because of John Holbrook's genius ship, which was designed to traverse air and the shallow water. Unlike in Spafford's time, they wouldn't have to trek through miles of jungle to reach it.

She had written John Holbrook's name on the back of the photo and in parentheses, the additional research she had found. It appeared he was a descendant of Spafford's. Why he was choosing this route was something he hadn't shared with anyone, but she at least had an idea. Were you hoping to find something out here? She thought at John's name. Then she flipped the photo over and looked at the pyramid. And what secrets, she wondered, lie within your walls?

3

———

RESORT MISDEEDS

Stuffed with caffeine and good food, Leslie opened the door of the restaurant. Thick clouds had coalesced, and heavy rain was drenching everything in dark colors.

"Señora, would you like an umbrella or boots?" asked a woman dressed in tan shorts and an employee polo shirt embroidered with macaws. Next to the door was a pile of identical black umbrellas and a collection of black rubber boots.

"An umbrella, please." Leslie knew it rained excessively in the Amazon, but being here intensified the feeling of humidity that clung to her skin.

When she stepped outside, the sound of the rain drowned out all other noise. Leslie personally preferred cold environs, but it felt good to be away from home and to be outdoors. She turned the opposite direction from her bungalow and walked down a flight of stairs onto a dirt path that was quickly becoming mud. Perhaps rubber boots would have been a good choice for an impromptu walk, but for now, the rain was warm, and the mud and water weren't high enough to get into her tennis shoes.

An open expanse of water, more walkways and trees greeted her on the other side of the main building. She walked across a bridge and peered over the side. Giant lily pads floated on the water's surface, and the rain beat rhythms around them. The tall trees reminded her of palms, only these trees were happily living in deep water, and there were batches of brownish fruit at the top.

She leaned against the rail and wished she could have shared this view with her friend Carol. Carol's face swam in front of her, smiling, but then changed. Dirt smears appeared across her forehead and a look of pain on her face. In Leslie's twenty-eight years, she had never had to live with guilt or worry and now she had both in quantities.

She thought she saw something move in the distance. She wished she could see better through the torrent of rain, but she could swear there was a figure standing under one of the trees in at least a foot of water.

There was a small human figure at the top of the tree as well, throwing something down for the person at the bottom. Then the person at the top fell. A child's scream followed.

Leslie ran around the bridge and to the edge of the water. She remembered bushwhacking through the Pecos Wilderness in New Mexico and walking through a wide river without hesitation. Of course, she'd been wearing waterproof hiking boots then, and she had no idea what might live in the Amazon waters.

She turned from the water's edge and ran to another bridge closer to the action. She could make out a small group of children. They were helping up the girl who had fallen. Leslie was relieved to see she was moving and wiping the rain from her face.

"Hola. Como esta?" Leslie called, glad to use her meager Spanish.

The children didn't even look over. They shyly walked away from her, except for the girl who had fallen from the tree, who took a second to wave at her and respond, "Bueno." Then they all disappeared into the jungle.

Leslie waited to see if any reappeared, but they didn't. From behind her came a clipped male voice. "Everything okay here? I saw you running."

"Everything is fine. I was curious as to what was going on over here. There were some kids in the trees."

He nodded. His dark raincoat was marked with "Security." "They come here from the town to strip the moriche palms bare of their fruit and fronds. Such a nuisance."

"Yes, I'm sure. It must be terrible that these children can get food for free." Leslie smiled back at the guard who looked at her. She nodded and walked away.

She stopped from a distance and saw the guard scanning the area, looking for movement. She was relieved that the children were probably long gone.

Walking toward her bungalow, Leslie paused to watch a small capybara forage in the open space next to the walkway. The rain was letting up now; it was just a light drizzle. The intimacy of the resort, the excitement of the jungle–if she weren't here on her own, this place would be quite romantic. She almost wished Devan was here, but their relationship had been over for a while.

The natural sounds were interrupted by the clicking of high heels stalking across a wood floor. It echoed through the open area, loud enough to mask the sounds in the jungle. To her left was a series of bungalows and moving onto a front porch was unmistakably Samantha Sorenson. Deep brown skin color, long black hair, and a face shaped as if it were perfectly chiseled from stone. A face Leslie had seen in entertainment news and once in a short-lived workout commercial. Along with a short, red dress, Samantha was wearing high heels. Leslie involuntarily rolled her eyes.

Samantha was talking to a tall, dark-haired man. Leslie couldn't see his face, but his hair was a bit long and tousled. Samantha pulled him close, and they kissed. Feeling like an intruder, Leslie headed for her place.

The beads of water on the wood made her shoes squeak. As she approached her bungalow, the silhouette of a man in black exited her room.

"Hey!" she yelled, and the shadow took off.

She threw the umbrella aside and chased after him. His direction turned and twisted around the buildings, and then he ran down steps into an open yard. She quickly followed. The shadowy figure dashed down a path that disappeared into the inky jungle.

She was closing the space between them when she splashed into a puddle.

The sound alerted him; he looked behind and stumbled slightly. She was on him quickly. She grabbed the back of his shirt and held on. "What were you doing in there?"

"Carajo!" his deep voice boomed. His left arm flew at her, nearly backhanding her, but she leapt back, letting go of his shirt and escaping the hit. The mud sent her sliding, and she stumbled back. He took off again.

"Damn," she cursed. He was putting more space between them.

She found herself on the outskirts of the swampy area, and the man was already racing over one of the bridges. As she rushed to follow him, a shape stepped out from the edge of the main building into her path.

Leslie couldn't stop herself and barreled into the man who stood before her. "Oopf," she said, her face was in the man's chest. She pushed away, but he maintained a grasp on her arms. "Hey, I'm–"

The handsome, blond-haired man she had seen earlier at the restaurant was looking down at her, his blue eyes flashing. "I'm sorry to stop you, but this looks a bit dangerous. It's never a good idea to go chasing after someone." He nodded in the direction the fleeing man had taken. "Especially some man dressed in black."

"He was in my bungalow. He might have stolen something."

"Oh," he said, releasing her. "Let me call security. They'll go looking for him. We'll also go with you and see if anything is missing." He stepped inside the building and pulled a walkie-talkie from a shelf. Stepping out of the rain, she realized she was drenched, and she realized with horror that the man's immaculate suit was now saturated with rain and various splotches of mud that had transferred from her.

He seemed oblivious.

While on the radio, he waived at a worker walking by them. "Please bring a towel for Misses—." He looked at her quizzically.

Leslie responded, "Miss Kicklighter."

"Miss Kicklighter." His conversations were quick. He talked to security first and then to the front desk to arrange a new bungalow.

Someone handed her a towel and Leslie gratefully wiped the dripping water from her hair and face. Her clothes were another matter. She decided there wasn't much she could do about her disheveled appearance and wrapped the towel around her shoulders.

The same guard from earlier came running in, his face impassive as his eyes brushed over her. He handed the man an umbrella.

The blond man held it high above them as they walked along to her bungalow.

"So you're the manager here?" she asked.

"Part owner, as well as being involved with other things." The rolling of his r's made her realize he wasn't American. "Simon Leverence, at your service."

"Leslie."

He stopped and reached out to shake her hand. His grip was strong and solid. "It is an honor to meet you." They continued on to catch up with the guard. "I must tell you, it is unusual for any crime to happen here. The locals help run the resort; they need people to come here and enjoy themselves. Although it's also unusual to meet a woman so brash as to chase after a possible burglar."

"Oh, well, I've been known to do brash things."

"Of course." He stopped once again. "Leslie Kicklighter. I thought I had heard the name before. I've seen you on some of the news shows from the States. You're an adventurer of sorts."

Her heart skipped a beat at the worry that he might bring up her last trek. She just smiled and nodded, moving forward.

In the bungalow, Leslie looked around. "Everything looks like it's in the right place." She dug into her purse. The important things were there: her passport, her wallet with cash, and all her cards. Even her luggage appeared untouched. She double-checked that the few pieces of jewelry she had brought were also in her bag.

"Perhaps you came back before he could take anything?" asked the security guard.

"I guess," she said, scanning the room again.

Simon nodded at the guard, and he headed out. A young boy appeared at the door.

"He's here to move your things to a new bungalow. It's a little closer to the main building, and the guard will keep a close eye out on your bungalow," Simon explained. He turned back to her as the boy took her bags and walked out.

"And Miss Kicklighter—"

"Leslie, please."

"Leslie, I'd like to offer you a complimentary massage. We have a wonderful in-house masseuse. It's the least we can do to make sure you enjoy your stay."

Yesterday had been a long day of travel, and her neck still ached from falling asleep in the airplane in a crooked position. The shuttle ride and the hour-long boat ride had not helped her muscles either.

"That sounds like a wonderful idea."

"Excellent. I'll let the front desk know, and you can take advantage of that whenever you want." He smiled and led the way out of the room. Once outside he held the umbrella for her again. She involuntarily shivered. "Would you like my coat?" he offered.

"No thank you. I'm not cold. It's just someone walking over my grave."

"Ah, yes, the saying from the States." He nodded and led her to another bungalow. He turned, and his blue eyes lit up from a strip of light from a nearby lantern. "Leslie, I hope I'm not too forward, but I was wondering if you would be interested in having dinner with me tomorrow night?"

Yep, I still got it, she thought. "I would love to, but I'm taking a weeklong trip on the *Toy of the Gods* that starts tomorrow. Perhaps when I get back?"

"I would like that." He took her hand and kissed it. A thrill ran through her arm.

She waited until the bellboy had left, then she caught a glimpse of herself in the mirror and stripped away the towel. Her tank top was sticking to her body; her hair was straggled and soaked, the bits of hair that had fallen out of the braid were plastered to her head in nest-like circles; and mud was splattered over her in a Jackson Pollock pattern.

On the plus side, she had just picked up a date.

She struggled out of her wet clothes and headed to the shower.

4

DAY TWO

Leslie navigated the walkways toward the main building, glad that the morning had brought a fresh, rain-free opening for today's trip into the Amazon. She had already enjoyed a relaxing massage and a tasty breakfast with a ton of coffee. She could feel that it was going to be a great day.

Entering the lobby, she blinked at the flash of light in her eyes. She stepped back as a woman reporter jumped in front of a photographer and sputtered. "Leslie Kicklighter! I'm so glad to see you. You're the first we've seen this morning. You've been out of the spotlight since your friend died in that cave accident. Are you ready for what lies ahead?"

The reporter pointed her phone at Leslie. Leslie assumed a recording app was running. She opened her mouth but wasn't quite sure what to say.

Jessup appeared at her side. "Members of the press, you'll have time to interview all of our passengers later, just before the launch." The woman looked disappointed but nodded to another, and they walked to the other side of the lobby, whispering together.

"Sorry about that Leslie," Jessup said, leading her toward the checkout counter.

She shook her head. "I should have expected them. You had mentioned in your emails that there would be press here. I just didn't think about what I might say to them."

"Well, be ready at the boathouse. They'll be arriving in droves. We seem to have gotten a lot of attention."

"Okay. Any statement we should be using?"

Jessup shook his head. "Nope. Feel free to talk about why you're here, however much you know about the ship's tech, and when they ask you about Iceland, feel free to tell them to take a leap."

Leslie smiled and nodded.

He waved and rushed away, disappearing through double doors behind giant vases filled with colorful foliage, probably cut from right outside.

She took a deep breath to enjoy the scent of the flowers. As she checked out, the clerk spoke in his heavy Spanish accent, "I'll call for a driver for you."

Leslie shook her head. She needed to feel some open air. "Oh no. That's Okay. I'm leaving early in the morning so that I can walk to town."

The clerk laughed, then stopped when he saw the seriousness in her expression. "Señorita, the walk is several miles over dirt roads. Certainly, you don't want to walk all that way." His hand was on the phone, but his eyes were glancing at a couple in the lobby arguing.

Leslie could feel her eyebrows knitting together. "Excuse me," she said to get his attention. He whipped his gaze back to her. "I need to get out and walk. I've hiked across the Greenland ice sheet. I know I can walk a few miles on a dirt road."

He took his hand off of the phone. "Yes, señorita. We'll make sure your luggage gets to the ship on time."

"Thank you," Leslie responded. She grabbed her purse from the counter and headed out the door.

The road turned and twisted and soon the resort disappeared behind the dark jungle. The smell of wet earth was even stronger away from the resort.

She could see why most people didn't walk the distance. Having come in by boat, she hadn't seen the road, but it was narrow, and the jungle pressed in on both sides. The sunlight wasn't even reaching the road. Instead, it was trapped above, touching the tops of the trees. That sky though, she thought. The trees were so tall it was like looking up from inside a slot canyon and made the sky seem even bluer.

She moved at a steady pace, her shoes creaking on the rough dirt. She carefully stepped over a line of leaf ants busily taking their booty across the road.

The occurrences of last night began floating through her mind, and although it had been crazy, she couldn't stop herself from smiling. So far this was the most adventure she had had for a year. During the past year, she had become a different person, someone she didn't like. After leaving Devan, she had just sat around her new apartment, taking no new presentations or writing assignments and absolutely no trips. She had thought that would be the answer, especially since her decisions had gotten someone killed. Instead, she had felt a little trapped but with no idea what to do next.

The depletion of her savings had finally given her a reason to step out, and the offer of the trip for free, and then her pitching the idea of articles to magazines, had given her a purpose. Plus, she could see making presentations to schools again about this new experience.

The rumble of a car sounded from behind her, and she

sidled as much as she could to the edge of the road. She expected the shiny black Jeep to keep going. Instead, it stopped, and the darkened passenger side window rolled down smoothly.

The man's voice from the interior was familiar. "Would you like a ride? I'm heading into town."

She leaned down to see the driver. It was Simon at the wheel. Although she was enjoying the walk, it would be good to spend more time with him before she departed.

The cool air wafted on her face, and she was happy she was wearing pants when she slid in on the leather seats. "Thank you."

"I am happy to help. Where are you going?" Simon asked.

"Well," she started as she pulled the information out of her purse, "the directions don't give an address. It just says to go to Nauta's dock and to find the boathouse."

He nodded but kept his eyes on the road. "Easy enough, there's only one dock in Nauta."

The jungle gave way to an open area with crudely made huts. Not like the smooth, wood bungalows at the resort but thin, knotty saplings of wood strapped together to form the building's circle. The only similarity to the resort buildings was the palm roofs carefully constructed against the rain.

"You don't have much of an accent. Are you from Peru?" Leslie asked.

"Yes, I was born here." He focused a moment as he angled around a deep hole in the road. "There is in the big cities of Peru, an excellent educational system. However, my father sent me to California for my education."

"What about this village of Nauta? I noticed children hanging around the hotel. Shouldn't they be in school?"

"Being in a small, remote village these children have access to school until they are five. After that, they would have to walk seven miles each way to reach the next level of school."

"I was afraid of that. I've seen this before in other countries," Leslie responded. It bothered her, these young people not having much of a chance to grow intellectually.

Simon nodded. "And considering high school, the closest one is more than a hundred miles away. So most of these children will grow up to do what their parents do. Women generally work for the banana plantations working in the fields; men as guards, guides, or vendors."

"Any chance of bringing a school here?"

Simon shrugged. "It would take more money than the village can afford."

"What about the money from the eco-resort? I thought I read that it goes to the locals."

"Yes. Because the resort is new, most of the money is still going toward its construction. Once that's paid off, we'll have to see what we can do." They glanced at each other and smiled. In her imagination, Leslie saw a beautiful new school built by the money from the resort.

The dock appeared next. Leslie turned to look out over the river. Here it was wide, and a swath of small, flat-bottomed boats were pulled up at the dock. The boat canopies ran the gamut of stitched together T-shirts, jumbles of cloth strips, or whole pieces of vibrant canvas. Locals were lined up at a few of the boats, buying bananas. The other boats had smaller items that people seemed eager to buy.

"What are those boats selling?" Leslie asked.

He glanced over as he pulled off the road. "It could be a type of ant, which is considered a delicacy, herbs or any of the other things locals might use from the rainforest. There are also a few that cater to the tourists from the resort, so some jewelry and other crafts." He turned in his chair a little to face her.

"Leslie, do you mind if I accompany you for a little while? I'm in no hurry to get anywhere this morning."

"Sure, that would be great."

As Leslie stepped out, Simon called, "Leslie, it looks like you dropped something." He reached down and picked up her compact from the floor.

"Oh, thanks." Leslie dropped it into her bag.

A group of young girls ran by them. Their faces, hair, and brightly washed T-shirts, and shorts looked very tidy in contrast to their bare and dirty feet. She wondered if any of them had been at the resort yesterday and quietly wished them good luck.

She and Simon strolled together to the boats and Leslie looked over a selection of beaded earrings. She picked out a pair of what she knew was made from a local seed, black and red. She looked to the vendor to ask for the price, but the man was looking behind her with a stare. She turned, but all she saw was Simon, smiling back at her. When she turned around, the vendor was smiling. Had he been fearful of Simon? Or perhaps the man was just a little off. She focused on negotiating, thrilled to use some of her Spanish, and paid him a nuevo sol.

When she was done, Simon pointed to the start of a trail with a sign that said "Boathouse." A narrow boardwalk wound its way through part of the jungle and over the river's lapping water. Leslie and Simon soon left the sound of the vendors behind them.

"Whoa," Leslie said as the boathouse appeared ahead. It filled the clearing with its two-story height.

Simon nodded. "I had heard the building was just as impressive as the ship. It is certainly like nothing else around here."

"Do you know John Holbrook?" Leslie asked as she continued toward the entrance.

"We've had dealings, yes."

"Anything you can tell me about him? Apparently, he asked for me to be on this trip, which makes me very curious."

"Really? That is curious. I'd say that the captain is very headstrong and," he hesitated a moment, "in fact, I'd say he is rather unfriendly."

A tall man with a chef's hat was just inside the building. His light brown skin, Polynesian, she thought, was set off by the bright yellow of his shirt. "Hello. I'm Cesario Gabriel, your chef for the trip." He stressed the word chef. "You must be passengers of the Toy?"

"Yes, I'm Leslie Kicklighter. This is my friend, Simon."

Cesario's long, tightly curled hair was tied back; the hair looked like it wanted to be free of the bonds, spreading out in a big puff. Leslie was surprised that on closer look, his shirt and hat were excessively stained. Daubs of color were in various locations and a little streaked as if he had tried to wipe the stains off.

"Please, come in." He handed them each a plate of appetizers and a glass of champagne; the liquid's surface was shivering due to his slightly shaking hands. "Feel free to take in the view of the outside of the ship. We'll be boarding once the captain is ready."

"We can't board it now? I would like a chance to look around," Simon asked.

"So, that's just not going to happen," Cesario said. "Not until the captain arrives. Plus, we'll have the reporters coming soon, and they'll want to interview everyone before we board." He looked at Leslie. "I'm sure you're excited about our meals." His face was earnest.

"Yes. I travel on my stomach, so I'm thrilled that you're

going to be our chef." Leslie had heard good things about Cesario but still felt like she was placating her nephew for his crayon artwork collection.

One side of his thin lips moved into a smile. "Thanks. So, perhaps we can talk about food during the trip." He picked up a tray from behind him and held it out. "I love talking food and cooking. Occupational hazard I suppose."

"Sounds great," Leslie responded, but she didn't feel as if he meant it. As they took their glasses and walked away, Cesario's smile disappeared.

They walked up to the dark gray skin of the ship. Simon glanced back. "He seems very proud of being a chef."

"He should, from what I learned he worked his way up in one of the toughest restaurants in New York," Leslie responded.

"How do you know that?" he asked

"Well, I'm not just here to be an adventurer. I'm also writing about this trip so I found out all I could about everyone."

The cruiser practically filled the inside of the room. In the front, it was shaped like a ship, but the sides and back had additional angles along the hull. Emblazoned in bold red letters was the name of the ship, *Toy of the Gods*.

The ship was tall, too. Looking up she could see the sides where bridge and cabins were probably located. She couldn't see all the way up, as the roof of the building was squared off close to the top. She wanted to touch the sides and feel the surface, but her hands were full, and there were two burly guards standing close by. "What do you suppose they're here for?"

"John's ship has been under very tight security in the last month. I think I heard that the ship was sabotaged and he's been guarding against future problems," Simon offered.

"Sabotage? Really. That seems strange, why would someone

sabotage it?" Leslie wondered aloud. She'd have to ask the captain about that later.

Simon shook his head. "Who knows? Another competitor for this kind of ship perhaps?" They moved out to a table that was just outside the building to sit and wait. "So what does one do as an adventurer, besides brash things?" Simon asked, a smile in his eyes.

"Find something either no one has done before or didn't do very well. Then go out there and do it better. Like the young man who followed the Amazon from beginning to end, although his trip was more treacherous than I would prefer." Leslie took a bite of the appetizer. The crispy bread with a warm layer of polenta and a shrimp exploded with flavor. So at least Cesario's culinary skills were not a lie.

Simon nodded. "I heard of him. The locals almost killed him. The drug smugglers didn't like him moving through their territory, and some villagers thought he was looking for somewhere to dig for oil. He's lucky he made it out alive."

"True," Leslie responded. "I tend to keep my travels far away from people, so I haven't had those sorts of problems."

She pulled the earrings out of her purse and started trying to put them on but was having a hard time with the unusual hooks.

"May I?" Simon offered.

She nodded, and he moved in to help. Leslie breathed in deeply because he smelled like cinnamon and expensive cigars.

"These earrings were a good choice," he said. "The huayruro seeds are considered good luck."

A man's roaring voice reverberated in the open space. "Simon, what the hell are you doing here?"

Leslie turned to see a big man, red-faced and staring, approach them in a rush. His was heading straight for Simon.

5

JOHN HOLBROOK

She recognized the man from her research as the captain himself, John Holbrook. John's hands were balled into fists and his face was red. Something about Simon had definitely set him off, but she wasn't going to allow her guest to come to any harm. She stepped into the way and John came to an abrupt halt.

"This man came with me," she said, attempting to stand taller to his six feet than her five-five.

"Are you a passenger?" he asked her.

"Yes."

He immediately took a step back which made her feel a little more comfortable. He spoke a bit more gently "Well, Simon needs to leave." He shifted his gaze to meet Simon's eyes. "Now."

Simon put his hand on her arm. "Thank you Leslie, but I should leave."

"Leslie? Leslie Kicklighter?" John asked. "I hadn't expected you to appear so petite."

Comments about her size always made Leslie bristle. "I am not petite." And say ridiculous things.

Simon continued, "We'll have to finish our conversation some other time Leslie. I look forward to it." He bent and kissed her hand. John snorted derisively but stopped when she eyed him angrily.

Simon smiled at him as he turned to go. "Excuse me," he said to her, then dashed into the boathouse.

John made a small bow toward her direction. "It's an honor to meet you, Leslie. I'm afraid I have to follow up on some things before we shove off, but I promise to explain more when we have the chance." He turned and disappeared back into the boathouse. She could hear him calling the chef in his loud voice "Cesario!"

Leslie inched toward the door, knowing she was being nosy but also very curious as to what had John in a hurry. She could hear him whispering something to Cesario, too soft for her to hear.

"Okay. But there might be a problem," Cesario answered, not quite so softly.

"Don't tell me there's something wrong with the galley?" John asked.

"No," Cesario said. "So, the police need to talk to you."

"What?" John asked.

What? Leslie thought.

"They were here earlier looking for you. They didn't say why."

John answered tersely. "Fine. I'll take care of it. Don't tell anyone else." Between the cracks of the door, she could see him stalk toward the exit but his demeanor changed at the door. She could hear him greeting a reporter with a cheerful voice.

Cesario picked up a flute of champagne and moved in her

direction. She stepped away from the door and pretended to be surprised when he stepped out.

6

———

THE LAUNCH

Simon was gone; the enigmatic captain had run off as if chased by a lion, and after plying Leslie with more champagne, Cesario had disappeared back into the building. At least Simon had slipped her his satellite phone number before he left. She would make sure to call him tonight.

"You. You come here." The shaky, stilted voice came from an old woman standing by the building. She waved at Leslie to approach her. The call annoyed her, but she figured she'd at least see what the woman wanted.

Even in this heat, the woman was wearing a scarf of red, lightweight material. It was a deep contrast to her brown dress with an imprint of leaves. The scarf wrapped around her throat, over her head, and cascaded down the sides of her face. One eye was masked over with cataracts; the other was clear brown. The lines on her face were like deep and wide rivers on a map. The scarf, Leslie thought, was probably the only fancy thing the woman owned.

As Leslie approached, her nose wrinkled at an odor of a heavy musk coming from the woman. "Yes?" she asked.

Fancy Scarf's teeth were bright when she spoke, and although it was shaky, her voice sounded younger, softer, and more authoritative than Leslie would have expected from such a frail body. "Take this. It will help with luck."

Fancy Scarf reached into the pocket of her dress and pulled out a small, round statue.

"Oh no, I'm sorry, I don't have any money to pay for it," Leslie responded, hoping to fend off any more offers for items she didn't want.

The woman shook her head, grasped Leslie's free hand, and then placed the statue on her palm.

"No payment," Fancy Scarf said. She jumped, making Leslie jump a little as well. "I almost forgot." She produced a small brown package. "You'll need this, as well." She placed the package on top of the statue.

"Well, thank you," Leslie said, not quite sure what need there might be for small trinkets in the jungle.

The scarf was slipping from the woman's head, and Leslie spied a headdress. Her eyes were riveted to the monstrosity. The headdress was lined with dead cockroaches, their bodies seemingly glued to the piece. Leslie found her heart pounding at being so close to it. *They are just dried up old bugs, right?* She tried to pull her hand away, but the woman's grip was firm.

Leslie held her breath. She didn't want to find out what dead cockroaches smelled like.

Fancy Scarf was looking at the ground and closed her cataract infected eye as she mumbled, "There is no guarantee, but without these, you would die." She was getting louder, the last almost at a yell. "No guarantee!" She finally relinquished Leslie's hand, and she gratefully backed away and took a deep breath of fresh air.

As Leslie watched the figure of the old woman diminish into the jungle, she wondered, was this woman a shaman? She had seen others of that trade wearing exotic things- like the man from a tribe in South Africa who liked to wear cowboy hats. He believed they would protect him from danger. But at least they weren't decorated with bugs, just teeth from a lion he had killed when it had attacked his village.

Leslie took a step back and looked back at the building. She could hear voices and new arrivals, then she looked back to see that the Fancy Scarf Woman had been swallowed by the jungle.

'No guarantee,' she had said. Leslie glanced at the items and wondered what the old woman had meant.

Leslie considered throwing away the statue and bag, but she couldn't just leave them lying in the open. It was against her beliefs since she was a firm believer of "leave no trace" ethics.

Pushing aside the feeling of creepiness, Leslie tucked the items away in her bag, put a smile on her face, and headed for the new arrival. She was glad to see that it was Jessup at the entrance.

"Who was the old-timer?" asked Jessup, glancing at where the old woman had been standing.

"No idea." Leslie shook her head. "She gave me some things for luck."

"That was mighty nice of her. Gotta love the Peruvians. Very friendly."

Leslie flashed back to the hard hold and crazy look in the old woman's eyes. "If you say so."

"How about coming inside with me and I'll introduce you to our group. We all arrived together." He eyed her for a moment. "Except for you. Always have to be different?"

She shrugged and winked. She liked being different. "Keeps people like you on your toes," she said and followed Jessup into the building. A small group was gathered in a corner, imbibing champagne and laughing.

"Where's all the press?" Leslie asked.

"We've got one early bird outside the front door. The rest will be here shortly. I put them on a couple of late shuttles so we'd have a few minutes. Before we head over there, let me tell you a little about each of our guests. The tall Navajo woman, that's AJ Bluehorse. She's made money by being one of the top computer programmers. The ginger, that's Frederick. He's another writer. Don't call him Fred. He's an anal little pipsqueak, but John wanted him here."

"Did he say why?"

"No. Just like you, he just said to make sure he was here."

Great, she thought, I'm lumped in with the pipsqueak.

"Then there is Samantha, of course. There's no mistaking her."

Samantha daintily held her champagne glass. Her blue sundress was topped with a matching blue hat with fluffy white trim.

"Wow. A bit over the top with the outfit, wouldn't you say?"

Jessup laughed. "She does that. Now, you've probably already met the cook, Cesario."

"Yes, he greeted me when I arrived."

Jessup continued. "He's been a friend of mine and John's for about ten years. We all met at a bar, cheering for the Peruvian rugby team."

Leslie looked at Jessup to see if he was joking.

"Seriously." He nodded. "We love our rugby."

"Sounds like an interesting bunch. The women are slightly outnumbered," Leslie noted.

"It will be more than slightly once we have our full contingent. We have one more passenger joining us here, Victor." He looked back at the entrance. "He should be here soon. Then besides our captain, there are our guides who've spent years exploring the Amazon; Sun and his brother, Miguel. Plus, as I understand it, we're picking up one more male passenger at the next stop."

"That's another resort, correct?" Leslie asked.

"Exactly, the last resort." He laughed and lightly elbowed Leslie, then said sheepishly, "Well, at least the last resort we'll come across on our trip. It's one of those eco-resorts, like the one we're staying at. It's just farther from civilization. We'll be there for dinner tonight. After that, it's the unexplored Amazon."

John came dashing in. "Hello, everyone. Glad to see you're all here." His gaze swept the room. He spoke quietly with the guards, and they headed to the front of the building. John continued, "We're going to let in the press and give them a tour of the ship. Please answer their questions if they have any. Then we'll shove off soon." He picked up a glass of water and gulped it down, pulled out a handkerchief and wiped the sweat from his forehead. "We need to get this trip on the road, so to speak." He was smiling, but it looked forced.

The press piled in the front door, excitedly chattering with each other. Leslie counted five reporters with their photographer or videographer counterparts. She also recognized a writer from Entrepreneur magazine making a beeline to John.

The woman reporter from earlier approached Leslie. "Leslie, I'm sorry I didn't introduce myself earlier. I'm Flo Rogers from the International Press Institute. I've followed your career ever since you were on that excursion in Alaska."

"Wow. Really? That was my first taste of adventure. That feels like a long time ago."

"Not that long ago. Eight years? You were the youngest woman to ever go on that route, and Ben Avenada, who was notorious for never taking women on his excursions, took you with him. I'd love to talk about that sometime, but more importantly, let me be direct. Those who do follow you know you've been tucked away for almost a year. Are you ready for this physically?"

Leslie nodded, the memory and excitement of her first foray into adventure and convincing Ben that she would be worthy flittered through her mind before she answered. "I knew this would be strenuous hikes into the jungle, so I started with a good, old-fashioned stair climber at home. Then, I spent some time at my local gym. I'm ready."

The rest of the questions went pretty quickly and soon John asked the press to follow him onto the *Toy of the Gods*.

"Hello everyone!" A new arrival with dark skin, a wide nose, and a big smile waved at the group. "I'm Miguel. It's good to see such a big group."

Jessup rushed up and shook hands. "Miguel, I'm glad to see you! Where's Sun?"

He shrugged. "If he's not here by the time we take off, he knows someone with a Jeep to take him to the next eco-resort. It will be his fault if he doesn't make it in time." His brow furrowed, he whispered to Jessup, but Leslie was able to make it out: "He's been acting a bit irrational since we came back from the site."

"Well," Jessup said cheerily, "at least we have you, and that's great."

Miguel smiled, nodded, and grabbed a glass of champagne from Cesario who was making the rounds again.

Leslie approached him. "Miguel, I'm Leslie." His handshake was quick. "I've been looking forward to meeting you."

"Good to meet you, Leslie."

"Thanks. I have to tell you that I've read a lot about you and your brother's treks through the Amazon basin. Besides stumbling on the ruins, any other surprises that you've come across?"

He barked a laugh. "When my brother and I first started exploring, everything was a surprise. He and I lived in California until we were in our twenties. Then we decided to come here and explore the land our parents loved. To tell you the truth, I'm amazed we survived at all the first couple of years. But now, after all we've seen in the last ten years, well, I'd have to say it's the stories we've heard from the indigenous tribes. We've heard everything from what really happened to the explorer Spafford, to stories of demons that roam the jungle."

"What? You know what happened to Spafford?"

"Well, I can tell you what I was told, and leave it up to you to decide if you believe it, but it's a long story. I'll have to save it for an evening in the lounge for everyone."

The sound of voices from the ship preceded the gaggle of reporters and cameramen. John was walking them speedily off the ship.

"Thank you, everyone, for coming. Please feel free to take images of the maiden voyage liftoff," John said. He pointed at the gangplank. "Time to board everyone."

The cameramen and video cameras swung their lenses at the passengers.

Jessup shook his head. "Neither Victor nor Sun are here yet."

"Victor is joining us at the next stop. Meanwhile, you should all get on board. Hopefully, Sun should be here before we leave," John said, still with a smile pasted on his face.

Jessup started, "John, that's not right. I spoke with V—"

"Jessup, I heard from him myself. Let's just get on board, and I'll give you the details later."

Jessup nodded. "All right. Well, everyone, you heard our captain. Follow me on board, and we'll take a quick tour."

The group followed Jessup up the gangplank into the belly of the ship. Leslie tried not to roll her eyes watching Samantha wobble up the open grate plank in her high heels, but it was kind of hard not to. She couldn't believe anyone would wear those crazy shoes in real life and certainly not on a voyage on the Amazon. She had learned on her many travels to travel comfortably and be ready for anything.

Meanwhile, cameras were flashing as they boarded. Someone called, "Sam! Over here!" Samantha paused and turned, showing her "good side", but she wobbled a bit.

The ginger, Frederick, brushed past everyone and offered his arm to the tottering celebrity. He was a bit shorter than her but only because her heels were so tall. She had to reach down to grab his arm.

"Oh yes. Thank you so much." Samantha's voice was soft. "Leslie!"

Leslie responded and turned to look, and the flashes from cameras went crazy. Samantha came up from behind her and put her arm around Leslie's waist. She whispered in her ear "The press loves us."

As they started into the ship again, Leslie hesitated. She let the rest of the group pass while she looked up at the hulk of the cruiser. Did she want to be stuck in this contraption with Samantha and the pipsqueak? The vision of her dwindling bank account numbers told her this could be worth it. Plus, what would the press say about her if she suddenly dashed out the door?

The captain was right behind her now. His voice came out much softer than his pleas for everyone to get on board, "Are you okay? Listen, about earlier. I'm sorry about all that. Simon and I don't get along."

She turned to face him. "How come?"

"Kind of a long story, but I'd love to tell you over drinks later."

She could tell he was turning on the charm; she felt partly annoyed and partly curious. His smile was almost genuine.

Jessup called from inside the ship, "Come on in Leslie. I can't wait for you to see what it looks like."

She was curious about this beast of a ship, and the ruins in their future beckoned to her sense of adventure. She climbed up the gang-plank and into the darker recesses of the ship.

As soon as they were inside, the captain waved the press off, lifted and folded the gangplank into a recess inside the ship and closed the door. It closed with the clunk of an airlock. Solid and final.

Leslie's eyes adjusted to the dark interior. The wood-paneled and carpeted floor hallways stretched out on either side.

John walked past everyone and disappeared through a door marked "Authorized Personnel Only".

"Wow. It looks so nice inside," Samantha said. "I was worried it would be as ugly as it is outside."

Jessup nodded. "Our cabins are on this deck. I'll show everyone to your cabins after we've taken off. First, let me show you around the place. Here, in the center of the ship is the entrance." He pointed at where the captain had disappeared. "That runs up two decks to the galley and the bridge of the boat. That area is off limits to all passengers, captain's orders."

"Are we going to see how this ship works?" Frederick's voice was deeper than Leslie had expected. "I understand the propulsion and the hovering mechanism are what makes this ship so innovative." Frederick's hand was resting on the handle to the "Authorized Personnel Only" door.

"John plans to share that information, just not right now,"

Jessup replied. "Everyone is free to use the stairs. They lead one deck up to the lounge and the observation deck."

The group followed him up the stairs. The lounge sported a curved wood bar along the back wall that had been worked to a shine. Expansive windows currently offered a view of only the inside of the boathouse, and plush chairs circled a few, round wood tables.

"You might want to watch our launch from here or from the observation deck." Jessup pointed at a doorway that led outside, then walked behind the bar, grabbed a glass and a bottle of dark, amber liquid and poured himself a drink. "We'll be taking off soon."

"Taking off? Isn't it 'shove off' or something?" asked Samantha who sat down at one of the tables and set a chunky gold purse down.

"Normally, but this isn't exactly a normal ship, but you'll see that soon. I promise you'll be impressed or my name isn't Jessup," he answered, then threw back his drink.

Cesario, who had been following the group, announced, "Lunch will be light, and it will be served in here after we are underway. You'll be having a large dinner at the Inca Resort."

Leslie followed AJ up the short stairs to the observation deck; the door behind them cut off the conversation from the lounge. She moved to the edge of the deck next to AJ who was quietly surveying the inside of the boathouse's giant double doors. From here, Leslie could look up and see the top of the Toy.

A cylindrical tube ran the length of the ship, attached by several steel cables. It reminded her of a huge, floating cigar. There was a loud thunk and then a sharp, motorized sound. The doors of the boathouse slid open, revealing the dark, muddy waters of the Amazon and the jungle beyond. She felt her skin instantly bead with sweat. The doors seemed overly tall, at least ten feet taller than the boat, as far as Leslie could gauge. Maybe it was to ensure that the appendage at the top wasn't interfered with?

"Interesting. I've never seen a ship liked this before." AJ's words were meticulous and soft. Her black hair was clipped short, which made her prominent nose strong, and a dark tattoo peeked out from under her short sleeves. She was wearing long jeans and boxy, black boots. "I'm AJ Bluehorse."

"Leslie Kicklighter." She reached out to shake hands. AJ just nodded and smiled back. Leslie wasn't sure if that was a Navajo thing or an individual thing. Some cultures didn't shake hands, and she didn't take offense.

"Leslie Kicklighter?" AJ said as she looked out to the river. "I like the name. It sounds to me like you mean business."

"Thanks. Yes, I guess it does."

Jessup, Samantha, and Frederick joined them on deck. "Looks like John is ready to get this trip going," called Jessup.

Everyone followed Jessup's eyes up to the bridge, nestled above the deck. John, standing near the front window of the bridge, was giving Jessup the thumbs up.

"Do we have to go sit down?" Samantha asked.

"Nah," Jessup replied. "Just don't hang over the sides, and you'll be fine."

Everyone turned to the view of the river, but Leslie continued to watch the captain. He was studiously working the mechanics of the ship.

Leslie glanced down at the deck and looked back up at a burst of red light, and a man materialized behind the captain.

Leslie moved around a little, trying to figure out if the glare from the windows might have been hiding him and made it look like he had pulled off a magic trick. She was sure no one had been standing there a second ago. The man was dark skinned, with a wide, flat nose, just like Miguel. She almost felt as if she should warn someone, but the captain turned then and shook hands the man.

"Oh, good. Sun's arrived." Jessup too was looking up at the bridge. Had he noticed the man's sudden appearance? He didn't look nonplussed. It had to be a trick of the light, she thought. People didn't just appear out of thin air.

A pinging sound came from the cigar-shaped cylinder overhead, and a quiver ran through the deck of the ship. Surprised gasps came from everyone on the observation deck. The boat was rising into the air. She glanced over the edge to look down as the ground slipped away. The press was madly snapping photos again.

AJ moved away from the rail while the rest of the group moved closer to the edge to watch as the ship rose a foot. The bottom of the ship was just barely touching the river's surface.

Leslie could see pods on the sides of the ship bottom, now revealed, that were also making pinging noises as they opened.

"So that's how this ship will travel along the Amazon?" asked Samantha.

"Exactly," Jessup replied. "John's been working on this idea for a long time. It can settle in the water and work just like a boat, but most of the time the river is too shallow for that. Other times, we can rise completely off the surface to get over obstacles."

The smooth, gentle hum of motors fired to life, and the ship moved forward- slowly at first, and then it picked up speed. As the edges of the ship cleared the tall doors, Leslie glanced up at the captain, impressed with his ingenuity. Then the ship was outside and moving along the river.

She felt that the moment needed more ceremony. Leslie looked ahead and raised an imaginary glass of wine and toasted to the future. Towards destiny, she thought.

7

INVESTIGATION

Jessup showed Leslie to her cabin.

"Impressive," she said as she inspected the room. It was decked out like a high-fashion hotel room with deep, plush carpet, a bedside table that edged out from the wall, a blue and brown quilt covering the double bed, and piles of decorative pillows. Her suitcase was already sitting on a luggage rack, ready to be opened and unpacked. A port window allowed some sunlight to land across the bed. The walls were a deep, soothing blue. "I'd bet the captain didn't design these rooms."

Jessup didn't answer. She found him staring down at the floor. "Jessup?"

"I'm sorry Leslie, I was just thinking about Victor. You're right; the rooms are downright charming."

"The guy who you thought was meeting us back in Nauta? Didn't the captain say he's meeting us at the resort?" she asked.

Jessup nodded. "That's the one. I just chatted with Victor last night. He was staying at the same resort as us. There's no reason for him to meet us at the next stop." He moved to go.

"I'm going to have to go talk to the captain about it and find out what's going on around here."

"While you're at it, maybe you can find out why he insisted on me being here?"

Jessup waved at her on his way out. "Will do."

She wanted to know the impetus behind John's interest in her, especially after hearing his charming words and attempting to make sure she stayed. Would Jessup tell her if he found out anything? Or maybe he already knew and wasn't saying. She and Jessup had known each other for years, but it wasn't like they were best friends.

She stepped out into the hallway. Jessup was turning into the center hall, probably to the bridge. Everyone else was still in their cabins.

Should she follow him? A thrill ran up her back.

Quietly and nonchalantly, she walked up to the center hall. Jessup was just closing the door. After waiting a moment, she opened the door. Just inside was a ladder. She quietly latched the door closed. Echoes of sound drifted down to her, but they were too faint to make out any words. She inched her way up the ladder until she could distinguish the voices.

She recognized Jessup's voice first. "You realize you're going to have to face the music when we get back?"

John responded, "There is nothing to face. I didn't do anything, and I'm not letting this problem hold me back."

"Problem? A man's death is just a problem to you? Victor was a friend of mine."

What, she thought, Victor is dead?

"That's not what I mean, Jessup, and you know it. Besides, there's nothing we can do for Victor now. My source says he had apparently been out exploring, got too close to a cliff, and the mud and dirt fell away underneath him."

"So we're sure it was an accident?" Jessup asked.

Why wouldn't it have been an accident, she wondered, but the silence from John was disturbing.

"Of course it was an accident," John finally answered.

Jessup evidently had bigger fish to fry than finding out as to why she was here. Leslie quietly crawled down the ladder and backed out the door. She breathed a sigh of relief as she closed the door and turned. She gasped and stepped back as a figure loomed from behind her.

"Say, what were you doing in there?" Cesario asked sternly.

"It was just." She took a deep breath to gather her thoughts. "I got a little turned around. I was looking for the way to the lounge."

Cesario pointed his finger at the staircase.

"Oh yeah, thanks," she said and went to the staircase, feeling Cesario's stare on her back.

She went up the stairs to the empty lounge and waited for a few minutes, her mind spinning about Victor. When she went back down, Cesario was gone.

A PASSENGER WAS DEAD, but accident or not, the thought shocked her. She hadn't known Victor personally, but she had heard of him. He had been an up and coming architect, and if she remembered correctly, he had a family. She didn't envy Jessup's position.

Even with the captain's strange silence, she couldn't imagine that it was anything other than an accident. What reason would anyone have for harming Victor? Although, Jessup had thought otherwise. She'd have to find out why.

She was a bit torn about this turn of events, though. On the one hand, it was a terrible incident to happen to anyone, sliding down a cliff face and dying. On the other hand, it would make an interesting addition to her story and drive home some of the dangers one could face in the Amazon. It made her feel a bit ghoulish.

She sat down on her bed, cross-legged, and took out the statue and package the old woman had given her. The statue was squat and chubby with the face of an owl and the body of a woman. Inside the brown paper-wrapped package was a cheap metal replica of a hut. On the bottom was scrawled "Nauta." She had noticed the same replicas in the gift shop of the resort. It seemed a strange thing to pair with the statue. She didn't believe in luck, but just in case, she tucked them into her daypack.

Coming up, she had one more opportunity to turn around. Then she imagined going home empty-handed. She'd end up living with her parents, or worse, going back to her old boyfriend.

She moved the luggage off the bed and lay down with the intention of resting before lunch. She didn't want any nightmares, so she conjured pleasant thoughts. The days with Devan surfaced.

He was at the kitchen table, hovering over his laptop. His cell phone was close. The sight of him had been bittersweet. Through two years living together, it was unusual that he was home. He rarely had time to talk, and lately, Leslie had desperately needed someone to listen, more than anything. She was sure about her decision and felt sad for what she would have to do. He was working, but she couldn't help wrapping her arms around his shoulders and kissing him on the cheek.

Unexpectedly, he whirled around and pulled her into his lap. Surprised by the unexpected attention, she let out a laugh.

"It's all working out," he said in his charming, slightly southern twang. "This time next week, I'll be running for senator. All those long days and nights will have finally paid off."

She maintained her smile, his words filling her with resolve. The resolve melted just a little though when he pulled her to him and kissed her, soft and deep. Her emotions were pulling her in different directions, and she couldn't stop silently crying.

Pulling back, he realized tears were rolling down her face.

"Damn," he responded, his distress dancing across his face as he wiped her tears away. "I thought I had talked you out of leaving, but you've made up your mind, haven't you?"

That distressed her too. He knew her well enough to figure it all out. All she could do was to nod. Any words she would try to say now would only make her cry more.

"I don't blame you. You've had a tough time since coming back from Iceland, and I haven't been here for you, and we both know I'll be even busier soon." He was telling himself the details she had already talked to him about. She felt a little sad that he was giving up and not going to talk her out of leaving.

"Well, if you're leaving, let's at least make this a night to remember," he said.

She nodded, smiled, and wiped more of the tears away. Wanting to remember every detail of him, she scanned his face while he closed his laptop and to her surprise even turned off his cell phone. She ran her hands through his short, dark hair as he carried her to the bedroom.

Gently laying her on the bed, he propped himself above her, kissing her softly. He pressed down into her and deepened his kiss. She felt her body relaxing, but her heart was beating fast and her breath coming faster. She kissed him back, and their tongues searched out for each other.

He lifted her shirt off and kissed her shoulders, using his teeth to move her bra straps out of the way. His mouth moved down and onto her breasts; she moaned. His hands wrapped around her body as he kissed her on the lips again, working at the catch on her bra, then he slipped the bra out of the way and focused on her nipples.

He moved back up her body, ran his hands up her sides, and pulled her close to him. His throaty groan in her ear and the feel of him against her made her grunt with pleasure. He rolled, so she was on top of him.

She didn't realize at first that he was trying to undo her jeans. She unzipped them herself and yanked them off, then grabbed his shirt and pulled it over his head. She tried to move so she could take off his pants, but he rolled on top of her again and smiled and kissed her hard.

He stepped back from the bed, capturing her eyes with his own while he removed his belt and tossed it to the floor. His eyes roamed over her naked body while he teasingly took off his pants, slowly. With one hand, he took her wrists, holding them above her head while he ran his other hand over her breasts and then followed up with his lips. He lay on top of her again, his lips on hers.

She wanted him inside her, and instead, he was teasing, making her wait. She struggled to move so he would know she wanted him since she couldn't speak with his tongue in her mouth, turning her on fire. He moved his leg in-between hers, moving slowly, and caused her to cry out.

He said breathlessly, "There's more where that came from."

Her laugh was cut short as he kissed her again. Moving his hand in between her thighs, slowly moving up, then plunging his fingers inside her to the same rhythm as his tongue.

She cried out against his lips, and he groaned. She pulled a hand free and stroked him. He was ready for her, but he still wouldn't let her move. He grabbed her hand in mid stroke and forced it back with the other, then went back to stroking her, deeper and deeper with his hand, her wetness making it easy, his hands, hard.

He finally slipped inside her, his moan exploded with hers.

Leslie sat up and gripped her arms, the clothing she was wearing reminding her that she was not in the throes of sex with Devan. That had been long ago and in a time that she would never get back. She missed him, that was true, but she also knew that it had been a relationship that wasn't going to last. Maybe she needed a cold shower, she thought.

Cesario's voice pounded over the loudspeaker. "Lunch is served in the lounge. That's the staircase for any of you who might get lost."

She blew a raspberry toward the speaker and then took some deep breaths. She padded over to her luggage and pulled out the necklace Devan had given her. This one had always been her favorite. A gold chain with tiny, sparkling links, and a simple gold pendant that hung in an elongated O.

If only every day had been an ounce of what they had on their last night together, the relationship would never have been an issue. The state she had been in back then, waking up from her nightmares alone, and looking for him for comfort but finding an empty bed while he was out working, had been worse than being on her own.

She put on the necklace, then spotted her satellite phone down in her luggage. Of course, she thought, she could call Simon and ask him about Victor's death. Perhaps he could keep an ear out as to what had happened. She turned on the phone and waited for the signal to capture a satellite.

8

SUN CASTEL

Walking through the empty, quiet hallway of the ship, she glanced at her satellite phone. The display still showed no signal. She should have realized her plan to keep in touch with Simon wasn't going to work so well. Satellite phones were generally reliable, but that all depended on satellite availability and location.

Entering the lounge, she found the rest of the group already there, mesmerized by a man dancing around the room.

It was Sun. Her research had told her that his parents had been from Peru, but he and his sibling had been born and grew up in the States, only to return to explore their ancestral lands. His brother, Miguel, was sitting quietly at the bar, seemingly ignoring the scene going on behind him.

At the moment, Sun seemed to be fighting an unseen entity. ". . . And there I was, fighting with that nine-foot eel with nothing but my bare hands. Those jaws could easily have taken off a hand, and even in death they are impossibly difficult to pry open."

Samantha covered her mouth to stifle a gasp, nearly

knocking her ugly gold purse off her lap; she quickly righted it again. "What did you do next?"

"Well, I came out just fine, didn't I? I'm wearing eel." He laughed and grasped the lapels of his black eel vest. His face looked gentle, which was a strange contrast to the intensity of his eyes and movements. A flash of gold caught her eye. He was wearing a gregarious gold bracelet, one-inch squares strung together.

Samantha smiled. "Oh." The rest of the group laughed.

"Welcome." Sun's voice boomed loudly through the lounge, and Leslie was suddenly in the shot of a spotlight. "You must be Leslie." Sun bounded over to her and reached out his hand.

His handshake was very warm and very solid, like shaking hands with an iron poker that had been sitting in a fire. He didn't seem to be sweating, but Leslie thought he probably should be if he was that warm. His short sleeves exposed sinewy muscles. He pushed back his ball cap that said, "I traded my buns of steel for buns of cinnamon".

"Pleased to meet you, Sun," she responded.

"Sun, I've known you for over twenty years. Since when have you fought giant eels?" Jessup asked him.

Sun moved fluidly across the room and waived off Jessup's question. When he didn't respond, Jessup continued. "Suppose you explain some of what we'll see on the trip then?" Jessup offered.

"Certainly." Sun moved back to his space that served well as a stage while he used his arms to accentuate his words. "Tomorrow we make our way to waterfalls that very few humans have ever seen. There is no trail, only us and our machetes," he deepened his voice "and all the creatures of the jungle." He whipped his arm back and forth as if he was wielding a machete. "The next day we make our way into the ruins once discovered by Benedict Cecil Spafford. No one, except for some of the tribes that live out there, has seen the ruins in a hundred years."

AJ leaned forward and quietly asked, "Are we intruding on any sacred areas while we're there?"

Sun paused a moment, staring at her, then said, "You're Diné, from the Navajo lands of New Mexico."

At this, AJ leaned back and crossed her arms.

"Your concern for disturbing our ancestors is appreciated, especially as these ruins are from my distant relatives. However, no one was buried in these ruins. The ruins are pre-Inca, created for the elite priests and to worship their god. A god that no one worships anymore. It's not sacred to anyone." Sun's eyes had lost their intensity.

"I thought all of the pyramids found in the Amazon were Inca?" asked Frederick.

Samantha chimed in, "I read that there were many pre-Inca civilizations. Most of those pre-Inca are responsible for the hundreds of pyramids and ruins that are scattered throughout Peru. Here in this valley, it was a series of tribes including the Huaru, Vinague, the Killiki, and then the Inca arrived."

Everyone was silent for a moment, taking in the sudden intelligent interlude. Samantha might be egocentric, but perhaps she did have some redeeming qualities, Leslie thought.

"Are there any dangers in these ruins?" asked Frederick.

Sun smiled. "We will have to be careful in the largest pyramid I'll be showing you, it's attached to a cave. But it should be very enlightening."

Her heart skipped a beat. "A cave?" Leslie asked, hoping that no one could tell she was trying to breathe normally. "That wasn't on the original trip plans."

John's voice brought her out of her flash of terror. "I'm sure that Sun will lead a very safe journey. Besides, it's up to everyone whether they want to go in or not."

Leslie moved to the bar and put some food on her plate. With her back to the group, she let herself take deep, steadying breaths. Then the captain was standing next to her. She hoped her face looked impassive. "Leslie, I was hoping I could show you around the ship later."

He was putting on his charming voice again; it helped a little because now she was more annoyed than afraid.

Frederick had followed the captain over. "Will you be showing her how the ship works? Because I want to be there for that too."

"Certainly, Frederick, I'll make sure everyone gets a chance to see some of the inner workings," John replied. He spied her satellite phone on the counter. "You brought a phone?"

"Yes. You never know when you'll need to talk to someone," she replied, although she hadn't meant it to come out quite so curt.

Sun continued in the center of the room. "Of course there are always dangers in the Amazon. Deadly snakes or meeting up with any of the tribes that hate the outside world." Here, Sun's eyes began to shine again. He sat down on the edge of a chair. "There were some loggers last year that went deep into the jungle. The company sent a scout because they hadn't heard from them. They were all dead from poisoned darts. They probably didn't see it coming."

I'd have to look up that story, Leslie thought. She hadn't heard about it, but it might be something to be aware of.

"True," John quickly stepped in. "But we aren't going to that area. That logging incident happened deep in the jungle, and we're staying close to the river. Sun, why don't you tell us a little more about the ruins?"

"The ruins were discovered by an explorer one hundred years ago. He and his crew cleared some of the trees from the city, made camp, and cleaned some of the jungle off of one of the pyramids before they disappeared."

"Disappeared?" The question came from Frederick.

Leslie stepped forward, glad to chime in with the research she had done. "In the early 1900s, explorers were looking for something new and interesting. Spafford was supposedly great with first contact with many of the tribes he found and felt that he was the right man to speak to hidden tribes and be able to find the hidden city he believed was somewhere in the Amazon. When he stopped sending word, many young explorers tried to find him, but they never knew the location. Many died from disease, killed by local tribes, or gave up. No one ever knew what happened to Spafford, but there were some reports that he and his team were kidnapped by a tribe. There was one explorer who swore he saw him from a distance many years later, but couldn't reach him."

Samantha looked perplexed. "So then, how do we know where it is now?"

Sun raised his hands in the air. "I found it again, a few years ago. I spend a lot of time in the jungle."

"We found it," spoke up Miguel, his voice a much deeper baritone than his brothers.

Sun nodded.

"Have you ever found any treasure?" asked Frederick.

Sun replied, "In life, there is more to treasure than gold. The hunt for gold is what killed my nation. My ancestor's nation, anyway."

The seriousness brought the room to a hush. Jessup was pouring himself another drink at the bar. Leslie added some more food to her plate and sat at the bar. She ran her hands on the smooth bar top. John, apparently troubled about the mood, pulled some boxes out of a side cupboard. "How about something different?" He displayed a stack of board games. "Meanwhile, I've got to get back to the bridge and get us moving again. We've got about another hour before we reach the resort. Then you all will have another hour to get ready. Don't forget, it's a dress-up affair."

Leslie was more interested in food at the moment and trying not to think about a cave, but found herself imagining a giant, dark mouth with sharp teeth.

9

―――――

DISAPPEARING ACT

From the lounge, the group of tourists had watched the dark jungle move by while they drank and shared small talk. Now Leslie and Jessup were the only ones left in the room when the ship settled into the river next to a small dock.

Jessup moved to go. "I better go get changed for this evening. Pulling out the best Hawaiian shirt I have."

Leslie laughed and followed, reaching for her satellite phone she had left on the bar. Her hand reached out into empty space. She looked around the room. "Jessup, did you see my satellite phone? I know I left it here."

He shook his head. "Can't say that I have. I'm sure it's here somewhere." He disappeared up the steps.

Leslie carefully retraced her steps through the lounge and up onto the observation deck. She came back into the lounge and checked around the tables and chairs and then behind the bar. Nothing. Someone had taken her phone.

She hated accusing her fellow travelers, but then what reason would anyone have to take the phone? They were free to ask to borrow it. She would be happy to loan it to someone for their use.

Now her blood was boiling. That phone was not just a connection to the outside world; her mother had purchased it for her during her first expedition. A considerable expense at the time, but something her mother had insisted she take. Not exactly a family heirloom, but it had sentimental value besides being practical. Maybe someone had picked it up thinking it belonged to the ship, but she wanted it back.

She needed to give this complaint to the captain. She dashed up the stairs, bent on finding his quarters. It took her a few steps before she realized she didn't know where it was. She thought back to the tour and remembered Jessup skipping over one of the staterooms. Perhaps that was the captain's room.

She had knocked only once when the door was yanked open. All six feet of him was steeled for a fight, tight jawline, and his eyes narrowed. He relaxed when he saw her, though.

"Are you ready for a problem?" she asked.

"Problem?"

"Yes, my satellite phone is missing. I had it with me in the lounge. You even pointed it out."

He nodded. "That's strange. Why would anyone take it?" He backed into his cabin. She followed. She had expected his room to be larger than everyone's with a bit more comforts. It was only slightly larger. The only main difference was a bulletin board. A black and white image of a familiar figure was centered on the board.

She glanced away so he wouldn't see her interest in the picture.

"I can promise to look into it," John continued, "perhaps have Cesario look through the cabins while you're all hiking out to the waterfall tomorrow?"

She shook her head at the idea of someone rifling through

everyone's things for her sake. It seemed a little too invasive, even if it was important to her. "No. Maybe just put it out there that if they return it, then they'll be forgiven. I just want to make sure that I have my equipment. Those phones aren't cheap."

"OK. I'll announce it at breakfast tomorrow. In the meantime, Leslie, you're welcome to let me or Jessup know who you'd like to contact. We can work out a schedule with our own communication equipment."

She nodded. "I appreciate it. Right now it's not an emergency, but I'll let you know if I need to contact anyone."

As she turned to go, she took another quick glance at the photo. She knew that face. It was Benedict Cecil Spafford but not a photo she had seen in her research. He stood with his leg on a square stone, hand holding a rifle, and his head holding up a British explorer's hat. It was none other than Spafford, showing off his manly physique. The stone was large and perfectly square. Behind him was a jungle, more than likely the outskirts of the Amazon.

"Is this a relative?" she asked.

John came up close to glance at the image as well; she could feel the heat through his clothing reaching out to her. He backed up a step. "I admire him."

"Who is he?" she asked. Will he tell me the truth?

"Just a man's man from long ago." His voice was sincere and apologetic, "Leslie, I hate to rush you but I have a meeting at the resort as soon as we arrive and I need to change." He took a step forward again.

It was her turn to step back. She walked out and almost ran into Sun standing outside the cabin.

Without a word to her, Sun walked into John's room and partially closed the door. Leslie decided to stand outside, if she happened to pick up more important information, it was worth being nosy.

She could hear John rustling around, presumably getting his clothing together for the meeting. His voice was low, "What the hell are you up to Sun? Where did this cave idea come from? You know I need this trip to stay together a little bit longer. Did you remember what we discussed about Leslie? Kid gloves and all?"

Kid gloves? What was that about? This man was so frustrating! She guiltily glanced down the hallway, glad to see no movement so far. She looked through the crack in the door. John was inspecting a suit, then pulled a couple of ties from a drawer.

Sun still hadn't answered so John turned and focused his attention on him. Sun was sitting in a chair across the small cabin.

"She'll stay," he answered matter of factly. "She wants a challenge, and she needs excitement. Don't worry. And I'd go with the blue tie."

Oh really, she thought.

"Since when do you know women?" John pulled out the blue tie.

She thought it was a good choice too.

"True. All women are mysteries of the world but believe me, no one is going to jump ship."

"I just hope the authorities don't know we are stopping at this resort."

Sun nodded. "Once we're away from here, we'll be far beyond the reach of any authorities."

John turned toward him again. "And since when have you been inside the pyramid? Did you find something interesting on your visit last month?" John asked.

Sun got up and moved toward the door. "Yes, yes I did."

She jumped back a little but paused when she saw John put out a hand to stop him.

"Sun, I need someone to keep an eye on the cruiser tonight. I'd appreciate it if you or Cesario would do that." John said.

Sun nodded and gave him a lopsided and low salute. "You got it. Hey." Holding out his hand, he shook John's and said, "Good luck."

She could make out John's face in the light; he was probably getting that strange, hot-poker-in-the-fire feeling from Sun, just as she had. Or at least his face looked like it. John shook out his right arm and nodded. It was her turn to get out. She dashed down the hallway at top speed for a second, then slowed to a walk, acting as casual as one could after eavesdropping.

She looked behind her but didn't see anyone. Happy that she wasn't being followed or watched, she slipped back into her cabin. Now she was definitely going to need to do some more research.

10

DRUNKEN MONKEYS

Leslie walked down the gangplank to the waiting golf carts, her stomach growling. She wished she could have eaten more at lunch, but she had been too wound up over the cave visit. She knew she wouldn't have to go into the cave, but she also thought that maybe it was the right time to face that horror.

"Well, what do you know? You clean up nice, Leslie," Jessup called from one of the waiting golf carts. Miguel, Frederick, and AJ, were waiting in the carts along with the two drivers.

Leslie did a careful twirl in the sandy soil in her high heels, her red dress glimmering with layers of silk in the setting sun. "Thanks. Is it my imagination, or are you wearing a suit?"

He stood a moment so she could admire his dark grey suit, underneath which peaked an incongruous orange Hawaiian shirt and bowed, then sat back down.

Leslie sat down in a cart next to AJ and admired her necklace. "Wow, I love your jewelry," she said, fingering her own necklace, the one Devan had given her.

AJ had dressed up in black jeans, a black T-shirt and a long silver and turquoise necklace that almost reached her waist. "Thank you, it was my mother's," she responded. "It's been in my family for many generations, since the late 1800s."

"Wow, really? That's amazing."

"Thank you."

"I hope you don't mind me asking, but I understand you're a computer programmer?"

AJ smiled. "Yep. That's me. I went to a coding bootcamp when I was young and when I realized I could create things with it, I learned everything I could. Not exactly what my mother wanted me to do, but since I got away from working for big corporations I've been very happy."

"Oh, wait for us!" Samantha yelled at the carts, although they weren't going anywhere. She sashayed down the gangplank in her black dress with spidery veins of silver. She had opted to carry her shoes with her, then used Cesario as a leaning post at the bottom to put them on.

Leslie involuntarily took a deep breath and sighed, as did AJ at the same time. They looked at each other and laughed. Leslie shook her head, "I'm glad you're on this trip, AJ. I think you're probably the most grounded person here. Well, you and maybe Jessup."

"I'm not sure I would call him grounded but I understand what you mean." AJ admitted.

"Let's go," Jessup yelled once everyone was loaded.

"What about Sun or John?" asked Frederick calling from a cart that also held Miguel.

"John went ahead. Sun is staying behind," Jessup replied.

The carts topped a hill, and a view of the expansive resort opened up before them. Short, trimmed grass covered the grounds.

"I'd love to hear more about your family if you wanted to share," Leslie said.

"Well, off the top I can tell you that my Navajo clans are the Towering House People Clan, the Salt People Clan, the Meadow People Clan, and the Bitter Water Clan. That's maternal, paternal, maternal grandfather, and paternal grandfather. My parents were Sandra and Daren Bluehorse of Gallup, New Mexico."

"Wow, thank you for sharing that. Gallup? I'm from Albuquerque. Small world."

AJ nodded. "I've been living abroad for the last few years. Sometimes I miss the desert."

They arrived at an open-sided building with a thatched roof, dark red stone floor, and fairy lights woven around the mosquito nets. They moved inside the building, and Leslie slapped her arm with the feel of a bug on her. She noticed others were swatting as well.

"I didn't want to put on bug repellent. Not while I'm all dressed up and feel so clean," Leslie said disdainfully, but then she pulled out the container from her purse and started applying.

"I didn't even think of bringing it with me." AJ slapped at something on her neck. Leslie handed it over after she was done.

"I don't see that these mosquito nets are helping much," said Samantha who was filling the air with the stink of Deet as she sprayed herself.

Jessup waived at the air and coughed, "Lord-a-mighty Samantha, we have to breathe this air." Then he noticed the approaching waiter. "Oh good, please tell me you are here to take our drink orders. I need a good, stiff scotch, straight up."

The waiter nodded and quickly gathered drink orders. Leslie admired the beautifully set tables with folded swan napkins. It must have taken a lot of trouble to not only get all of these items to the resort but also build it. She could hear a generator running in the distance, probably the only way to get electric power out this far.

"Jessup, how about telling us about the ship?" asked Frederick.

Jessup raised his glass of liquor as it was being delivered and drank it back. "It's a combination ion craft, hovercraft, and riverboat. The ion system allows us to move quietly and it's good for slow, precise movements. The hovercraft system is more of a backup; it's not as exact as the ion system, but it has more power.

"The tank on top of the cruiser, as well as the nacelles on the bottom of the ship are part of the ion system. It allows us to hover over the water's surface. So we can travel over shallow river bends and sandbars without blinking an eye. When we want we can also travel on the river, but that slows us down."

"Wait, ion lifter? Never heard of it," Leslie said.

Jessup set down his glass. "I'm not a scientist like John, but I can tell you that you can create a smooth surface and a sharp surface that are charged with ions, one negatively and one positively. When they're working, it forces ions to collide which creates a force that lifts or pushes."

"I've heard of that," said AJ, "but I've never seen it used for something this large. There must be one hell of a battery on board. Is that safe?"

Jessup nodded. "I know he went through a lot of testing to get it right and make it safe. I can tell you without a doubt that the *Toy of the Gods* is a safe ship."

"So what's in the tank?" Frederick smiled and leaned forward.

Jessup shook his empty glass at the waiter. "Besides a huge ion lifter? Even I don't know that. It's a trade secret of John's."

A waiter rang the bell at the buffet table. Frederick dashed up, apparently even hungrier than Leslie, but he called back to the tables. "Samantha, would you like me to get a plate for you?"

"That's so sweet of you, but Cesario already offered."

Cesario was bending over Samantha and whispering in her ear. It was the first time Leslie had seen him with his hat off, and his hair hung down in long, black tresses. Seeing his hair without the chef's hat reminded her of the tousle-haired man from the other day. Was it? He looked like the same man she had seen kissing Samantha at the resort. But then, just yesterday they had pretended not to know each other as if meeting for the first time. That would be strange, she thought. They wouldn't have a reason to hide a relationship, would they?

The growl from her stomach reminded her that there were more important things than possibly secret relationships right now. She made her way into the line.

"Dinner for tonight includes celery soup, pork chops in Cocona sauce, chicken with rice, fresh salad, and bread," announced a waiter.

Leslie happily piled her plate high and made her way back to the table. Her drink was waiting for her. Everyone was starting to dig in. She loved the light, refreshing taste of the celery soup, but the bread was tasteless. Although, she had yet to have good bread ever since she had arrived in Peru. She had heard it had something to do with access to the right ingredients.

Samantha exclaimed, "Oh, how cute."

A monkey was sitting on an empty table. It was looking at everyone with innocent, doleful eyes. Leslie's immediate thought was of her basset hounds. They had those same innocent eyes. The same dogs that had found a way to push their dog stairs over to the kitchen chairs so they could get up to the chairs and swipe the muffins that had been cooling on the table. She eyed the monkey closer.

Another monkey leaped up to the table where Frederick had vacated to search for a restroom. Leslie looked around at the netting. Now that the sun had fully set, the darkness around the building was absolute, but she could see a monkey standing at the doorway of the netting and yet another lifting the edge of the net to enter the building.

Taking his eyes off the first monkey, Cesario scooted back in his chair a little. "Shoo, monkey, shoo."

"Oh, Cece! Don't shoo him away. He is so cute," Samantha said.

"Careful, Samantha. These monkeys can get mean, and they aren't here just to be friendly," warned Cesario.

The monkey reached for Cesario's beer glass, licked at the beer and then tried to lift it. It was full and a little too heavy. The glass promptly fell and shattered on the floor. The monkey shrieked, and suddenly several monkeys were circling in from all around them.

AJ stood and moved back from the tables. She exited the room through the netting. The monkey that had lost the beer picked up a handful of Cesario's food and threw it at Samantha.

"Ehh!" she shrieked.

A pork chop was now sitting on her shoulder, dripping sauce onto her dress.

Everyone stood from the tables and away from the monkeys. Jessup jumped up and ran over to Samantha, took a napkin and flung it at the monkey. The monkey ignored it and made a cackling, laughing noise that had Leslie's hair standing up on the back of her neck.

She felt a tug at her hand and realized she was holding her drink. A monkey was attempting to take it from her. She didn't want to seem desperate for alcohol, and she also knew monkeys could bite, and bite hard.

She relinquished the glass, and the monkey bared his

teeth, in a disconcerting smile. It took a sip, shrieked then promptly threw it at her, splashing her dress and shoes. The glass crashed to the floor. She stepped back from the gathering of monkeys. "Critic, that was a good glass of wine." She tried to wipe the drink from the fabric of her dress but knew it was a lost cause. A cacophony stopped her. The few monkeys were suddenly turning into hundreds. Without warning, food began flying in the air. The group ran for the outside of the building, but it was too late. Leslie lamented the fact that a blob of soup was gooing to the front of her dress.

A gunshot ripped through the air. The monkeys stopped in mid-throw like someone had pushed pause on a video. The sound of dogs baying accompanied another gunshot and the monkeys ran at full speed out and under the netting. A man carrying a long-barreled shotgun appeared in the light. Four dogs looked up at him. He pointed his gun where the monkeys had gone, and the dogs took off at a run.

The man came inside and looked around at the mess. Out of breath and in a heavy British accent, he exclaimed, "I'm terribly sorry for all that. I'm supposed to put the dogs out before meals, but I did forget. Those rotten monkeys are a bunch of alcoholics! They get a taste of fermented fruit in the jungle, and now they go in search of it."

A familiar voice boomed out "What the hell kind of outfit are you running here?"

Cesario responded quietly, "I believe the captain has arrived."

Sure enough, John walked into the light and surveyed the group. "David." It was part question and part accusation in one word.

"I'm very sorry John. The hotel will make reparations." David spoke to a waiter who was standing by his side, staring at the scene with wide eyes. "See to it that they get shown to the open bungalows to clean up."

Everyone jumped at the crack of a gunshot not far in the distance.

"Bloody hell!" David exclaimed. "I'll go see what that's about."

Jessup reached under his jacket with one hand and wiped his face of soup with the other. "Want me to come with you?"

"No Jessup," John replied, pulling a gun from under his jacket. "Just make sure everyone here stays safe."

David started off with John right on his heels. John glanced back as they faded into the night, "Cesario, make sure they are taken care of!"

Frederick walked into the building "What the . . ."

"Frederick you missed it," Samantha said excitedly. "The monkeys went crazy." She had found a clean chair and was sitting, fooling with her purse, a smile on her lips.

Leslie moved that direction, curious at what could make her so happy, but Cesario put a hand on her arm and called to everyone.

"All right everyone, we'll be showing you to some bungalows so you can clean up."

As she walked by the still clean AJ, Leslie said, "Next time you see disaster coming, maybe you could take me with you?"

AJ smiled and nodded, "I promise."

Once inside a quiet bungalow, she shook her head at the sight of herself in the mirror.

She stood in the shower a long time before finally stepping out and realizing she had nothing to wear. With the towel wrapped around her, she went into the bungalow's living area and found John, his back to her, standing in the room with dresses hanging from his hands.

"Excuse me?" she asked.

11

TROUBLE IN PARADISE

John whipped around. She had never expected to see the stalwart captain at a loss for words. She found the grey suit with blue tie to be very fetching on him but left her feeling a bit underdressed with just a towel.

He lifted the dresses in his hands, still at a loss for words. Then finally he said, "I brought these. I wasn't sure which one to leave." He dropped them both on the chair and headed for the door.

"What were the gunshots about?" she asked quickly.

He paused with his hand on the doorknob. "Someone shot one of David's dogs. It looks like they found intruders near the river. One of the dogs came back with a piece of someone's clothing."

"Oh no." Leslie walked toward him. "That's terrible."

He turned to look at her. "David's a bit devastated at losing Jag. He's raised all his dogs from pups." John looked down at her bare feet and then inspected her towel. She found her temperature warming up despite her wanting to dislike the captain but figured she should use her time wisely.

"Captain, why am I here? Why did you want me on this trip?"

"Please, call me John." He put on his warm smile and shrugged. "I asked Jessup to find a writer for the trip, and he found you."

Leslie shook her head and took a step closer. "Jessup mentioned that you wanted me by name. Why?"

"Oh, well." He cleared his throat. "I had heard about how, well, you were, are an adventure writer and you seemed like the perfect fit."

He was trying to be careful about what he said. "So you know I haven't worked for a year?"

"Yes. Jessup told me though that you had no problem selling the upcoming stories to some magazines."

Leslie smiled at that. "True. My reputation in writing doesn't seem to be tarnished, just rusty."

His eyebrows knitted closer together. "Tarnished? Why would you think it would be tarnished?"

"I just." Now it was her turn to be slightly flustered. "I feel very guilty about what happened in Iceland, and I feel that it might have tarnished my reputation a bit."

"I think you must see yourself much differently than the rest of the world."

Leslie could feel herself blushing this time, and she pointed at the dresses. "Thank you for the choice of wardrobe."

He opened the door and said quickly, "Thank the hotel. They're the ones that screwed up the evening." Then he stalked out, closing the door soundly behind him.

"Well," Leslie said under her breath, "fine then."

～

Changed and ready for dinner, again, Leslie stopped in the lobby to see if there were working phones.

"Certainly," replied the clerk at the front desk. "While we have our generators working, all the phones are available. You can use any of the house phones to call out."

Now the phone was ringing on the other end. "Simon here."

"Simon. It's Leslie." She felt a sense of relief at hearing his familiar voice. "I hope this isn't an inconvenient time?"

"Not at all. It's good to hear from you. Where are you?"

"I'm at the Inca Resort. We'll be heading out in the morning, I think."

"It sounds exciting. I wish I could go with you."

"I wish you could too, but I wanted to find out something. Before I continue on the ship, I had heard that someone who was going to take the ship died and I was wondering if you had heard anything."

"You must mean the tourist, Victor Nuslend?"

"Yes, you know about that?"

"This is a small area. News of this kind travels quickly here, and I get reports from the police of unusual instances. It appeared that he was exploring on his own without a guide and found his way to a cliffside. The cliffs in that area have been known to have mudslides. He was there at the wrong time."

Hearing it from Simon made it all feel less threatening. The man had died in an accident. The captain was just overly cautious.

She was already writing her story in her head. 'Mysterious Death and Troublesome Captain.' "Thank you, Simon, I appreciate the information."

"Just please be careful yourself, Leslie. I expect to see you in a week for dinner."

"You bet. Talk with you soon."

Leslie spied AJ, her unmistakable cropped hair sticking out

in the back. She was sitting at another house phone, leaning over and whispering. Leslie continued, walking by the restaurant, then noticed John at a table with men, all in business suits.

One of the men was facing away from her. From the color of his hair and the wave-like form of gray, he looked like the man she had seen with Simon yesterday. The one who had stormed out of the restaurant.

She wanted to see the man closer though. What would it hurt to introduce herself?

She walked into the restaurant feeling just a bit conspicuous. The silky blue dress clung to her body down to her hips and then flared out and down to the floor. Her long, brown hair was still a little damp, so it was falling around her face in soft curls. Her shoes were just a pair of slippers that someone had dropped off, so her footfalls were quiet.

She was close to the table when she heard the man say to John, "We're impressed with its speed, having arrived so quickly from Nauta. We're looking forward to our trip."

John opened his mouth to reply but stopped when he noticed her approach. He stood to greet her.

"Leslie."

"Hello, John." She mimicked his warm tone.

He looked over her dress as he had inspected her towel, but his brow was wrinkled.

"Are you gentlemen joining us on the *Toy of the Gods*?" Now that she was close up, she could tell this was definitely the man she had seen with Simon.

The men opened their mouths to reply, but John stepped in, "No, they are not joining us." Then to the table, "We'll be right back." The man with the graying hair stood and bowed slightly to her as John gently steered her away from the table.

"Have a good evening." She waved on her way out the side

doors that led to the open air and an outdoor patio, with only a few couples and people out at this late dinner hour. John quietly closed the door behind them, his hand still gently on her arm.

"Leslie, I'm sorry. I'm trying to conduct a meeting."

"You know, Simon was meeting with that same man with the gray hair yesterday. Except he was mad with Simon and stormed out."

John's brows knitted together again as he glanced into the restaurant, then back at Leslie. "Why are you telling me this?"

"Because something seems to be going on and I'm trying to figure it out, and you are obviously the key."

John put on his charming smile again. "Nothing is going on. I'm just trying to find some future investors."

She opened her mouth, and her stomach chose that moment to let out a loud gurgle. "Sorry. I haven't eaten much today."

"The hotel is setting out some new food for everyone at the building." He pointed at the light of the building. "Perfect time to take care of that hunger." He paused for a moment, then finally let go of her arm. The heat from his hand lingered.

"Before you go, I know that you also specifically asked for Frederick to be on this trip. Why is that? Why two writers?"

"How did you know that?"

She shrugged. "Jessup mentioned it the other day."

"Yes, well, Frederick has some connections that you don't have." That seemed to be enough for him. He turned and headed back in. He paused before closing the door. "You look great in that dress, by the way."

"Thanks," she responded.

She thought of heading for the building, but here on the outdoor patio was a small bar. She didn't feel like approaching the scene of the former monkey frenzy. Instead, she saddled up in front of the bar and ordered a drink, pulling the bowl of snack foods closer. She'd have one or two drinks before going back. It wasn't like she had to drive anywhere. Besides, what kind of trouble could she possibly get into all the way out here?

SHE HAD DRUNK TOO MUCH. She could feel her equilibrium was gone; things were spinning slightly. She had carefully made her way to the lighted building, walking like she was on eggshells, but mostly to keep her feet from going off in the wrong direction. She had safely made it to the building and sat at a table. Now she leaned over to the man next to her. Was that a man? She wondered. Through her blurry gaze, it looked like one.

"Hello, Leslie." The voice sounded familiar. The face was starting to come into focus.

She laughed out loud. She was definitely drunk. There was no way Devan would be found alive or dead in the middle of the Amazon. She had been thinking of him, and here he was, in her drunken buzz. She leaned closer to the man to try to see if she could discern who he was, but he still looked the same.

"You're a little drunk, aren't you?" he asked and kissed her forehead.

It even smelled like Devan, the soft scent of cologne and manly soap. "Yes. Maybe." she answered, her words carefully formed, but she wasn't sure if she had actually said the words. "Who are you?"

He smiled and moved in closer, his lips almost touching her ear. "Devan, you remember, your old boyfriend for a few years, who loved you."

She laughed and leaned back in her chair. "No. I know it's not you. I was just thinking about you."

He leaned toward her. "You were thinking about me? When was this?"

"Devan?" She thought it might have been Jessup's voice.

She leaned away from the hazy man and turned to look at Jessup.

It was definitely Jessup.

"Jessup, is this Devan?" She pointed at the man seated next to her.

"Yes. I'm sorry about that. I didn't know it was him we were expecting."

Her heart was beating faster, and it helped her to get a little clear headed. Her vision cleared a little, and she scooted back from Devan. Long-ago boyfriend. She had made the right decision to end a not so perfect relationship. She could feel her cheeks burning and stood to go.

"I think I need some air."

"Are you sure you are up to walking around?" Devan asked.

She ignored the question and willed herself to walk straight. When she got to the stairs, she grabbed the handrail and slowly lowered herself down to each step. She stumbled on the last step and Devan was suddenly there to catch her. She pushed him away. "Cut that out."

He stepped back and disappeared up the stairs. "I only want what's best for you," he said quietly, where no one could hear but her.

She felt her cheeks burning more and kept walking. Where to, she wasn't sure.

All she wanted right now was a simple, calm, relaxing trip. A time to reflect. This thing was getting more complicated by the hour. What was Devan doing here?

She started looking for a way out. The resort had to have a way out. She'd be happy to find a vehicle and drive herself out of here. Her things be damned; she'd leave them behind.

She walked around to the front of the resort, her eyesight growing blurry again; it was hard to see in the dark. There was a single light burning at the side of the building. She thought she could see a few vehicles parked out in the darkness. She slipped in some mud but kept moving.

She finally reached a Jeep and climbed in. She was searching for a push-start button and found none. She moved to the next vehicle, but her eyes were getting so heavy. She couldn't figure out where the starter might be.

"What are you doing in there?"

She closed one eye and used the other one to try and focus on the man who stood next to the Jeep. "John?"

"Yes. Now, what are you doing?"

She blew out air and shook her head, almost falling over. "I'm leaving. This is crazy."

"I don't think you're in any shape to be driving," he said.

She immediately wanted to argue but then realized he might be right. She scooted over and patted the steering wheel. "You drive me then."

"Oh no. I have enough things to do without driving you around." He opened the door and reached for her hand.

She slapped it back.

"Leslie, come on. I'll take you back to the ship."

She wanted to argue, but she was so tired. She let him pull her out of the Jeep. When they started walking, she slipped again. He scooped her up and kept walking.

12

THE MORNING AFTER

She opened her eyes with a groan. There was a massive net across her face. She grabbed at it and realized it was a mat of her hair and flipped it to the side. She regretted that as the light from the small porthole set her eyes hurting. A glance at the clock next to her bed said it was still early morning.

She was in her bed still wearing the blue dress from last night and was sad to see it splattered with mud, probably ruined, but she couldn't remember how that happened. She didn't even bother to check the mirror but placed the dress on her chair and made her way to the tiny shower stall. She felt almost human after the hot water, change of clothes, and a couple of ibuprofen.

She started up the stairs to the lounge, the smell of coffee tempting her to walk faster. The strands of laughter reached her, and she stopped midstep. She recognized the voice. That couldn't be right, she thought. It can't be him. Why would he be here? Then a tiny flash of memory from the night before.

"Leslie, are you okay?" Samantha was coming up behind her wearing skin-tight, pink leather pants and a tank top.

"Sure. I just was thinking I forgot something." She grabbed the necklace that Devan had given her. No time to take it off. It would feel strange, letting him know that she still thought about him, but there was nothing for it. She continued up the stairs.

The laughter up ahead had stopped. Someone was walking across the room and coming to the stairs. The silky, southern twang greeted her. "Leslie, I thought I heard your voice. I hope you've recovered from last night."

Devan reached out as if to hug her. She side-stepped the hug and held out her hand. Without missing a beat, he shook her hand and gave Samantha a warm smile. "And you are no doubt Miss Samantha Sorenson. Pleased to meet you."

Funny, she had expected to feel a thrill from his touch, but there was nothing.

Samantha gushed. "You're Senator Yale! Leslie, you know Senator Yale?"

"Devan. I'm just Devan today."

Smooth as always, she thought. "Excuse me," Leslie said, grabbing a mug of coffee from the bar and joining Miguel and Frederick sitting at a table. Outside, the trees were moving by slowly, so slowly Leslie didn't feel movement. Devan and Samantha joined them.

Frederick was talking with Miguel. "What's the area like?"

"For today's hike? We'll be going to a waterfall with a beautiful pool."

"Any locals around?"

Miguel shook his head. "Probably not. The tribes that live out in the reserves stay farther out. They don't generally trust outsiders. We may see or meet some when we visit the ruins tomorrow, but not yet."

Samantha was more interested in Devan. "Devan, what's a senator doing here? In Peru."

Devan glanced at Leslie and said something about wanting to see the Amazon, but realization struck home for her. I must be an idiot, she thought. He had to have something to do with why she was here. She knew she wouldn't get any direct answers from Devan now. She could see it in his eyes that he had his politician's mask on. Sincere and helpful, but not strait-laced.

She downed the cup of coffee, set the empty mug down and walked out, feeling Devan's eyes on her as she exited.

Where would I find the captain? Probably on the bridge, since the ship was in motion. She didn't hesitate this time at the "Authorized Personnel Only" door. John was watching the river and the switches in front of him.

"I want off," she said.

John turned to look at her and shook his head. "We've been sailing all night. We're already two hundred miles from the resort, and that's the only place you could have gotten off."

"Then turn around. We can't be too far away," she insisted.

"You're talking about eight hours in the wrong direction. I honestly can't turn around now; it would devastate my future." John's voice was almost pleading.

More of last night came back to her. The ill-fated attempt at escaping in the Jeep. He must have left the second everyone was on board because he knew she wanted off.

"That's it isn't it?" She paced back and forth. "He's the real reason I'm here. I could just slap someone."

"And I would deserve it," John responded.

His sincerity stopped her pacing. "At least you're not putting on your charming smile that you were using on me yesterday. Why?"

"I need help from the senator. He was reluctant to come unless you were here. That was the deal."

"Great. I'm a deal. And what exactly is Devan going to do for you?" she fumed.

"Some of the materials I need are from Peru, and this first voyage is significant. He's here to smooth the way, as well as to expedite the materials for exporting. I'm sorry if him being here makes you uncomfortable. He insisted that you not know of him being on board until, well it was too late." He turned and adjusted something, then turned back around.

"Did Jessup know?"

John shook his head. "No. Just another thing he's going to hate me for."

"Good, so I won't be the only one. Captain, I would appreciate it from now on if you were straight with me."

John crossed his arms and leaned against a console. "While we're talking straight, perhaps you can tell me how you know Simon."

Surprised by the question, Leslie paused for a second. "We met at the hotel. Someone was in my room and might have stolen something. I needed help, and he was there to help me."

John's brow wrinkled at that. "Was anything taken?"

"No. Just my feeling of security," she responded.

Sun came up the ladder.

"John, we're coming close to the beachhead for our hike to the waterfalls," Sun said.

John nodded and turned back to the console. "If it's any consolation, Leslie, I'm sure the senator has your best interest at heart."

She knew that, and that more than anything annoyed her. She was somewhat flattered that he had gone to this much trouble. At the same time, Devan had once again smoothed the way for her. Helped her out of her stupor, where she hadn't been able to do it for herself.

"Damn him," she whispered under her breath.

LESLIE MADE her way back to the lounge for more coffee. Everyone had left, presumably to get ready for today's hike where they'd get a chance to swim or soak in a hot spring. Miguel was the only one left standing on the deck.

She stepped outside; the sun and heat immediately made her feel heavy. He was looking out to the jungle. The Toy was setting down on Sun's beachhead. It was a thin sandbar that reached out to the river. All anyone had to do was put down the plank, and they could walk across to the edge of the jungle.

Leslie thought that even the colors here seemed drenched in humidity. The green of the jungle was dark, as well as the brown of the river and the deep blue of the sky against the clouds.

A new sound began to emerge above the normal noise of the jungle; it sounded to Leslie like wind being sucked into a huge wind tunnel, loud and mournful. The sound was repeated from several different locations and continued to get louder.

"Miguel," she asked. "What is that?"

"Howler monkeys. They're putting out a warning that there are intruders."

"Monkeys?" Leslie repeated and tried to see if she could spy them, but the edge of the jungle was too thick.

"I'm sure we'll see a few today."

"It is amazing and beautiful here, even if it is hot and humid."

"Ah, yes. It is indeed beautiful. I can't wait for you all to see the waterfall that we're hiking to today. It's not the tallest in the Amazon, but some things are just too difficult with tourists."

She smiled at that and nodded. "I know what you mean. I had some rich couple ask me to take them on a long-distance hike in Alaska. I was sure I was going to regret it. It turns out we were only a few hours in when they decided roughing it wasn't for them. Some people just aren't cut out for really toughing it out."

He replied, "It's the tough kinds of trips that make me appreciate the things like a real bed or to sit down and relax without having to pick a centipede off my pants."

Jessup came and joined them on the deck, ready to hike with his daypack in tow. "Centipedes? We have centipedes somewhere?"

"Not here at the moment," Miguel said. "But you will need to be on the lookout for the bugs that will want to come home with you tonight." He nodded toward the jungle.

"What about people?" Jessup asked. "Are we far enough out to be away from everyone?"

"Primarily, yes." He pointed to the opposite side of the river. "My brother and I once came across some dirt roads in that area, barely passable, but well used. We don't know whose road it is, but we stay away from anything that looks like it's in use."

"Why?" Leslie asked.

He sighed heavily. "The problem is that some drug runners like to hide in the jungle. Cut down what growth they can and grow drugs. They have been known to mine their fields and have men with guns guarding their territory. We'd rather explore the Amazon than become a permanent part of it."

"That seems to be a lot of work to go to hide some cocaine," responded Jessup.

"Hmm, the penalties here are tough for drug smuggling, if

they are caught. But those who can grow their crops and get them sold will make quite a profit."

"Any indigenous tribes?" she asked.

He nodded. "The way I like to describe it is there are different levels of tribes that live in the Amazon. There are the natives like those who live in Nauta. They've come to terms with living in a more modern world and even interact with it. Then there are the tribes that live out past the ruins. They will visit Nauta once in a while for supplies, but they are wary because drug dealers and illegal loggers have killed some of them, forcing them off some of their lands. Then there are the tribes that live even farther out. They have no interest in knowing the outside world. They are far more dangerous, but we won't be going that far into the unknown territory."

"You call it unknown, but you know most of it?" asked Jessup.

Miguel responded, "Yes. But two men exploring doesn't make that area known. Besides, my brother and I can't keep doing this forever. We're getting older, and although our blood is from Peru, we are still a bit North American, and all of the sickness and injuries we've had are taking their toll."

Jessup nodded. "I know what you mean."

"Ever hear from any of the tribes about the final whereabouts of Spafford?" Leslie asked.

Miguel nodded. "The Mic Pachu tribe members say they shared information about a lost city. They're sure he disappeared on his way to find it from the pyramid ruins. "

"A lost city?" she asked.

"According to what Sun and I have figured, there was a city not far from the pyramid. Unfortunately, the knowledge of the location of the city hasn't been passed on to the current tribe members. Or, more than likely, for some reason they aren't willing to share the location anymore."

She felt the clank of the gangplank opening. They watched it slowly lower and then sink into the sandbar. Sun walked out, accompanied by everyone who wasn't on the deck. He looked up, his neck craning to see them and waved them down.

"Come on!" he said excitedly. "Let's go."

They turned from the edge and grabbed their things. "I don't know," said Jessup. "I don't see that he's slowed down any."

Miguel sighed again. "I don't know what's going on. He's been so different since our last trip. It's like he's a different man."

Leslie dashed down the stairs, ready for an adventure. A different man? She needed to be a new, different woman. Maybe he could teach her how.

13

THE WATERFALL

Leslie hacked at the branches as she followed behind Sun into the jungle. He had promised it would be a short hike to the waterfall and springs, but she wasn't sure how long she could be his backup for making the trail more comfortable for the rest of the group following them. Her arms were screaming, and the heat was beginning to be suffocating. Although Sun was doing the hard work, cutting through the thickest parts, and she only had to follow up and make sure everyone could get through. She figured that was what she got for dashing up to Sun and asking him questions. This was probably his way of keeping her from bugging him.

It was beginning to be a rhythm. Hack, hack, step, step.

She tried to take her mind off of her discomfort by thinking about Devan. She wondered if this elaborate plan was just to win her back. Either way, she was sure that Devan would drop the bomb soon. He was patient, but he also knew she was not.

Sun stopped and turned with a grin, tugging on his hat that was an ad for "Bob's fries, we heart carbs." "We're almost there." He turned back the direction they were going and continued.

His whacking with the machete picking up steam. Everyone else was following behind. She could hear the panting of breath at the labor.

Devan chose that moment to catch up to her. "Leslie, I'm sorry. John told me that you're pretty angry, and I don't blame you. I just thought that you'd take this a little better."

Leslie swung around and lowered the machete. "So you admit that it's because of you that I'm here."

Samantha and AJ were not far behind, and she didn't want anyone to overhear them arguing. She turned back around and followed Sun through the thick branches, now broken by his swings. She thought she could hear water, but it was so like the sound of the wind through the tops of the trees.

She almost kept walking when the scene opened up, but the difference in going from the dark jungle to the light opening was blinding. Water cascaded from over a hundred feet above their heads, and droplets created a rainbow halo.

Below the waterfall was a pool surrounded by rocky outcrops and bright flowers. The place looked like it was from a Hollywood film.

"Yes," answered Devan quietly in her ear. "I'm responsible for you being here."

She rolled her eyes. "We'll talk more about that later."

Jessup was the last one to emerge from the jungle. "Hallelujah." He ambled up to the edge of the water and walked in, boots, clothes, and all. He floated in the water on his back. "Ah."

"Is it safe to get in the water?" asked Samantha.

Sun shrugged, "No tourists have been lost here yet."

"So, we aren't the first tourists to see this place?" asked Frederick, taking snapshots of the scene and attempting to angle his camera to keep Jessup out of his nature shots.

Sun laughed. "Yes, you're the first tourists, so my statement is in fact true." He turned to go.

"Sun, where are the hot springs?" Leslie asked. Not that she was sure she wanted the hot springs, but she wanted to be a little farther from Devan.

He pointed up to the top of the waterfalls. "Up there. The easiest way is to go through the jungle, up and around."

That sounded boring to her. She approached the rocks that skirted the waterfall. They were slightly stepped, enough that it would be simple to climb. The far edges were out of the mist so they would be dry. It would be hard work to get to the top, but she felt the need to do something strenuous.

She was planning her route up when Miguel rested his hand on her shoulder. "Thinking of climbing up?" he asked.

She nodded, and he handed her a pair of gloves. "The problem here is that centipedes, ants, and spiders, they all like to hide in rock crevasses. Many of them are poisonous or at the least have very painful bites. I highly suggest you use these."

And that was what was nice about having guides, she thought. She had never considered that. Climbing in New Mexico, the worst thing you could find was a rattlesnake, and luckily they didn't hide on cliff walls.

She started her climb up, the sound of splashes and swimming going on behind her.

"Leslie, are you crazy?" The call came from Samantha. Leslie focused on her foot and handholds as she steadily climbed.

Devan laughed. "Her aunt told me once about when she took her as a kid to this steep walkway around a river. When they got to the top, Leslie went beyond the sign warning people to stop and climbed up on some crevice. She just about gave her aunt a heart attack."

Leslie smiled at the memory. Her aunt had taken a photo of

the moment. Leslie had stood as close to the edge as she could. She had only moved back only when her aunt begged her.

Halfway up the rocks, she spied a break behind the waterfall. There was a cave behind it.

Her heart raced a little faster. Tomorrow there would be a big cave.

Today, she could at least stand outside this cave and test herself.

She made her way closer to the water, then slowly found foot and handholds that weren't too slimy until her boots touched down on the inside of the waterfall on a broad ledge. Her towel was on the top of her backpack, so she pulled it out and wiped her face and gloves. The mist had felt wonderfully cool. Here inside the waterfall, and next to the cave, the air was nearly frigid.

Stepping up to the edge of the cave, she placed her hand on the opening, and pulled out the flashlight from her bag. She wanted to go in the cave, but as she passed the light over the entrance, it made only a small dent in the darkness.

It wasn't enough to see part of the cave. She needed to see it all at once, to take in the normality of it and feel that it was just a natural piece of the earth. She leaned in on the entrance, resting on the wall, one step inside the chilly cave. She wanted to see inside.

She looked behind her. A large rock obscured her view of the pool, and the sound of the water hitting rocks echoed loudly. She looked back at the cave, and for some reason, she could see into it now. She glanced up. There was no sunlight coming through the falling water, so where was the light coming from?

A few more steps into the cave and she could see it was getting brighter. Another step and she could see that the light was coming from the rocks. They were glowing. She took off a glove and touched the rough surface. They were cold and damp to the touch, like any other cave rock. She aimed her flashlight deeper into the cave, in case this unnatural glow suddenly ended.

It was strange, but it didn't bother her. She could see in this cave, and it was just like any cave. There were no rocks in the ceiling ready to fall. A sparkle at the back of the cave drew her in further. Behind a small pool of water were bunches of tiny crystals clustered tightly together.

She pulled out her camera and took some photos of the crystals and the glowing rocks, without the need of the flash. As she stood, she disturbed a tiny, light green frog in one of the gathered pockets of water. It hopped resolutely toward the other side of the cave.

On her way out of the cave, she ran her hands over the rocks again. She remembered coming upon that cave in Iceland. Neither Carol nor her had hesitated to go exploring. They had pulled their headlamps out and had been wonderfully surprised to find the cave was at least the size of a football field, with nooks and crannies to explore. The colors throughout the cave and on the stalagmites were a mix of browns and blues.

By now, the glow in the cave was beginning to fade. She moved to the exit, checking to make sure her camera's memory still had the pictures. They were still there; it hadn't been a dream.

Now she could count this as a win. She had walked into a cave. She went to leave but turned back and walked to the edge of the cave. One step into the darkness and she could feel the anxiety, but it was still a win.

She gathered her things and threw the backpack on. Outside again, she climbed out the way she had come in. When she was out in the sun and farther from the water, she found an overhang that she could sit on. She got out her towel and wiped down her wet gloves and boots, glad to see and hear everyone enjoying the pool below. It felt normal.

Ready to move on again, she looked up at her path through the rocks and spied Sun sitting at the top. She wondered how he had climbed up there so quickly.

He was eating something and threw a piece of paper over the side of the waterfall.

Her brow furrowed as she watched the paper fall toward the water. But then it disappeared in midair. She looked at Sun, and he gave her a salute, then stepped away from the edge. She wasn't quite sure what to think about it all. But suddenly she realized that nothing about this trip was normal. She looked back to where the paper had disappeared. There wasn't anything to see but empty air. Maybe it had just turned where she couldn't see it. That could explain it.

She climbed up and out. She would contemplate the weirdness about this trip in the hot springs. She was looking forward to opening her sack lunch that Cesario had packed for everyone and pull out a can of cold beer she had brought. Everything would hopefully look better on the other side of lunch.

14

A TEST

un was curious about what the woman would do with the power he had given her. Being able to manifest one's great desire without knowing they had the ability to do so could have interesting effects. So far he wasn't impressed with what the captain had inadvertently used the power for; it said something about him.

For now, though, he was hungry. He found that he liked eating, but the idea of eating the pitiful lunch in a sack from Cesario didn't appeal to him. He needed something a little more extravagant.

He walked into the jungle, listening to the sounds of the humans behind him enjoying the cool water. He could also hear the heartbeats of all the creatures within a fifty-mile radius, plus all the wraths and vapors that humans couldn't see. Like him, they were a dying breed. He could pick out only a few, all of which were hibernating through the day. The heat of the sun always put them to sleep.

He could also feel the forces building up against this group he was with that had nothing to do with him. A human with an army of bandits was worried about them, concerned about discovery. But as long as he was testing them, he would hold those forces back and spin the universe however he needed to find a successor.

As soon as he was out of sight from the group, he willed his being to the new location. It was a little harder, bringing human tissue to the other side and back, but until he had found everything he had been looking for, he would continue to use this shell to interact with the others.

He walked up the steps of the restaurant. What remained of the host's memories recognized it as his favorite spot. He liked this location as well. As a god to the South American people he hadn't had the need or interest to travel, but he found the cool air and the yellow and red leaves that represented the season to be fascinating. He found he liked this Pennsylvania.

"Hello, Sun," said the cheery waitress. She didn't bother to grab him a menu, just pointed him into the dining room. She giggled and pointed at his hat.

He smiled back; he liked this hat particularly with the words "My other hat is just as awesome."

Luckily, his favorite table was available. The waitress immediately brought him a dark beer and two cans of beer for his friends and then walked away.

As had become a habit, the two women who were always at the bar moved to join him. The blonde called out as she approached the table, "Sun!" This one he liked the best. Her clothes were similar to what his people had worn. Small pieces of cloth that barely covered her top and a short skirt.

"Terry, good to see you. How is the business going?"

She grabbed and opened one of the beers left by the waitress and took a couple of gulps. "Not too bad. Tabatha and I have made some great sales today. We work well as a team."

He found it fascinating that humans would sell access to their bodies for gold.

"We can't hang around this time Sun," the tall redhead said. She grabbed her beer, glanced at the door the waitress had gone into, and tucked it into her purse. "We've got some business. You enjoy your meal."

Terry gulped down the rest of her beer and slammed the can on the bar on their way out.

He wondered for a moment if he should try somewhere new; he had the whole world to choose from and so many types of food. But the smell of greasy beef met his nostrils, and he decided to stay put.

The waitress appeared, the steam rising from the fajita beef sizzling on its dark pan. The image reminding him of priests carrying offerings to the altar. Then a flashback of the reason he had become so disheartened with his followers, turning on each other for the sake of the new arrivals.

He brushed away the thought and the wave of emotion with it and breathed deeply of the fajita aroma, then noticed that there was a hint of flowers in the air as well. The waitress was wearing perfume. He glanced at her again. Her name, "Parker."

"You enjoy," she said and walked away, sashaying to the front of the restaurant. This was how a king should be served. He watched her go then began to dig in but then felt the pull.

A tug of his power was calling him back. The woman, Leslie, was using the powers he had given her for something. He materialized funds and threw them on the table, he didn't want Parker to go without compensation. He put together a fajita, wrapping it in the napkin and stuffing it in his pocket.

Time to see what the woman was up to and if she was the one he was looking for.

15

HIDDEN DANGERS

The soak in the hot springs had felt fantastic but had not brought any ideas about Sun or the strangely lit cave. Leslie also knew that there weren't always scientific explanations, as far as she knew, for some of the things she had seen in her life. Now they were heading back. Maybe there was something that Sun or Miguel knew about the cave. She'd have to ask them.

Sun was ahead of the group, leading them back to the ship. Frederick, Samantha, and Devan were in front of her and the rest were coming up behind her with Miguel at the end to make sure no one got lost.

They arrived at the ship fast; at least it felt quick, probably because she hadn't had to swing a machete. When they emerged from the jungle onto the sandy edge of the river, the ship was a short distance downriver; they had an unfettered view of the expansive, muddy rushing water.

AJ approached the edge of the river. "Impressive," she said.

It wasn't hard to see what she was referring to. A bird with a bright orange head and shoulders sat on the limb of a tumbled over dead tree sticking out of the river. The bird's lower half was a vibrant, deep blue. The bird would have matched perfectly to a Chicago Bears jersey.

AJ pulled a computer tablet out of her bag, pointing its camera toward the bird. The screen of her tablet showing her zooming in.

In the open space next to the river, Cesario was sitting next to a folding table. A few green coconuts were sitting nearby, and he had a machete in his hand.

"Hey everyone," called Cesario. "Come on over and have a fresh coconut. AJ?"

John was setting up folding chairs in a circle. Sun went straight for a chair to sit down, and Miguel joined him.

AJ continued to take photos, stepping closer to the water. "Right there," she responded.

Cesario pulled the machete out of its scabbard and quickly hacked off the top of a green coconut in one swift motion, handing it to Samantha, then handing her a straw. Leslie's mouth watered at the thought of cool coconut water, especially as she felt the beads of sweat rolling down her back.

"Come on everyone. It's very refreshing after a hot hike," Cesario called, glancing again at AJ who was joined at the riverside by Jessup. Cesario hacked at another coconut and handed it to Frederick.

Jessup pointed toward the bird. Loud enough so the whole group could hear he said, "That's Peru's national bird, the cock-of-the-rock."

"Ha!" Samantha laughed. " I know a few guys who think they're the Cock-of-the-rock."

Leslie gladly accepted the next opened coconut and wandered toward the river. The tang of fresh coconut washed over her tongue.

The bird spread its wings and took off upriver. AJ focused

on getting photos of the bird in flight. From the corner of Leslie's eye, she saw part of the river's edge move.

A sharp intake of breath from Samantha was the first thing to tell her it was more than just some dirt moving.

An oily, black alligator was clambering toward AJ, who was unaware.

Leslie called "AJ, get away from there!"

AJ turned to look at her then looked at where Leslie's eyes led her. She wasn't quick enough; the monster was going to get her.

Jessup moved faster than anyone. In the time it took AJ to turn around, he had run to the backside of the alligator, approached it from behind, sat on its back and grasped its jaws.

"Someone, bring me something to keep his jaw shut," Jessup said. "It's easy enough to keep them shut, but . . . "

The scream drew them all to Samantha's stricken face. She was pointing back at the river. Another black alligator was coming out of the water, just feet from where Jessup sat on top of the first.

Leslie froze. Cesario ran by. He swung his machete at the alligator that was moving toward Jessup. He swung twice and stepped back. It wasn't moving. The machete had cut through its tough skin just as it had the coconuts.

John dashed over and joined Jessup in holding the living alligator. Its tail was thrashing like a giant, angry cat. "Cesario, bring me some rope, quick!" he called.

Cesario ran into the ship and luckily was out quickly. Miguel helped Cesario wrap the alligator's long snout. "Let's stake him down for now, so he doesn't walk away until we can set him off," said John, and the three of them quickly tied the creature down.

Jessup walked up to Leslie with a smile on his face. "I hope that's the last time I have to tussle with an alligator. I'm getting too old for that sort of thing."

"How did you know how to do that?" Frederick asked.

"I know," Samantha said, leaning forward and pointing at Jessup. "I was on the radio show with him the day he was going to go wrestle some alligators."

Jessup nodded. "Luckily, the alligator's muscles are mainly tied up in shutting its jaw on its prey, and it has only a few muscles for opening its mouth. Not that I want any of you to try that. I've been trained by an alligator specialist in Louisiana."

John walked up to Jessup, taking a hold of his arm. "Jessup, are you okay?" His face was etched with lines.

"I'm fine. I was just telling everyone I'm getting too old." John glanced at Leslie, his expression unreadable.

"Is that normal?" asked AJ. "For alligators to come up like that?"

"These are actually black caiman. They're the distant cousin to the alligator. A little smaller, but more aggressive." Samantha answered. It still made everyone pause when she came out with these gems.

"Yes, what you'll find in these waters are the black caiman. I've never seen them come at someone like that," John said, "but then they don't normally see people this far out. I'd also feel better with everyone on board."

"We might want to take the dead caiman and cook him up. They make for a delicious meal," Sun said.

"You tell me how to cook it Sun, and I'll offer it as an option for dinner." Cesario nodded. "I like the idea of not leaving it behind like this. Although I'm sure the other predators in the jungle will make quick work of it if we left it."

"Well," said AJ moving toward the boat, "I've never tried caiman."

John nodded, "You all head in. Cesario and I will get the

equipment. Make sure to stay on board. I'll untie our friend carefully before I head in last."

"Why not just kill it too?" asked Frederick.

John shook his head. "The caiman is an endangered animal. Too many people are hunting them for their hides. Besides, I'm not going to kill it unless I have to. As soon as we load everything back on the ship, we'll move on to our next location. The ruins tomorrow should be what everyone has been waiting for."

With that, the group headed in. Leslie took one last look toward the river, but there was no other caiman that she could see, and no brightly plumed birds to lure them to trouble, at the moment.

16

THE TRUTH

A shower and finishing off the coconut water had revitalized Leslie. Now she wanted some of the snacks that Cesario had left in the lounge; she thought she had seen some roasted salted corn and some churros with her name on them.

She took two steps up the stairs and heard a heated conversation up ahead. It was Devan and Jessup.

Jessup's tone was angry, "Pretty slick trick, Devan."

Then came Devan's soft, southern twang. "I didn't want to trick her, but you know she's been tucked away in her apartment. I had to do something!" That was the other thing that annoyed her about Devan. His southern twang made him sound more innocent than he was.

Jessup continued. "I can see finding a way to get her out of the house, but did you have to come on the trip too? Certainly, you could help her keep her dignity intact. She was so happy when she arrived. Now, you can tell she's upset," Jessup said.

Dignity wasn't quite the right word. She felt as if her pride was dinged. And now, a bit more while she heard people talk about her.

There was a heavy sigh from Devan. "I know. I could have left well enough alone and made sure she knew nothing about my involvement. However, I had to be in Peru earlier this week anyway. And who knows if the Toy will make this journey ever again. Maybe I'm selfish, but I wanted to see these ruins. They're famous, yet no one has seen them."

"What do you mean 'Who knows if the Toy will make this journey again'? I know that's John's goal to make this a standard trip," Jessup said.

"True,"Deven replied. "But I also know that John's paying through the nose for insurance. If he wants to make this business a success, he's got to rein in the expenses. I also know that he has to pay for some additional materials for his next version. Personally, as an investor, I can't support this trip in the future."

"But you authorized this trip?"

"Yes, but that's because of all the press and investment opportunity. If we had done this as a trip down the Rio Grande, who would have cared? Without that, this excursion is a waste of time," Devan responded.

"So you're going to pull the rug out from under John?" Jessup asked.

"Don't blame me for any changes. He's seen the numbers. He knows that this is an expensive and dangerous deal. Just imagine how much the insurance went up when they heard, 'unexplored Amazon'. But you wanted to know about Leslie. Yes, I'm here, and I care about her."

Leslie rolled her eyes.

"If you had seen how happy she was at the beginning, you'd realize exactly how selfish you are," Jessup said.

"Look, I'll talk with her. I don't want her to be upset."

Leslie could hear the sound of a chair moving. She backed up and headed to her room.

Moments later, there was a knock on her door. She threw it open, fully expecting to see Devan.

"Can you help me?" asked AJ.

Leslie covered up her surprise. "Sure. What's up?" She noticed that AJ wasn't standing straight, she was leaning against the frame of the door, her boots were off, her feet in black and white striped socks. Her dark eyebrows were furrowed, and she looked to be in pain.

AJ hobbled into her room and sat on the chair. She looked down at the floor. "I hate to be a burden, but my feet are killing me! I don't understand. Those are supposed to be good boots." She peeled off her socks to expose her blister laden feet.

"Ouch. That looks painful. How long have you had your boots?" Leslie was aghast at the raw feet she was seeing.

"I just got them before the trip."

"Did you break them in?"

"No. Should I?" AJ asked. Her earnest face made Leslie feel terrible at being the one to have to tell her.

"Yes. Wearing new boots isn't good for your feet, especially for hiking." Leslie pulled out some Epsom salts, but took a look and realized that many of AJ's blisters were torn open from so much rubbing. Salts weren't going to help here.

"I'm going to need to apply some first-aid ointment, then cushion the blisters that haven't popped yet, and bandage the ones that have. Is that okay?"

AJ nodded.

Leslie pulled out her first-aid kit, put on some gloves, and got to work. "Well, as a computer programmer you probably don't go outdoors that often."

"I'm a little embarrassed actually. You'd think that I'd be a bit more knowledgeable about the outdoors."

"Why, because you're Native American? I don't think that automatically requires you to understand hiking. I mean, it's not like all Native Americans are great hunters or trackers like in the old movies. Right?"

AJ laughed at that. "Sure. But I am an expert at tracking down code."

"Exactly."

AJ shifted in the chair and grimaced.

"Sorry. Your feet are going to be uncomfortable for a while. If we keep the blisters cushioned and covered, it should help a little." Leslie continued working, methodically surrounding the blisters with moleskin and covering them with band-aids.

AJ asked, "What inspired you to come out on this trip?"

"Jessup asked me to come on board as the storyteller. I'm writing some articles. And you?"

"Jessup invited me to come and check it out. John is still looking for more investors, and they're trying to talk me into this as an investment."

"What do you think so far?" asked Leslie.

"The technology has its advantages. I could see them going in several different directions with this and being profitable. However, if they plan on continuing the tourist bit, I think they need some cruise director touch or something. These men are all brisk, no-nonsense."

Leslie nodded. "You know, you're right. This trip is more like a serious excursion than a tourist exercise." She finished covering up the last of the blisters. "Tomorrow, if you have a different pair of shoes, you might want to wear them. Otherwise, your hiking boots are going to rub these same places. And definitely, do your best not to let the blisters pop anymore. It increases the chance of infection, and out here in the Amazon, you don't want to get anything like that." It made her think about what Devan had said about the insurance. Something as simple as this could grow into a serious problem in the jungle. Luckily, they could get back to safety relatively quickly in their speedy transportation.

AJ nodded. "Thank goodness we're not too far from civilization on this boat. I'll be glad to get back at the end of the week."

AJ hobbled to the door, trying her best not to land on the bad parts of her feet, which Leslie was sure had to be difficult considering blisters were everywhere. As she opened the door, AJ turned, looking up at the ceiling while she considered something. She finally said, "Did you notice that both John and Jessup were carrying guns last night?"

The question surprised her. She thought back. John had shown up with a gun in his hand, and she did remember Jessup reaching inside his vest but not taking anything out. "I guess so."

"My instinct is telling me that something more is going on here than what we are seeing. I wouldn't call this a disaster, but you should keep your eyes open."

Leslie nodded. "Thanks. I will. And this might sound a little crazy, but if you want to get some ideas about what to do about your shoes, you might want to talk with Samantha. I saw an episode of her show once where she was talking about how to keep your new shoes from 'causing a scene,' as she called it. She had some tricks to break them in."

AJ smiled, "Okay. Couldn't hurt."

Leslie checked the corridor as AJ walked out. There was no Devan on his way. It was empty. So, it was time for a churro, she thought.

17

___

DISCOVERY

Walking up into the lounge, she reveled in the cool air against her skin from the air vent aimed at the stairs. She assumed she'd find Jessup behind the bar, pouring himself some more whiskey or perhaps playing chess with anyone who would say yes. Instead, Frederick was at the bar, a fizzy drink in his hand, the other hand playing with the chess pieces.

She nodded a greeting at Frederick who registered her presence with a wave. She nabbed a mini churro and then hesitated at the door to the observation deck. Did she really want to step out into the humidity after she had just showered?

The trees were moving by slowly, and she did want to look out at the scenery. She opened the door and felt the humidity, but the breeze created by the cruiser's movement kept the deck feeling somewhat comfortable. She popped the churro in her mouth. The sweet cinnamon on the crispy shell with a hint of cream melted in her mouth. It was a good thing they were doing so much activity on this trip otherwise all of her clothes would stop fitting.

Several feet below the floating cruiser, the muddy, murky waters of the Amazon looked almost too much for the riverbanks. The water went right up to the edge of the bank and in many places the plants dipped down and touched the waters. Up ahead, twin spires of thunderstorm clouds were building above the trees.

Leslie loved the feeling of the breeze and being up in the air. It was a bit like being in a hot-air balloon but with some directional controls. She walked around the perimeter of the boat; the deck was strips of a dark wood that angled up slightly at the rails. Beyond, birds were fluttering from treetop to treetop, and she caught glimpses of monkeys. She brushed her hand along the railing and was almost to the very front of the ship when she noticed an old rope. It was tied to the inside of the deck and hung over on the outside. Being curious she wiggled the rope. It wouldn't budge it.

What could the rope be for? She looked over the edge but couldn't see where it went. She leaned over farther and thought she could see something hanging from the end. She leaned out a little farther, making sure to keep her hands on the rail so she wouldn't slip. Leslie could then see what was hanging from the end.

"What the hell are you doing? Are you trying to fall off?" John's voice rumbled from above.

She righted herself onto the deck and glanced up. He was standing outside the bridge; the bridge window open.

Leslie pointed over the side. "I was just curious as to why there is a piece of meat hanging over the side."

"What?" he asked, but didn't wait for an answer. "Sun, watch the wheel," he called out behind him. Then, he climbed down along the outside of the ship and dropped from the bridge deck. He grabbed hold of the rope and pulled it up.

"That's not normal, right?" she asked.

He looked at her, scanning her face, then went back to the slab of beef now lying on the deck, tiny drops of blood dripping from the thawing meat. "Definitely not normal. And exactly the kind of thing that could make sure caiman are around and hungry, at least while the blood was still dripping."

John pulled a knife from his pocket and cut the rope, then with a grunt tossed the meat far out into the muddy water.

"Why would someone do that?" she asked.

"Maybe trying to get us to turn the cruiser around?" he said, not looking at her, coiling the old rope around his elbow and hand.

She felt her blood boiling. "You're accusing me?" How quickly this man could make her crazy.

"I'm not accusing anyone. I'm just saying that could be a likely possibility."

A thunderclap in the distance echoed her own rumbling feelings. Then she thought back to the riverbank experience. "Cesario seemed worried about AJ being near the edge. Maybe he knew about the meat?"

Now John looked at her. "I've known Cesario for ten years. He's not going to put anyone at risk like this. If you're going to try and pin it on someone, pick someone else."

She'd had enough. John was back to wrapping up the rope again. She walked up and placed her hand on his arm to get his attention and waited for him to look her in the eyes. "John Holbrook, we talked before about being straight with each other, and I can tell you I had nothing to do with hanging a piece of bloody meat over the side of the cruiser. Got it?"

He sighed and placed the rope over his shoulder. "It's interesting that you mentioned Cesario. He told me how you were acting fishy the other day and that it looked like you were coming out of the authorized personnel only area."

She shook her head. "I was lost. It was a new ship to me." She looked briefly away from the captain's eyes.

"I'm sure that a woman who's been in charge of so many expeditions has a problem finding her way around a small ship." His sarcasm was undeniable. "However, I don't think you did it. But I don't know of anyone interested in stopping this cruise and making us turn around, other than you."

She had to admit that was true. "Okay. Yes. I asked for us to turn around. But I'm enjoying the trip, most of it anyway." He was right, of course. No one else had shown an interest in doing anything but enjoying this trip. "What are you going to do about this?"

"I'll start asking questions. It seems more of a nuisance than anything else. No one was injured." He shrugged his shoulders.

"But what if Jessup hadn't moved so quickly? Couldn't AJ have been killed or seriously injured?"

The captain's expression changed, his eyes looked darker. "Yes. AJ could have died if Jessup hadn't moved so quickly. We would have had to turn around, get AJ help or just end the trip. But it also might have been something else. This was the first time we've seen any caiman on this trip so far; what if someone was just trying to see them in the river? They wouldn't have necessarily known that someone would get chased."

Leslie took short paces back and forth in front of John. "So you don't think anyone is in danger?"

"I honestly don't think so." He looked at the rope pensively. "There's no guarantee that there would have been caiman close by, and there's no way it was targeting any one person. Let's at least get everyone there to see the biggest part of this whole trip; meanwhile we keep an eye out for anything else happens, I'll be willing to turn around after the ruins. We can always get back to civilization in about twelve hours."

That sounded acceptable. She nodded.

He turned to go, smiling over his shoulder. "I'm glad to hear you say you've been enjoying most of the trip."

She smiled back. Hopefully, she thought, things would stay smooth until they could turn around.

18

SPAFFORD'S SECRETS

Leslie popped another churro into her mouth as she headed back to her room. She'd do a little writing before dinner. She had heard that Cesario was cooking one of the caiman and a choice of spaghetti and sausage. If the tasty scents in the ship were any indication, she might have to try the caiman.

A sound stopped her; it was the faint sound of minions laughing. She had chosen that ringtone for her satellite phone because she loved the characters. It was hard to tell which direction the sound was coming from. She walked hurriedly through the halls, trying to zero in on its location while it was still ringing.

She didn't hesitate at the captain's door and walked into the room, quickly shutting the door behind her. The sound was coming from in here. She could tell it was coming from the corner of the room, but the sound of the last minion faded away. She'd have to search.

She knew the captain was busy at the controls of the ship. He had gone straight back to the bridge, and she knew he preferred to be there at any time the ship was underway. Right now she could see through the portal that they were still heading toward their next destination.

She glanced at the photo on the bulletin board. Benedict Cecil Spafford looked dashing in his day. But then she turned to the task at hand. The captain's bed was neatly made with a tightly tucked blanket. In one corner of the room was a pile of dirty clothes, and bits of electronics scattered throughout the room but in the far corner was a small chest. She knelt down and opened it. The scent and mustiness of old cedar and leather greeted her as she surveyed the objects inside. And there it was. Her bright yellow satellite phone sitting between books, Peruvian snacks, a map, notebooks, and a camera. So much for being straight with her—Although, she was surprised that she didn't feel angry. John had been suspicious of her contacting Simon, and he had honest concerns. But she did feel relieved that she had her phone back. The number that had called her was her friend from Albuquerque. Leslie dialed up her voicemail.

"Hey Leslie, everything is good here. I just wanted to catch up. The beasts are doing fine. Enjoy!"

Thank goodness, she thought. The last thing she needed was an emergency back home. She was glad the beasts, aka her basset hounds, were okay.

Now that she was here with time to snoop, she picked up a book that looked suspiciously like the old journals she had seen in her research on Benedict Spafford. It was bound in dark brown leather and in gold lettering were the words 'Day Book.' Opening it, she immediately recognized Spafford's swirling cursive handwriting.

She wanted to read it all, but should she? She felt as if the captain owed her, and the more she knew about the ruins, this trip, and the captain, she'd be better off. Besides, turnabout was fair play. She wondered if this journal spoke of the last days of Spafford. Although she imagined him still alive, his young self kept alive by some magic elixir. Still moving through the jungle in his explorer outfit; bossing his men around; preening over his youngest son, who was the closest to him in stature and personality.

But that was not realistic. Most likely he had died from being bitten by any number of dangerous animals or insects, or even something as simple as an infection.

She tucked the book in her purse and turned to go.

The room and its contents though were interesting. She didn't really want to leave. The captain was an enigma, and she wanted to know more about him, why he was so secretive about things. The piles strewn about the room were too disorganized to reveal any clues about the man. Besides, the longer she was here, the more likely she'd get caught.

She peered throughout the peephole to the hallway. Nothing was moving as far as what she could see. She took a deep breath and barreled out the door, shutting it quickly behind her. She took a few steps toward her cabin before she looked back. No one was around to see her.

She wanted to read as much of the journal as she could before dinner and try to return it to the captain's cabin before he noticed it was gone. Her heart was racing as she entered her cabin. She couldn't move fast enough to sit down and crack open the book.

Today was a hard day. I have been to this small town on the Amazon river many times, but it is difficult to watch the changes happening. The need for rubber from the rubber plants is growing in Europe, so Nauta is practically filled (although I suppose five isn't filling up a town. However, here it seems so) filled with English chaps trying to vie for workers and hunting for the plants. The town has grown slightly since last I was here, but it is still a backwater place. No real running water, and holes in the ground for a sewage system. Still, it is better than what the jungle will give us. Already some of the men I have hired are complaining. My manager tells them to stash it. My son is as tough as I am. He just shakes his head at the complaints.

Tomorrow we set out with our canoes. My local guide has said the river is running well, but we'll be required to haul our canoes at times. It is a hard trek to make with so many supplies, but the times we will be able to take the river will shorten our trip by days.

The old shaman that I talked to last year told me to look for a sign along the river for where the ancient city was hidden. He had said that demons walked there, angry demons that didn't like to be disturbed. The sign along the river was a giant snake that had been spit out by the demons. Of course, talk of demons is tosh. There are no demons. The primitives that live here simply don't understand the world as I and my civilized brethren do.

We head out tomorrow into the deep jungle. I am looking forward to it, and I know I have missed being here. It is a constant struggle to stay above the heat, humidity, and the depth of poison that the jungle has. I also look forward to meeting new tribes. My constant testing of my first contact protocol has worked beautifully. Others have died approaching these primitives.

LESLIE SKIPPED over the talk about the tribes, flipping pages until she found the last pages filled out by Spafford. The handwriting was more scribbled than before.

WE HAVE CUT *down the surrounding trees and knocked back the jungle as much as possible around the largest of the pyramids. It is amazing. I have not seen anything made of gold, but this was a significant civilization that worshiped here. We finally found a way into the pyramid, but many of the men will not go in. My son and I only explored a small portion. Luckily we found a booby trap and have shored it up to keep it from being set-off.*

THEN FARTHER DOWN ON the page, it started up again.

I FEEL *as if something is watching us. This jungle has been my home longer than England, so I am trusting my instincts. An eerie silence has settled on the jungle. I have put my men on high alert; everyone is sitting with a gun at the ready. I am also sending this journal back with a runner. My wife, when you read this, know that I miss you terribly and Leonard has been exemplary. I can see that he will take on my role of expedition leader long after I am gone. If anything happens to us though, know that I love you and the children.*

I plan on calling out and attempting to talk to whoever is watching us. We'll see if I can draw them out.

THERE WAS A DRAWING, similar to the one Leslie had, of the pyramid with men clearing the area for their camp. This one was different though. Benedict had drawn a large moon over the pyramid and a giant eye in the jungle.

That explains it, she thought; Maybe, it was an angry tribe that killed or kidnapped Spafford. At least, it seemed that way. Not a lot of information, but at least she knew a bit more than she had before.

But Spafford had found an entrance. In all the reports from Sun and Miguel, they had never found a way in. Although now Sun professed to knowing a way in. Tomorrow was looking more exciting. Outside, the jungle had stopped moving by the ship; they were obviously stopped, so her chance of returning the journal without getting caught was riskier. She carefully placed it in her purse and decided to carry it with her to dinner. The second she had a chance, she'd put it back.

19

____

HALLPAQUIRAO

Dinner was fantastic. Leslie tried both the stewed caiman and the spaghetti with sausage. Now she could barely move. Cesario might be moody and strange, but he made an excellent dinner. It was evident that Sun had liked the caiman; he was up getting fourths.

John and Jessup were setting up a chess game. "What do you mean I'm an old man?" Jessup said to John.

John replied, setting up the black pieces, "I mean you shouldn't be pouncing on alligators at your age."

It looked like it had the possibility of upgrading to an arm wrestling match. Thunder peeled outside, and a spurt of rain hit the window as the wind whipped into it. John had moored the ship before the storm hit, and it felt safe. Leslie was thankful the ship was too massive to sway even in the strong wind. Sheets of rain blurred the darkening, stormy skies.

Across the room, Samantha, AJ, Sun, and Frederick were starting a game of poker.

Leslie wondered if she should try to sneak away to the captain's cabin while everyone was busy. Except Cesario was missing. She didn't want him to catch her doing something suspicious again; if anything, she wanted the captain to be less suspicious of her.

"When it rains here, it's no cats and dogs. It's more like cows and elephants," Miguel said, sitting next to her at the bar. "What do you think of the Amazon, so far?"

"A bit too hot and humid for me, but I do like this feeling that we are in the middle of nowhere."

"It's not just a feeling. We are well and good into no man's land." He got up and went behind the bar to a stylish map on the wall. "The resort we passed was back here." He pointed to a spot on the map next to the river. "That resort is the last bit of civilization on the river. Once we left there, we were in no man's land. We've been traveling now two days. We're about here." He pointed far down the map of the twisting river.

"When you say no man's land, what exactly does that mean?"

"Consider the south side of the river, on our right as we're traveling. It is extensively unexplored by modern man, except for my brother and I, and is inhabited by a few indigenous tribes that prefer to be on their own. That area is about the size of California."

Samantha added, "The whole Amazon basin runs 2,700,000 square miles. Isn't that crazy; that's huge!"

Miguel nodded and continued. "The north side of the river has been known to be inhabited by some drug runners, but far from the river and far from the resort, so we won't come across any out this way."

"So the ruins we'll see. It was a city?" Leslie asked.

"No," Sun spoke while laying his cards on the table. "It wasn't a city."

"Sun, that's just speculation. We don't have any proof yet."

"Miguel, I feel it in my bones."

"So if it's not a city, what is it?" asked Samantha, watching her betting money being collected by Sun.

"It was a place of worship," Sun responded. "The city was farther away. Priests, sacrifices, and honored leaders traveled to Hallpaquirao in order to pay homage to their gods."

"What?" Miguel gave Sun a hard stare. "Since when did you give it a name?"

"Brother, I promise that before we leave there tomorrow, I'll show you how I know."

The tension from Miguel quieted the room, except for Sun who got back into the poker game with fervor, excitedly dealing out the cards for the next game.

Leslie felt she needed to change the subject. "Okay. Today, I had a weird experience. Behind the waterfall, I walked into a cave. The rocks all glowed like they had light bulbs in them. But it only lasted a short while."

"Trick of the light maybe?" said John, his eyes focused on the chess board.

"There was no light. The sunlight was obscured by the waterfall and the rocks. All I had was a small flashlight."

"Well," Devan thought for a moment and then answered, "perhaps your being in the vicinity activated some sort of moss that was growing on the rocks and it created a phosphorescence."

"A plausible explanation. I guess I should have taken a rock sample," Leslie said. And the idea had true merit. Maybe it hadn't been as miraculous as she had thought. "Although," she continued, "it almost seemed as if the light was coming from inside the rocks."

"Were you scared?" AJ asked.

"No." Leslie shook her head. "It was a good thing. It was what I needed at that moment."

"Do you need an answer then?" She placed her bet on the

table. "I would look at it as a gift, something to just be accepted."

"I like that answer. Thanks, AJ," Leslie said.

"Hurray!" Samantha squealed as she gathered the chips on the table to her. "Leslie, Miguel, you should join us. Let me see if I can beat you too."

"She's probably a card shark," Leslie whispered to Miguel as he stood to move over to the table.

"Well, if she has a perfect memory, as I suspect she does, she's probably a card counter. So I wouldn't put in real money." Miguel said.

Leslie considered joining the table, but Spafford's journal was on her conscious. She wanted to read more, but she also didn't want John to find it missing.

Cesario entered and approached the dumbwaiter. He pulled out a magnificent looking layered cake, obviously different layers of chocolate and set it on the bar. "I'll be back shortly with ice cream. No one cut this cake until I come back."

That meant he'd be busy between here and the galley. She'd have a few moments to return the journal without John or anyone knowing. She grabbed her purse and slipped out of the room. She was back before Cesario returned with the ice cream.

While they were enjoying dessert, lightning cracked outside, and the rain burst against the front windows.

"I'm glad we're not out there," said Samantha.

Miguel nodded. "It can get miserable out there in the rain. Sun and I spent many nights in our tents trying to stay dry."

Leslie held on tight to her cup of coffee and was thankful that she wasn't an explorer of the Amazon. She was happy right where she was.

20

NIGHT WALK

Sitting on her bed in her cabin, Leslie had written as much as she could in her journal, but she had drunk too much coffee to go to sleep now even though it was close to midnight. She washed up and headed for the lounge to grab a drink, hoping she would find some company.

Instead, she found it deserted. The rain had stopped, and there was only the soft, white noise of the air conditioning running through the vents.

She wandered behind the bar and checked out the refrigerator; inside was an apple, some cheese, and a few cold beers. She only needed one. Taking large crunches of the apple, she sat in a comfy chair and stared at the dark windows. Then a shadow moved by the stairs.

"Hello?" she called. Silence.

Leslie set the beer down but kept the apple in her hand. Tiptoeing to the door, she found no one on the stairs. She walked down to the bottom. The doors to everyone's cabins felt so far away from here.

Clunk! The sound of a door shutting somewhere in the hallway.

Leslie called out just a little louder. "Hello?"

She turned into the long corridor and jumped when a tall shadow appeared before her. She dropped the apple.

"Damn it, Cesario! Why didn't you answer when I called?"

"I just heard you. I was coming to see if you needed anything." In the dim light of the hall, his hair and long nose sent shadows across his face.

"I don't need anything. I thought I saw someone wandering around." She looked behind Cesario, but the corridor was empty. "Were you just out here a moment ago?" she asked him.

"Not me." He shrugged.

She grabbed the apple from the floor and headed back to the lounge. "Never mind. I must have been imagining things." Yet she was sure she had seen something. Had it been Cesario watching her? Or someone else?

She took two long swallows of beer and savored the flavor of the cheddar cheese on her tongue. Although it was hot outside, she headed out onto the observation deck.

The lights inside the bridge came on. Leslie looked up and could see John working at the controls, bringing up the lights on the outside, and getting the ship ready to move again. Tomorrow would be the ancient city; the idea was thrilling. She held onto that thrill as she took her things back to her cabin.

As she made her way past the other cabin doors, she saw a light from under what she was sure was Jessup's room. In the middle of the door was taped a hula dancer. He did like his Hawaiian things. She knocked softly just in case he was sleeping.

"Come in," he called.

He was sitting on a yoga mat on the floor, his hands palm up on his knees. He was sporting stretchy pants and a purple Hawaiian shirt.

"Yoga?"

"It's what keeps me as limber as I am." Jessup gestured her to the chair.

"Thanks."

"And what can I do for you, Leslie?"

"Well, you can tell me about John."

"Anything in particular?" he asked.

"Did he know there might be any danger to us, the passengers?"

"Oh hell no." He shook his head. "He's not out to get anyone hurt. No, he's just been concerned about getting this project off the ground without any interference."

"You've been friends for a long time?" she wondered aloud.

"Definitely." Jessup continued, "I knew him when this was just an idea. He had dreamt of this cruiser for as long as he could remember. He redrew it a million times. Came here to Peru because it was the only place he could find what he needed for it. When you get to know this boat," he said, tapping on the floor, "you get to know John."

"Let me guess, mysterious and tough as metal?" She smiled.

Jessup laughed. "I think you hit the nail on the head."

"But there's more to Peru, right? Isn't he related to Spafford?"

"Spafford? That adventurer? If he is, he's never really talked to me about it."

Leslie stood up from the chair. There were a plethora of framed pictures stacked tightly together on his dresser. She picked up one of a young man with Jessup's smile. He was holding a surfboard.

She regretted it when she realized who it was. "Your son?"

she asked quietly, remembering the information last year about Jessup's son being all over the news. Killed in a head-on collision with a drunk driver.

He nodded. "That pile is everyone I've outlived. Two wives, three best friends, and a son."

She put the photo back. It was a sad pile to carry.

"I'm getting tired," he said as he moved to sit on the bed, and Leslie thought he looked like he had a few more lines on his face. "I think I want this to be my last adventure."

"What? No more traipsing around? Don't you think you'll get bored?" Leslie asked.

He shook his head and smiled. "I don't think so."

"So you think John is a good guy?" she asked.

"Yes. I think it might help to know; he's worked hard all his life. His mother was poor and worked hard. When he was thirteen, he got his first job. He's been working ever since. He's driven, but he isn't destructive. Although he was a bit devious to hide the Devan connection from the both of us. But that has to do with materials, not lives."

"Okay, I believe you." To herself, she thought that obviously, he didn't know everything about John, but she figured he was mostly right.

He saw her to the door. A hula hoop was laying in the hallway.

"Dag gum him," Jessup said.

"Who?"

"The devil, John. He keeps leaving these things. It's a private joke." He grabbed the hula hoop and threw it into his room. It bounced off of a wall and landed on the floor.

"Goodnight Jessup."

"'Night," he said.

Could John have heard them while they were talking? She stood outside Jessup's door, but he wasn't making any noise so she moved down the hall, trying to see how much someone could hear outside one of the cabin doors.

She paused at another door and could hear Samantha. "Oh, Cece." Oops, she thought and kept moving. Now she was more certain that it had been Cesario at Samantha's room back at the resort. And now she knew that it was possible to hear outside. But did it matter if John heard her asking about him? He had to know already she was curious about him. Oh well, soon they would be heading back home, and there would be few opportunities to try and get to know the captain.

Leslie silently slipped into her cabin. She went to sleep dreaming of ancient ruins.

21

SUNRISE ON THE RIVER

John appreciated early mornings, especially on the ship. It was quiet, and no one else was up and about. Although when he glanced out the window, he half expected to find Leslie folded over the railing, trying to give him another heart attack. At the moment, the view from the bridge was only the mist ascending through the trees and up from the river as the sun began to rise.

John sipped on his coffee while he walked through the bridge, checking the instruments. He had moved the ship in the night, as soon as the rain had stopped, to their next location. He gently raised the ship up in the air so he could reposition it for passenger disembarkation later. First, though, he wanted to view the jungle from the unusual vantage point, just above tree level. He could see over the tops of the trees, and the light from the sun was beginning to spread over the horizon, layered by the morning clouds and mist in colors of pink and yellow.

John did a turn around the bridge. Across the river from where they were going to touch down, he thought he saw an open expanse. It was an area free of trees. Which was pretty much impossible out here. Could it be another lost city? It would almost make sense, being not far from the other ruins. He'd have to ask Sun about it later. He could check it out after everyone was on their way for the day's trip and after the mist had burned away. He had wanted to go on a short hike, and because he didn't want to be too far away from the ship, a hike into that area wouldn't be far.

John had to wonder; had it been worth it getting Leslie onboard and keeping her here, or was she more trouble than she was worth? He knew Devan would keep his promise. He had proven he was a man of his word. At least the others weren't too much trouble, although Frederick's avid interest in the workings of the ship was starting to bug him. But he would show him around today.

But then did he really think Leslie was causing trouble? He hoped she wasn't, but so far she was the only one he could connect to Simon. It bothered him that he had yet to find out Simon's reason for continuously sabotaging him, but he was glad that their partnership had fallen apart. He had heard rumors about how cruelly Simon treated his banana plantation workers. He preferred not to do business with someone like that.

Cesario walked onto the bridge, wiping his hands on a towel. "I'm about ready to start sending breakfast down to the lounge. Where do you want yours?"

"I'll take it in the lounge. Thanks, Cesario." As Cesario turned to go, John stopped him. "Cesario. How's everything going in the galley?"

"Fine. It's one of the best kitchens I've had to cook in."

"Has any food gone missing?"

"No." Cesario shook his head.

"There was a side of beef hanging off of the cruiser yesterday. Do you know anything about that?"

Cesario's eyebrows shot up. He looked at the floor and took a step back. "No. I'll have to check the storage, but anyone could have gotten into the kitchen." Cesario turned and walked out.

Damn, that had been a strange response, thought John. Now he suspected Cesario, and Leslie was the one who planted the idea. Of course, it didn't help that Cesario wouldn't look him in the eye.

Looking out the window, this time Leslie was there, walking around the deck with a cup of coffee in hand, taking in the sunrise.

He would be happy to lower the Toy again to conserve energy, but he also wanted to enjoy the sunrise. He kept the ship afloat until the sun had come over the horizon. Then he carefully lowered it into place.

He was glad to see she was still on the deck. He needed to ask her a question.

22

———

VEILED MORNING

The sun was partially hidden behind thin clouds, just peeking through as it touched the morning sky. The pale light reflected in the fast moving river.

Leslie strolled along the deck, curious to see if any more ropes were tied to the railing. She stopped to inspect a long-horn beetle sitting on the rail. It was so big it would have barely fit in her hand, if she were willing to touch it.

She moved on to where the rope had been yesterday. Nothing there. She set her coffee cup on the rail and leaned over the side to look down. The rain had done a good job of washing away the blood.

"I already checked. Nothing is hanging from the sides today," John said as he came through the lounge door.

"That's good," she said, turning to face him.

"I wanted to ask you. I want to go on a short hike later today, but I didn't bring a daypack. Any chance you have an extra bag? I assumed with so much hiking experience, you might have one."

"Well," she thought a moment, "I'm using my daypack

today, but it comes with a larger backpack that I brought. You're welcome to use it."

"Perfect. Let's go take a look at it, if you don't mind."

She took a deep drink of her coffee and then led the way with John following close behind. So far the rest of the cruiser was quiet.

He followed her into her cabin, and he seemed to fill up the room. She pulled out the bigger backpack from her luggage. "Are you coming with us today?"

"No," he said as he took it. "I have an enigma to check out on the other side of the river. I appreciate the loan."

Her closet was open and John looked at the blue silk dress. He reached out and touched it.

Leslie shook her head. "It's a very nice dress, I'm surprised that the hotel was willing to give that away, no matter how much they messed up."

He turned toward her, he looked uncomfortable. "The other day I heard you say something about glowing rocks."

"Yes. I swear the rocks were glowing in the cave behind the waterfall." She figured he was going to tell her that she had to be mistaken.

"That night, at the resort, they handed me that ugly brown dress to give you and I was thinking how much better blue would look on you. The dress, this dress," he held the material, "materialized in my hands."

"Wow." She hadn't expected that.

"Yeah, there's no explaining it. But I thought you should know. Peru is a place of many mysteries and we may not find out how these things happened."

She smiled, "Well, it is a lovely dress." John nodded and walked out the door.

She followed him back to the lounge where AJ and Frederick were piling on breakfast.

Samantha, Devan, and Jessup appeared up the stairs.

Devan was talking with them. "It's not like I sit at a desk all day. I do have to take on a lot of activities and meeting people. Plus, I always like to get out."

"Yes, a senator's work is never done." Jessup's sarcasm was obvious.

"Hey, just because I'm a politician doesn't mean I'm lazy." Devan responded with a laugh.

As they approached the breakfast buffet Samantha cut in. "If you ever need someone to host activities for you or to go with you to any of those activities, you just look me up Devan. I'm a great hostess."

Sun practically pounced into the room, bright eyed. Today's T-shirt read "Jesus loves this hot mess." "Everyone, I can't wait until we leave for today! 10:30 a.m., and we're going to have a fairly short hike and a long day of exploring. Cesario will have lunches ready. Everyone make sure to be back here at 10:30." He bounced out the way he had come past Jessup.

Jessup grabbed his cup of coffee and stalked back down the stairs, sloshing it on the carpet a little as he made his way out of view.

Leslie addressed AJ, "Are you going to make it on the hike today?"

"I will make it. Sun suggested wrapping my feet in duct tape, and I'll do it if I have to. Plus, Samantha helped me spray down the inside of the boots and mold them to my feet a little better."

"That was nice of her," Leslie said, glancing over at the table. "Why do you think she carries that ugly purse to breakfast?" She nodded toward the puffy gold purse sitting squarely on the table.

AJ shrugged. "Something valuable to her I'd guess. Well,

I'm going to go see what I can do about these feet." She got up slowly and ambled her way to the stairs.

Leslie dove into the food and glanced up at the view. The mist had finally burned off and far down the river she could see storm clouds building. She could feel that something was going to happen soon, something big. Was it the ruins? The storm? Or was something else lurking on the horizon? She brushed aside the foreboding and drank down the last of her coffee.

23

A LOST CIVILIZATION

Outside the lounge window to the deck, a curtain of mosquitoes danced in the sunlight. They moved in what looked like up and down motions but in lines in the air, like they were part of a dancing show.

"I hope everyone has their bug spray on. We're all going to need it," Leslie said. She pulled her collar up and her sleeves down. It was about eighty degrees outside and getting hotter, but better to sweat than worry about where a mosquito could land. The last thing she needed was to catch dengue fever or anything else from the mosquitoes here. Although she had shots and pills that were meant to ward off anything dangerous.

Samantha, dressed today in a light blue T-shirt and pants complete with cowboy hat with blue edging, came to look at what had prompted her comment. "Oh my God, there are millions of them out there."

"The farther we hike away from the river, well, it will be a little better," responded Jessup. "But it is the rainy season, so there's a lot of still water for them to breed in."

Leslie was glad to see that Jessup was wearing a long-sleeved T-shirt under today's shirt choice, a yellow and pink concoction with a hula dancer.

AJ was sitting down, her feet elevated.

"Get them all wrapped?" Leslie asked.

She nodded. "I walked around the ship a couple of times. It seems like this will work, but I'll probably be at the back of the pack."

"Oh, I think she'll be fine. We worked on her boots yesterday, together," said Samantha.

"I don't blame you hobbling in on those blisters. I'm pretty excited about going," said Jessup. "I've been to different ruins, and it always gets me when everything is so restricted as to what you can see. Here are some ruins that we'll have the run of."

Devan sat down next to Leslie. "All ready for today?"

"Sure, why not?"

"There's a cave involved. You're not worried?"

"No." She shook her head, and inside she knew she almost meant it.

"Just remember, I'm here for you." He reached out and put his hand on hers. "As a friend of course."

"Of course," she responded and stood up. She glanced at the bar where Cesario was cleaning up the breakfast foods, placing dishes in the dumbwaiter.

Sun appeared at the door and waved his hands toward the exit. "Let's go, everyone. Time to see the past." He led the way off the boat.

John was standing by the door as they all made their way out.

"I wish you were coming with us. This is going to be amazing," Leslie said.

"I know, but I'm going to stay and keep an eye on things.

And Cesario will be here, working on a big dinner for everyone. I'll probably head out on my hike when you all are almost back. Stay safe out there," he said.

Strange, it was the first time his concern didn't feel condescending. Leslie reached out and put a hand on his arm. "Don't worry. We'll be fine."

Cesario had already given everyone their box lunches and bottles of water. They all had backpacks and made their way down the gangplank.

Frederick was hanging back with AJ. "Sun, will we be able to follow you if we get behind?"

Sun looked carefully at them, then nodded. "Yes. Just follow the broken branches. It will be easy to follow us."

Sun led them along the river's edge, which was muddy from the recent rain. They had only been walking ten minutes when he pushed aside some small trees so they could see the five-foot-high snakehead statue.

Leslie figured it must have been the same one that Spafford had spotted.

"There's another one about twenty feet that way." He pointed farther out. "This marked the territory of the Inca as an entrance and a warning. The jungle has since decided to hide it from the river's view."

He continued into the jungle. Leslie passed her hand over the fangs of stone as she walked by. It felt dead cold.

This time, Miguel was following up Sun with his machete. Luckily, she'd get a break. Even so, the going was a lot tougher than yesterday. Beads of sweat quickly gathered on her face. The act of stepping through branches and over trees and vines was a lot of work. Last night's rain had left its mark with thick mud dispersed throughout their path. Leslie tried not to step on the worst of the mud so she wouldn't have to struggle with pulling her boots back out, but she soon realized it was impossible to tell which spots were better than others. Limbs and vines were also determined to reach out and snag her, whether it was her hair, her backpack, or her sleeves.

This time a branch had somehow caught her back pocket. She reached behind and broke the branch. When she pulled the end out of her pocket she heard a rip. Oh well, she thought, at least it was just the pocket.

Leslie checked on AJ. Luckily the going was slow for everyone, so AJ wasn't far behind, and Leslie liked that Frederick felt the need to hang with AJ.

Devan stumbled, and Leslie reached out a hand.

"Thanks," he said, taking it and she helped him up and out of the mud. They moved along a few more steps. She was so relieved when Sun and Miguel led them to a small clearing and were setting their things next to an old fire pit.

"Wow!" Samantha exclaimed as she reached the clearing.

"Wow is right," Jessup said.

A towering pyramid loomed ahead of them. Seven-foot tall gray stone blocks were placed together at each level. In the center ran a narrow and shallow set of stairs.

"Thank goodness we're out of the mud," said Samantha, trying to wipe her boots on the grass.

Leslie looked around; even the fire pit was dry. "How is that possible? It must have rained here too."

Sun pointed around at the ground. "You can't see them, but the people here created intricate waterways. They would reroute any water either away from the area or to a fountain."

"Who did you say built this place?" asked Frederick as he emerged from the jungle, tripping over a mound of dirt. AJ came through just after him, marveling at the site.

"Many peoples built this place. In the end, it belonged to the Inca." Sun's voice was somber. "Imagine what it would have been like to come to this jungle in the beginning."

With his words, Leslie felt a sense of moving in time, and suddenly it was as if her imagination was real. The jungle grew, and the pyramid disappeared. She reached out a hand to steady herself from the strange sight. Devan grabbed her hand and seemed to need the support as well. The experience made her heart race a little, but she could hear Sun's voice.

"The Vinaque came to this region. It was well protected, safe from their enemies, or so they thought."

She could picture them. A hoard of men, their heads elongated in strange shapes and wearing loincloths. They had hollowed out this valley for a couple of square miles. In the distance, the clear-cutting had unmasked a vast cave entrance.

Then the waterways appeared—small, narrow tunnels in an immense network that covered the ground in all directions, some reinforced with stone. It reminded Leslie of mole burrows. The tunnels disappeared as they were covered with earth.

"Then they built the first pyramid to hide their treasures and to demonstrate their love to the earth and their gods."

She could see a pyramid slowly unfold brick by brick over the mouth of the cave with small, square blocks of mud. Soon, there was no telling that a cave was standing in that location.

"Then they built their pyramid to their god."

Small bricks could be seen making their way up in a huge mound. The walls of both pyramids were covered with clay that hid the bricks. Gigantic tapestries suddenly hung from the buildings, folding over the pyramid steps like icing on a cake; bright reds and oranges outlined the intricate weave work. Men in tall headdresses walked with their heads held high and climbed the stairs of the pyramids, while the men with bare heads worked in the fields and on the buildings. Small buildings began appearing throughout the area. A circular enclosure appeared, lamas were led in.

"Then the Killiki and after them, the Inca came. They took on the same worship of the earth and the gods, but they brought their own building methods."

Next, stone statues of giant serpent heads on top of the bodies of lions appeared on either side of the pyramid steps. Then, huge pieces of stone were carried into the valley; handholds were etched in the pieces and men were using logs underneath to move the stone forward. These blocks were piled in front of the building's original structure, replacing it. Then the facades of stone were covered with a new layer of clay and painted.

"Then, the locals say some of the god's own people turned against them."

The scene had turned dark, and a few men were coming down the stairs pulling a woman with them. Her dress of gold pieces shimmered in the moonlight. She struck at one of the men, and he flew back as if by an explosion. The other man struck her hard. She collapsed. He carried her to the bottom and disappeared into the jungle.

"And that, they took one of their gods to the Spaniards who were in Nauta and gave them some secrets, but they never found their way back here. The one god left saw to that."

Suddenly the field was back to the overgrown jungle and a partially exposed pyramid. The clay and colors had long since been removed by time and erosion.

The things she had seen had felt real. She looked around at the others. They too were looking as if surprised, except for AJ who had tears in her eyes, and Sun who looked disappointed.

Samantha's voice broke the spell. "I read that the Inca treasures have never been found, that Benedict Cecil Spafford thought he had discovered their last stronghold, but no great treasures were ever revealed. Could the hidden treasure of the Inca be here?"

Leslie and Devon released hands. She looked in the direction that the other pyramid had stood in her imagination, but too many trees were in the way to see if any of it was still there.

Sun shrugged. "Perhaps." He smiled. "First, let's go have a look at the temple pyramid."

24

___

OF GODS AND TREASURE

Sun started up the stairs. "This first pyramid is the temple. There's an entrance at the very top where we can see where they worshiped their gods." A huge head of a serpent lay on the ground in front of the steps, broken off from its body. "This was in honor of their god." Sun ran his hand over the stone facade and then walked up the steps.

Frederick stopped to take a picture of the serpent head. Each scale was carefully detailed in the stone. Leslie looked up but couldn't see that there was an entrance anywhere.

"I'm so glad I've been doing the Stairmaster," Samantha said and started up behind Sun.

"AJ, are you going to need a hand?" Frederick asked her. She was looking up the steps with a wary eye.

"Thanks. I'll make it." She started gingerly moving up with Jessup walking not far behind. Miguel was quietly taking up the back.

Leslie tried to get into a rhythm on the steps, but they were too close together and worn. She would get into a quick tempo and then start to trip when the next step wasn't at the same height. She settled for a slow set of stepping.

When she finally reached the top, she looked back. They were almost at the same height as the treetops.

"This pyramid was built to honor and pray to their god. Only royalty would enter here." Sun pointed at the entrance, a tall trapezoid opening that gaped blackness. "They would funnel the beliefs of their people, commune and pray to their gods, and then be the gods' messenger. Everyone will need their flashlights to enter."

Everyone dug in their bags for flashlights and Leslie pulled out her headlamp. Sun walked through the entrance without a light and Samantha hurried in behind him, shining a light for him.

Leslie waited for everyone and entered last. It wasn't a cave, but the dark opening made her heart skip a few beats. Leslie spoke to no one in particular. "I've heard," as she walked in, lowering her voice so that it wouldn't echo so much in the small space, "that these types of buildings can withstand earthquakes?"

Samantha responded, "I've been to the ruins at Machu Picchu. That's what I heard there. They've withstood dozens of earthquakes without a stone moving. The stones will shift slightly, but then settle back into their original positions."

Leslie had been in caves that were a cooler temperature than the outside, but she hadn't expected the room to be quite so cool. On the floor, a few long, black centipedes ran on the smooth, shining stone surface. Their little red legs were moving fast to escape the light. Leslie checked her boots to ensure none were on her.

Leslie spied a trapezoid shelf carved out of stone. She ran her hands over the stone surface. "Such amazing work to get this stone smooth. And look at the shape. At least with the human eye, it looks like a perfect trapezoid."

AJ made a soft exclamation as she tripped. Everyone turned as she knocked into the stone pedestal in the middle of the room. The tabletop fell to the ground, cracking on a corner.

"Oh no," AJ responded as she stood.

The sudden oohs and aahs from around her told Leslie that something could be seen inside the wide base of the pedestal. She walked over to join the group, the gleam of gold in the flashlights temporarily blinding her.

Frederick reached down to lift the item. "Can someone help? It's heavy."

Leslie stepped up to assist. Its surface was smooth and cold. She bent her knees to help lift the heavy gold item. Everyone's flashlights shown on the statue.

It was a squat figure. He had a face like a serpent and a man's body.

"That's amazing," said Frederick. "Look at the detail."

Everyone's eyes roamed over the angered expression in the serpent's eyes.

Leslie admired the work. However, the statue looked a bit evil with red jeweled eyes and pointed fangs.

Samantha reached out to touch it. Devan and Jessup took out their cameras.

After a few minutes, Leslie was ready to put it back.

"Should we just leave it where we found it?" asked Frederick.

"Yes," Leslie and AJ said simultaneously.

"But what if grave robbers find it? Wouldn't we want to take this back to the archaeologists?" asked Frederick.

"So are you a grave robber or an archaeologist?" AJ asked.

Sun spoke up quietly. "It may be a long time before anyone

else ever finds this place again. Who knows who will get here first?"

"Please, I'd prefer it stays where we found it," Miguel said.

"Then I say we put it back," Leslie said. It reminded her of the many times she had found artifacts in remote regions. She had taken photos just for her memories, then left the items where they were.

Frederick took another minute to look at the surface of the statue, then together Leslie and Frederick lowered it back into its hiding place.

"Help me, Devan. Please," AJ said as she grabbed the edge of the stone top. The two of them lifted it on top of the base and slid it until it clicked into place.

Leslie checked underneath the table. "There's no visible seam. Unless someone else knocks into it, they'd think it was a solid piece."

AJ smiled. "Good."

The group went back to looking at the niches and a few markings on the walls. The wind whistled past the door, bringing with it a scent of flowers. Leslie had seen enough. She made her way outside; the wind was blowing harder, but the warmth felt good after the cool darkness of the pyramid. On her way down, she paused to inspect large, drooping purple flowers that clung to the side of the pyramid. From this vantage point, she could see the myriad of purple, yellow, and white flowers scattered on the pyramid and grounds.

"Well," Sun said as he stepped outside of the temple entrance, "let's get down and have some lunch." He sprinted down the steps, scaring Leslie as he came running close by. She watched as he made it to the bottom in record time.

She wondered if Sun had a death wish, or maybe he was just foolhardy. "Miguel." He paused on his way passing her.

"Maybe your brother needs someone to talk to. He doesn't look, well completely sane. He also looks a bit upset."

Miguel nodded. "I'll talk to him. Thanks."

The others were coming out of the entrance and slowly making their way down.

Sun waited at the bottom until they were all together. "You might all want to grab your things. We're going into the regrowth of the jungle between here and the second pyramid. We won't have to deal with mud, but it will be a hike."

"Oh," Samantha said as she stumbled over something. She reached down and picked up a long piece of brass colored metal. One end was a large, thin crescent shape. The other end was a smaller crescent and attached to the center by a thin, ornate piece of metal.

"What is this, Sun?" she asked, holding it up higher.

Sun snatched a huge leaf from a nearby plant and opened his hand for Samantha to drop the item into. "Pretend you were a priest and you had to make a sacrifice." He clasped an imaginary sacrifice in front of him and wrenched the larger crescent up and away from him as if cutting a throat. "Very sharp, even now." He held the leaf up and brushed it with the crescent. It left the leaf cleaved in the middle.

"The marking in the middle is the face of their god." He raised the metal next to his face making a grimace that matched the image. "Any resemblance?" Sun didn't wait for an answer but threw the knife far into the jungle.

"What I don't understand is how is this clearing still here? If Spafford was the last person to have this area cleared, why is it still clear. Shouldn't the jungle have reclaimed this place?" asked Frederick.

Miguel answered, "Since Spafford and his men cleared away the trees, the local tribes move through here and use it as a place to worship their gods. They dance and sacrifice here."

"Sacrifice? What do they sacrifice?" Jessup asked.

"Animals. The tribes don't sacrifice humans anymore. The tribes have grown so small, and life is so hard, they can't afford to sacrifice anyone. Unless it's an enemy, but there's very few of them, as well."

Leslie wondered if perhaps the sacrificial knife wasn't quite so old. As she gathered her bag, she turned to AJ. Softly so that only AJ could hear her, she said, "AJ, earlier, did you see, well I don't know what to call it?"

AJ nodded. "I would say it's the magic of this land. The people who lived here felt strongly about what they built."

Leslie was intrigued by the idea that a land could hold magic. However, she was more worried about the size of the cave she had seen in the vision. Just the entrance had appeared immense. If the vision was true and the cave was immense, it didn't make Leslie feel better.

The call of a bird came from above. A hulking black vulture flew in a wide circle overhead, its shadow crossing over them.

25

TREASURE PYRAMID

W hile waiting for everyone to grab their things, Leslie rested back on a smooth tree to take a photo of a toucan. Even with its bright colors and long beak, it was almost hidden in the foliage, but she could easily hear it squawking.

"I wouldn't lean on this particular kind of tree," Sun said and motioned her forward. Leslie moved away.

"The priests would use these types of trees for punishment. Men had many wives, but if a woman were with more than one man, they would tie her to this kind of tree." He rapped on it a few times with his knuckles and stepped back. AJ, Frederick, Jessup, Samantha, and Devon joined to watch.

She hadn't noticed the tiny holes that riddled the tree. Small, red ants began pouring out by the hundreds. Within minutes they covered the surface and were fanning out to cover every limb and leaf. Everyone took a few steps back.

Devan whistled. "Those are fire ants. When I was a kid, I was standing in a fire ant hole back in Georgia. Didn't realize it until my feet were covered. Most painful bites I ever went through."

"Well, just in case you want to know," Miguel added, "The most painful insect is the bullet ant. It lives here in the Amazon and has a sting that rivals that of a bullet wound. It's about the size of your finger. They prefer hunting small frogs, but do be careful if you're reaching for a tree or a branch that you're not grabbing a bullet ant."

Sun turned toward the jungle. "Follow me. Time to see the second pyramid."

Everyone gave the tree a wide berth; the ants were still swarming. Leslie followed behind Sun and Miguel, feeling as if she should keep her hands in her pockets and looking at every tree and trying to tell the difference in which trees had ants.

"Damn it." She stumbled on a branch. She found it hard to believe that most of the jungle they walked in was once clear-cut, even if it had been a hundred years ago. Although, when she looked up to the sky she could tell the trees weren't as towering as she had seen near the river. But looking down, the ground was just as treacherous.

They soon approached a facade of stone. The steps were covered with moss, vines, and flowers.

"This is a building?" asked Frederick.

Sun nodded. "They all look like this until they're cleaned up."

"I don't see an entrance," Leslie said.

"It's up here," Sun said and walked up a few paces and pulled out a moss-covered rock. The sounds of roots breaking and rocks scraping were accompanied by two doors slowly swinging open.

Miguel had his hands on his hips. "And why didn't I know this?"

Sun turned toward Miguel. "I met with a local; he told me everything. He's the reason why I know the name of this place. He should be here when we exit and you'll have a chance to meet him."

"I think I'll be right here," said Frederick. He moved down and away from the entrance and sat.

"We'll be back in an hour," said Sun.

"Frederick, are you sure?" asked Samantha.

Frederick pulled off his glasses and cleaned them. "I'm sure Samantha. I just don't like, well, there's only so much adventure I can take in one day. AJ, please be careful in there."

AJ nodded in his direction.

Everyone was pulling out their flashlights. Leslie put on her head-lamp and grabbed the flashlight. She waved Devan through in front of her; again, she wanted to go in last and not have anyone behind her, wanting her to rush in.

She was surprised to find that the entrance led to a dark, downward staircase. Before she followed, she stepped back from the entrance, went to the rock that was currently out of place after Sun pulled on it and wrapped her handkerchief around it.

"Frederick, just in case this door closes, this is the rock to pull."

He had his handkerchief out, wiping the sweat off of his brow. He nodded. "Understood."

She made her way down the stairs, echoes of voices reaching her from below. When she reached the bottom, she leaned against one of the walls and thought "Glow."

It had been worth a try, but the cave was still dark. Sun was at the far end, at least a hundred feet away, and the dismal light from the flashlight and the headlamp did a poor job of illuminating even a fraction of the space.

Leslie focused her light on the ceiling and smiled. There

were no stalactites here, just a jutting, rough ceiling that extended high above them.

Everyone was following Sun, their echoes of conversation making the room sound strange.

"Leslie." The grip on her arm made her jump.

She turned, her headlamp shining in Devan's face. "Devan. You scared me." She moved the lamp from shining in his eyes.

"Well, you didn't answer."

"I was taking in the scenery." She panned her flashlight around again.

"Well, Sun is getting antsy to keep moving; has a room he wants to show us," Devan said.

She followed Devan to the other end of the cave. A set of carved stone steps led up. They made it up fifteen steps when they found Samantha sitting down, leaning on the cold stone wall, face down in her hands.

"Samantha?" Devan asked.

Her voice came out chokingly. "I looked over the edge. There's no railing here. I could just fall over into. . ." she took a hiccuped breath, ". . . an abyss."

Devan knelt down. "I can help you."

Leslie assessed the narrow width of the stairs. There was no way around Samantha. Either they helped her up, or they all needed to go back down.

"How?" Samantha asked.

"You lean against the wall; I'll stand close. If anyone falls, it will be me."

"Oh. I wouldn't want you to get hurt." She stood. "I'll try."

"Don't look over the edge. Stay focused on each step," Leslie said.

"It doesn't scare you?" asked Samantha.

"No. I'd have to say I've been on narrower ledges than this," Leslie replied. Which was true. The narrow passages high in the Andes mountains were barely a foot wide. She had also been on knife-edge mountain trails.

"Really?" Samantha stood and carefully turned. Her left hand on the wall and her right clutching her flashlight she went step by step, very slowly.

Devan kept his hands on her back. "Leslie told me once about one of her first trips with a group in the Grand Canyon. They had only a five-inch wide path in places."

It hadn't been quite that thin, but luckily he left the part out where a donkey had lost its footing and dropped over the edge and sadly died seventy-five feet below.

Leslie looked around while Samantha edged forward. She had to admit the drop from the steps seemed pretty intense. Not only were they moving up, but with each step, the bottom of the cave was dropping down. She figured there had to be a thirty-foot difference already.

On the wall that Samantha was clinging to, up above their heads, the stone had been chipped away to create a ledge. Leslie wondered what it was and reached into it. She could feel water running through her hands and a smooth surface of the indentation. To the left, it went up to the top of the entrance of the cave and disappeared; the other direction it went around the corner, ahead of them. Another piece of the extensive drainage system, she figured. When they rounded the corner, Samantha let out a sigh of relief. It was a top landing that opened into a tunnel. There was no sign of the rest of the group, but there was nowhere to go but follow the tunnel ahead of them.

The waterway was now below eye level, still on their left side. Something gleamed under the water. Leslie reached in and pulled out a tiny, gold, frog-shaped idol. She appreciated the smooth lines and then dropped it back in.

They had moved fifty feet into the darkness when they

heard voices and saw light moving in a room off of the hallway. Old wood doors were open.

Inside, everyone's flashlights were illuminating a hundred square foot room with shelves carved into the walls. Pots filled each shelf.

"What is this place?" asked Samantha.

Sun spread his arms wide, "This is a storage room. Because of the cold, they stored food items here."

Large jug-like pots were at one end of the room. Leslie walked up to a shelf and softly ran a hand over a pot decorated with colorful lines that looked like a maze. A thin film came off on her finger, showing the even brighter original color underneath.

Sun lifted down a plain pot from a shelf. "This is an older pot. They were smart; they didn't want to waste anything." He turned the inside of the pot towards the room so everyone could see the bands and zigzags of color inside.

"Amazing," Jessup said.

Sun nodded and carefully placed the pot back in its place.

"Look at the painting on this one," said Devan.

Leslie glanced at it but turned to see AJ admiring pots shaped like animals. One shallow pot was shaped like a turtle, another like a chicken. "I wonder if they put turtle meat in that one and chicken in the other?" Leslie asked as she took some photos.

"Leslie, have you done much research on these people who lived here?" AJ asked.

"A little, though mostly about the current culture."

"You should write about these people," AJ continued. "The Navajo have handed down their histories and traditions through word of mouth. These people never got that option. I have to wonder how much of their history they remember."

"That's a great idea." The image of the young girl in the

pink T-shirt passed through her mind. But would any of the remaining members still hold information about their history?

Leslie walked outside the room and dug her notebook out of her bag. She jotted down some notes.

Jessup headed toward the stairs. "If anybody is looking for me, I'm heading outside with Frederick. These old bones have to go sit down."

Preferring more exploring than walking back into the small room, Leslie walked farther into the tunnel. It appeared up ahead that it dead ended. There was a small, rough, natural-shaped opening that could have barely fit a person crawling through. Leslie got down on her knees and looked through. The irrigation channel continued along the one wall it as far as she could see.

Leslie stood up and turned, a flash of light surprising her. She panned her flashlight back. Something was tucked inside a narrow crevice in the wall. On closer inspection, she found it was a gold disk. It was tall, almost her height, and the same width. She could just stick her hand inside the crevice and run it over the surface. It was covered with symbols.

In the crevice above the disk was a tiny, natural shelf. It held a few idols and one of the ceremonial knives that Sun had shown earlier, all in gold.

It was tucked away as if someone had tried to hide it. "Anything down there to see?" Devan called down the tunnel.

Leslie walked towards him, "There's a tiny opening, hardly enough for a person. They carved the waterway through there, so it keeps going. I'd say this is the end of the tunnel though."

She figured some secrets were meant to be kept.

26

SUN'S ESCAPE

"Sun, is there anything to see in the big cave?" Leslie asked as everyone waited at the bottom of the steps for Samantha and AJ.

He shrugged while he watched Samantha scoot down the stairs on her backside. "Not really."

"I'd like to just walk around a little if that's alright. I'll be out soon."

"No problem. Leslie, what is she doing?" He pointed at Samantha.

"She's afraid of falling."

"Oh."

Leslie headed out to the back of the cave, the sound of footsteps behind her. "Devan, you don't have to follow."

"I want to. This has been interesting."

She moved forward until she found what she was looking for; the ledge for the waterway came out of the ceiling, about where she had found it above and it climbed down the wall at an angle. She followed it around the wide turn of the cave.

Around a few more turns the cave became smaller, only ten

feet wide and ten feet high, that's where she found where the water was going. There was a confluence of another waterway from the other direction. The two were being directed through four pieces of stone worked together, and she could hear the water rushing into the floor beneath them.

Next to them was a trapezoid doorway made from rock. Unlike the smooth, joined rocks at the other locations, this doorframe was made of small, uneven rocks with wide swaths of plaster in between.

"I was hoping for something more than this."

"Like?" asked Devan.

"I don't know. A magical water fountain, maybe," she jokingly suggested. "This is strange. And why a door in the middle of nowhere?"

Devan walked through the door and looked from the other side. "Nothing different over here."

Leslie peered through the door into the darkness beyond. "Looks like the cave goes a long way."

"You're not going to keep going, are you? Even I'm getting tired."

"No. I'd hate to keep everyone waiting." She took one last look around and joined Devan. Then it hit her: She had just explored a cave without even thinking about being nervous.

They climbed out of the pyramid, the sunlight not too blinding with it filtering through the trees.

Sun picked up the rock and unwrapped Leslie's handkerchief and pushed it back into place. The doors slowly closed together. He turned and said a few words in a foreign language. Leslie saw movement in the jungle. A dark-skinned local, with deep lines on his face, wearing nothing but a strip of fabric across his stomach and holding a spear, seemed to unfold from the surrounding trees.

Jessup stood up. "Was he here the whole time? I never heard anyone approach."

Miguel nodded. "Probably. The locals have a lot of experience hunting in these jungles. You have to be quiet if you're going to sneak up on a jaguar or a wild boar."

"Is he safe?" asked Samantha.

Sun nodded, "He's here on my request to speak with Miguel. I promised Miguel I would show him how I knew of so many things."

Sun spoke a few more words to the man and pointed at Miguel.

Miguel went over and started a conversation with the native.

"Miguel, when you're done, can you take everyone back? I'd like to take some time here." Sun said and walked into the jungle toward the other pyramid.

Miguel walked with the man as they talked, leading everyone out and Devan pulled closer to Leslie. "Leslie, I think we should talk."

"Now?"

"No, how about later? After we've had a chance to relax, come meet me at my cabin?"

Here it was, what she had expected. "OK." She might as well get it done with and find out what scheme he was up to.

27

SUN'S TRIP

Sun needed something to lift his spirits. He waited until he was hidden from view before disappearing and moving through the ether. He reached out to the world to find a place with positive energy. He found himself materializing on a park bench. Around him, people were dashing around and in the distance were tall buildings that were definitely not made by Inca hands.

It had been a long time since he had seen his wife, his light. She had just taken a human form on the day she was kidnapped, her powers not yet complete. If she had at least been able to communicate with him, he would have killed those men in their tracks. But once he realized she was gone and he couldn't find her, he made it so that even his own people couldn't find their way back to Hallpaquirao. His priests had packed what they could and left, realizing that something was wrong, especially as the trees and plants began to grow before their eyes.

Maybe he should just end it all, he thought. Everything. Forget the search for a successor, someone to carry on. The empire his people had built was gone, their DNA scattered to the four winds and so much culture lost. Although not all. He had seen it in Nauta and heard about it. But he wanted to leave something behind. He wanted to know that when he left this world that someone was crafting good things with what powers he could leave.

Meanwhile, testing them one at a time was becoming time-consuming. He needed to get this done faster. He didn't have the patience, and he didn't want to continue to live with this sadness. As a god, he knew he felt more than others. He knew his sadness was beyond measure to any other creature's suffering. He reined in his energy a bit, the clouds overhead had thickened, and the bushes with big red flowers had grown a few inches since he had arrived.

A young girl was walking by, her hand held by her mother. "Mom, I want to go back to the castle."

"Later honey," she told her.

"But I want to see the princess again."

"Later."

Sun looked over at the structure that apparently was a castle. It was tall, almost as tall as his pyramid. He knew that a princess was a human equivalent to a god or something like it. He decided it was a sign. He would go to this castle and find the princess. Perhaps she would have some wise council, even though she was only a human.

He could appreciate this place. It seemed a good city. The grounds were green but trimmed and well-kept. Except, he could hear screams and strange noises in the distance. Perhaps that was where they kept captured warriors from other tribes. If so, there were many.

He found the castle to be a strange sort of building. Not a place to live because a large tunnel cut through the middle. There were several women standing near the opening, dressed in long, flowing robes. He chose to approach the one who looked the wisest. Her long black hair and simple garb spoke of strength.

"Are you the princess?"

"I'm Pocahontas. It is a pleasure to meet you." She spoke as if he should have known her name. She was obviously someone of importance.

"I'm having a crisis, and I need some council."

"Oh, you poor man." She tucked her arm through his arm in a familiar way and led him a short distance to a low stone wall. She sat and patted the space next to her.

He sat. "I'm the god Viracocha, and before I end my existence, I am compelled to find someone worthy of my powers."

"Oh, I get it. Method. Totally get it. I mean, yes, I understand."

He didn't know what "method" was but felt it wasn't important enough to ask. "I know there will be someone worthy in a group that I'm testing, but it's taking awhile, testing them one by one, and seeing how they react. I need to get it done quickly. Unfortunately, I do not have the power for time travel."

She nodded, "When you say 'test', well, can you just test the whole group at once?"

Sun thought about it for a moment, then stood and knelt for a second in front of the princess. "Wise councel. I know just how to test them all." He considered for a second, to test Pocahontas, but destiny told him that the person he was seeking was already in the group in Peru. "By sometime tomorrow, I should have my champion."

"So, are you writing a script?"

Sun knew the word, it was in his memory, but the question didn't make sense. He just shook his head and walked away. He moved through the crowds, feeling the positive energy and feeding off of it to make himself feel better. He approached a food vendor and ordered the same as the people in front of him: two hot dogs, a Coke, and a bag of cotton candy. He loved the hot dogs, especially with mustard, and the Coke was a strange sensation in his mouth. He didn't like the cotton candy though and handed it off to a child as he passed.

He had come up with a way to test everyone and in a way that would feel normal. He'd be able to keep an eye on all of them and give them a taste of power in a more controlled setting. He would have to play it normal for now, and "throw the switch" later. As soon as he had the opportunity, he would put his plans into action.

He turned a corner to hide from view and sent himself to Peru. He felt better now and could make it through the rest of the tour. He would find his champion through a trial of fire if he had to.

28

SIMON REVEALED

S imon woke in a bad mood. It had taken several days of rough road to get to the farm, and no matter how much stuffing used or work his maids did, there was no making his bed comfortable. He stood and stretched from the bed while Miranda brought his coffee to him straightaway.

He wished there was a way to get a mattress out to this remote farm, but that would mean a lot of bribes, delivery help, and work for his men while they had other things to do. In any case, he had to keep this farm going for just two years to reap the full rewards of the coca fields; then he'd abandon it and take his money with him. If he didn't want the money so badly, he'd burn it all down today, along with all of the employees who he kept here to run his house and work the farm. He hated this house and all the buildings on the property. It was so primitive like everything in this part of Peru, except his own modern house back near Nauta. He missed the crisp straight lines of his home.

He drank down the first cup of coffee. "Miranda!" She appeared, coffee pot in hand. At least she could make a decent cup of coffee over a fire, one of the reasons he had hired her. The power from the generators had to deal with processing the coca, not amenities.

Fernando entered the room. "Simon, Stevens is here."

Simon nodded. "I'll be out shortly. I'll need you and one of the men at the special tree."

"We'll be there," he responded and then disappeared into the next room.

Simon put on his shorts, polo shirt, and shoes. The heat would be sweltering today, so he had to keep it cool. He walked into the next room, really just another small building connected by a small round hallway. The best his indigenous builders could come up with.

Stevens jumped up from one of the wicker chairs the second Simon walked in. "Simon, why are we out here? Couldn't we have met in town? It took over a day to get here!" asked Stevens, his long gray hair slicked back. Steel gray eyes were hidden by his dark sunglasses and his forehead looked high with its receding hairline.

"I have something I'm keeping an eye on out here," Simon said. "Now, let's take a walk." He normally liked Americans, especially ones who had helped him in one way or another. But not this time.

Stevens continued his tirade. "Well, I tell you, that road was atrocious. So much mud and holes, it's a wonder your men can make it here." He was shaking his head, following Simon down the steps and onto the jungle trail.

"The road was difficult to build and has to stay rough to make sure no one follows my Jeeps into this terrain."

"Hey man, I appreciate the chance to come out here and see the facility, but" Stevens stepped into mud that splashed onto his black pants. "couldn't someone have warned me about the mud? I'm wearing my good leather shoes. Let's turn around and go back where it's dry."

"Not yet, we're almost there."

"Where?" Stevens looked up ahead and stopped when he saw Simon's men standing on either side of the trail. "What's going on?"

Simon stopped next to his men, then turned to look back at Stevens.

His men moved quickly, grabbing Stevens by each arm. Stevens walked with them without fighting. "What's going on?"

"I simply expect you to tell me something. A DEA agent is somewhere here in Peru and has been sniffing around. His name and a description would be sufficient."

"Why would I know anything about that?"

"I have it on good authority that you've been talking."

Now Stevens started to struggle against his men. "No, man, you've got it all wrong. You know I'd never mess up a good deal."

Fernando wrapped a rope around Stevens' hands; the other man tied a rope around his legs. "Look, Simon, I don't know anything."

"Really? Then when you were arrested recently, why were the charges dropped? Don't you know I have friends every-where?" Simon asked.

His sunglasses fell off as the men pushed him back. His eyes were wide.

Simon had known Stevens for many years. He could tell from the vacant look in Stevens' face that he couldn't think of a good answer.

Stevens stopped struggling as the men tied him to the tree. "Stevens, have you heard how they tortured women for infi-delity in the old ways?"

"No, but I figure you're going to tell me."

Simon smiled and tapped his gold ring on the tree, enjoying the surprising solid echo. He waited until the fire ants crowded onto Stevens and begun to find skin.

Stevens shrieked.

Simon nodded at Fernando. "If he talks, report back to me."

"If he does, do we cut him down?" Fernando asked.

"I know he was the one who was working with the authorities, so whether he talks or not, leave him there." He walked back up the trail, sidestepping the mud pools, then closed the door on the screams. "Miranda, start up the generator."

She jumped a little at the sound of Stevens' screams but only nodded and disappeared into the next room.

At the hum of the generator, he went to the small table, woke up his computer, and activated the GPS program. Leslie's compact was still sending out a good signal. It appeared that the Toy was stationary and fairly close to the farm.

As soon as Fernando was done, he'd send him out with some men to the river to find the ship. If they couldn't stop John, maybe they could take the ship and use it for their own purposes. Unfortunately, he didn't see a way of keeping Leslie out of harm if her group spotted the farm. That would put this whole operation in jeopardy.

This situation was all John's fault for putting her in this danger. Simon slammed his fist on the table. There might be no way to ensure the young woman's safety now. Plus, he'd have to put safety nets in place to make sure no one escaped.

He'd have a man plant an idea into the small band of locals that any visitors were only looking into the land and that their intention was to kick the locals out and burn down the forest. That way, if anyone escaped Simon's men, they would not escape the villagers.

29

DEVAN'S SCHEME

Leslie put on a pair of jeans, flip-flops, and a tank top for dinner with Devan. She was sure he'd be dressed to the nines, but she wanted to be comfortable after such a long day of hiking. She picked up the book that Samantha had handed her when they had come back from the hike. The Title: *Peru before the Incas.* A thick, scientific book. She'd rather have Benedict's journal so she could read everything about his journey. What it must have been like in the jungle back then, she wondered.

Oh well, time to go hang out with an ex-boyfriend. On her way out, she realized it was starting to get dark outside and that a storm was approaching. The telltale thunderclouds were building all around them. She decided she should check on John to make sure he had arrived back safely. And maybe she was procrastinating, a little.

John wasn't in his cabin, so she made her way to the unauthorized door. This time, she figured he wouldn't mind if she was worried about him. She climbed up the ladder and came out into the hallway behind the bridge. She was relieved to see a figure bent over the instruments, writing something down on a pad of paper. Until she realized that it was Cesario.

As soon as he saw her, he shoved the paper into his pockets. "What are you doing here? You're not allowed."

"I'm just here to check on John. He went hiking, and I thought he'd be back by now."

"He's not back yet."

"Maybe we should go after him, make sure he's okay?"

Cesario shook his head. "If we left now, we'd get caught in the storm. Besides, I'm sure he'll be back soon. John's done a lot of backpacking in his day."

She figured he was right about the storm, she just hoped that John would get back before it hit, or she would head out as soon as the storm broke. She climbed back down the ladder and headed to Devan's cabin.

John was topmost on her mind when she knocked on Devan's door. When he opened it and showed her in, that changed. The bed had been moved back to make room for a table, complete with candles, two covered dishes, glasses of wine, and a vase with flowers. Even though the dishes were covered, the tasty scent of hot food filled the room.

"Whoa," Leslie said.

Devan smiled wide. "Glad you like it. I had to do a little wheeling and dealing to get this to happen."

"How did you convince Cesario to do this?" She said it jokingly.

"Ha, I'll have you know that I set this up with the captain since before the ship left."

He held out her chair, looking dashing in his dark blue suit.

"Thank you."

"You're welcome."

She didn't know what to talk about. She picked up the glass of wine and took a few sips, and was glad that he continued.

"I'm glad you agreed to come meet with me, Leslie. There are a couple of things I want to discuss with you."

"Okay," she said. She was ready for whatever he had to say.

He reached across and took her hand. "I wanted to tell you that I'm engaged."

"What?" Leslie pulled her hand back.

"Yes, to a wonderful woman. She owns the health club that I've been using."

"Engaged?"

"Yes. I hope you're not too disappointed. I was worried that my being here might have given you the wrong idea, especially since I was flirting with you the other night. That was a mistake on my part."

"Well, I was also pretty drunk," Leslie said. It was never easy to deal with the feelings for an ex, but in this case, she was okay. "This is great. How come you didn't bring her with you?"

"No way. She's not the outdoors type. I'm glad you're okay with it though. Now that that's covered, let's eat." He lifted the metal covers from their food. The scent of beef Wellington filled the small cabin. He had had Cesario make her favorite.

Leslie took a bite of the succulent beef and prosciutto wrapped in a puff pastry. Cesario had outdone himself; it was superb. Even a bite of the green beans, roasted and mixed with slivered almonds, was excellent.

"By the way," Devan continued, "you know that I'm smoothing the way for John so he can get some important materials exported out of Peru."

"Yes."

He put on his charming smile, and his voice had turned softer. Ah, here it is, she thought. The real reason for the dinner.

He continued, "You see, when we return on this trip, there will be a lot of press. The Peruvian government likes that, and they want to keep good press. Especially after the United States warned people to be on the lookout for possible kidnappings due to the recent scare in the Cuzco area. That warning scared away a lot of tourists and money."

"Uh, oh," she said.

"What?" he responded.

"You're using your politician tone with me. Which means I'm not going to like what I hear. How about I just say no now and save us the time."

"It's not that bad." He spoke faster now, "After we get back, we'd just like you to announce that you'll make a solo trip through the jungle."

"Jungle? Hmmm, bugs that carry malaria and other diseases, dangerous animals, heat, humidity, not to mention the toll this environment would take on equipment. Rotting boots, wet and sweaty clothes that would never dry, and talk about stinking after awhile. It would be amazing if I came out alive."

"You wouldn't have to go through all that, just make it look like you did it. Film sections of you in a jungle setting but having a great time." His charming smile was still glued on his face.

"Devan, are you asking me to put on a fake trip?"

She gripped her utensils, trying to decide where she was going to stick the fork. In lieu of getting arrested for forking a senator, she used it on the beef.

He glanced down at the table. Certainly he knew this wasn't going to work.

"Not fake as much as safe. I don't want you in danger. Remember that show we watched, that guy traversing the Amazon from beginning to end?

You were so mad about how he did it. You could do something like it, make it look a whole lot better. The world-famous

Leslie Kicklighter makes her way through the Amazon jungle. It would make great press.

You could announce it when we reach Nauta. So, you have some time to think about it."

"Devan, I don't do fake, and I don't camp in hot jungles." She stood to go.

"You haven't finished your dinner. At least stay for that."

"I've lost my appetite. Goodnight Devan." She moved to the door and thought better of it.

She approached the table, and Devan's face lit up. She almost hated to, but she lifted the cover onto her plate, grabbed the utensils and the plate and carried them with her to the door. "Thank you, Devan, for the great meal."

She was glad for this meet-up; she knew now more than ever that walking away from Devan was the best choice she had ever made.

30

VIRACOCHA STRIKES

Leslie balanced everything in her left hand while she opened the door to the observation deck. She sat cross-legged on the deck and started eating, a light wind cutting across the ship and the smell of ozone in the air. A tear rolled down her check, and she wiped it away. She knew she was feeling a weird mix of emotions- her sadness and disappointment in Devan, and her worry about John.

The thunderstorm was getting closer, the seconds between the flashes of light and thunder getting shorter. Somewhere in the jungle, she could hear a toucan calling.

Well, she thought, at least she had this great meal. She swallowed the last bite, almost sad to see it go. Then she hurried into the lounge to pour a glass of wine.

It was quiet tonight. Everyone had chosen to have their meals in their rooms and relax after their long day. Leslie was glad to have the lounge and the deck to herself.

She went back out and sipped the rich red wine. She looked out over the river. There was movement on the far side of the river and she was relieved to see John, walking quickly toward his inflatable canoe. Thank goodness, she thought, he was going to make it back in time.

She yawned, and the sound suddenly seemed loud. The sounds of the jungle had stopped. No toucan, bug, or anything was speaking. That's strange, she thought. She remembered how Spafford's journal had mentioned the lack of sound right before strange things had happened around them.

Leslie moved toward the door into the ship, but reflections of red sparks in the water drew her gaze up to the sky. She watched curiously as more red sparks flashed through the clouds. She had seen lightning travel from cloud to cloud before, but this looked different. Tiny red sparks were moving from place to place.

The red sparks began to come together and move down toward the boat. Was this what they called St. Elmo's fire?

The sparks coalesced into the outline of a man with a head, arms, and legs, standing on top of the cruiser just above the bridge. Leslie backed up to the edge of the deck and gripped the handrail. It felt real and solid. What she was seeing couldn't be real.

The vision had in its hand a glowing spear. It raised the spear in the air, and Leslie expected to hear the sound crack when it landed on the metal. Instead, there was no sound but twin sparks of red light were flung from both sides. They elongated and moved toward the back of the boat, snaking their way around until they met again.

All the light from the cruiser went out. The red sparks disappeared.

Leslie was left in the utter darkness of the Amazon.

Suddenly, the sounds of bugs, animals, amphibians re-established themselves and spoke from the jungle once again. The sound reassured her that some things were normal again.

"Normal," she said out loud to hear the sound of her voice. "What the hell around here is normal?"

She reached out her hands and walked in the direction of the door. Her eyes strained for even a pinpoint of light, but there was nothing. She slowed down when she felt she was near the door, but it took a few more tentative steps before her hands found glass. She felt around to find the handle.

She found plenty of noise inside the dark ship. She could hear voices down the hallway talking excitedly. She felt safer knowing that everyone sounded okay.

Then one of the snakes of red light rose from the floor below her, stopping her in her path. It came to head height. She swore it looked at her with small, glowing eyes. It lashed out toward her face, and she jumped. Her back against the door, she felt herself slip into blackness.

31

A NIGHT IN DARKNESS

John turned over the compress on Leslie's forehead and then went back to pacing. More than anything, they needed to get out of here, and here they were stuck with no power. Meanwhile, he wouldn't mention the danger they were in to anyone until they could do something about it. At least he had brought a couple of wind-up flashlights; they seemed to be the only things he could find that would work.

More than anything though, he wanted Leslie to wake up and be okay. Finding her on the floor of the lounge had his heart racing and his mind spinning. Had there been a strike of lightning? He checked again to make sure her chest was rising and falling and that she had a pulse. He had known lightning strikes to stop a person's heart. But she appeared to be fine other than being unconscious. She lay on his bed so still.

He could see a flashlight coming down the hallway toward his cabin.

Cesario poked his head in. "Any change?"

"No, she's still out cold. How's everyone?"

"So, everyone's okay. Although they're of course a bit

worried about getting out of here. They want to know the status of the ship."

"I know. I won't feel comfortable until I know Leslie is conscious. If there's no change in the next hour though, I'll do more investigation."

"Okay. It's starting to get hot in here."

"There isn't any air. I'd say suggest everyone go to the lounge. We can open the doors. And that way we can keep an eye on everyone. Plus, check to see if anyone else has some wind-up flashlights. We could use some more."

Cesario nodded and walked away. John could see the worry on his face. Damn it, he thought, this was not how this trip was supposed to go, his ship and all of these people in danger. If only he could get a message out.

He knew Leslie must have taken back her phone; it wasn't in his room anywhere. If they could find it, they could see if it worked. Although he didn't have much hope of that at this point.

The sound of stirring from the bed gave him a second of relief. Leslie was touching the cloth on her forehead. He flashed the light toward her face, looking for any other signs of injury.

Leslie raised her hand to block the light.

"Hey you," he said. "Where does it hurt?"

"What—" her words came out more like a croak. She cleared her throat.

"What happened?" He guessed that's what she was trying to say.

She nodded.

"Damned if I know. One minute everything was looking fine, the next my cruiser is disabled, and you're unconscious. Scared me, you know, and that doesn't happen often." He turned the rag over on her forehead again.

"I'm surprised that you're so concerned for your passengers," she said.

He smiled. "Only for ones that can sue me."

She smiled back.

"How do you feel?" he asked.

She took the compress off of her head and sat up. "I've got a tiny bit of a headache, but otherwise I'm fine. What did you make of that snake thing?"

"Snake. What snake?" he asked.

"The snake made of light that crawled around the ship."

"You must have hit your head harder than I thought." He sat down on the bed and ran the light over her face again. "Keep your eyes open. I need to see if you have a concussion."

"No, really. There was a strange red light, and then everything went dark."

He held his breath while shining the light in each eye and was happy to see everything was normal. "Your eyes look okay. I'm just going to do a quick check for any other damage. Let me know if you feel any pain." He brushed his hands over her head, putting equal, soft pressure all around her skull. "How bad is that headache?"

"Not too bad. I feel fine, other than my pride and my nerves."

He brought his hands to the back of her neck and looked into her eyes again. He felt a surge of heat through his hands from her body. He stood up and stepped away. He was not going to take advantage of this kind of situation.

"Come on, I'll walk you to your cabin. You wouldn't happen to have a wind-up flashlight, do you?"

"No, why?"

"A regular flashlight won't work. Everything with a battery is dead. The only flashlights we have working are the wind-ups, and we only have two of those."

He walked briskly out of the room and then paced in the hallway while Leslie moved slowly out of bed and gingerly joined him. He felt terrible about being brisk, so then he offered his hand to help steady her. She took it.

By the time they had reached her door, she was moving more smoothly.

"Could you check your satellite phone and let me know if it works?" he asked.

She stopped in mid-move and turned to give him an annoyed look. "Oh. My phone that you took off with?"

"Yes, and you then went into my cabin and took, I'm sure. I think we're even."

"Not really. This is my property, and I only went in your cabin when I heard it ringing." She pulled the phone from her luggage and sat on the bed, pushing buttons to attempt to turn it on.

"Look, I was just worried that you might be contacting Simon. He's done nothing but put up roadblocks for my project, and I can't pin it on him, but I think he was responsible for some sabotage to the ship early on. I just wanted to make sure he didn't know our location, especially when we were still close to the resort."

She looked up at him. In the dim light, he could see her eyes looking to the side and her mouth drawn into a frown, an expression he hadn't seen from her yet.

"Why didn't you tell me that before?" She asked.

"Why?"

"I called him from the Inca Resort phones. We talked for a little while. But I'm sure there's some logical explanation for some of his actions. As for the sabotage, if he was responsible for the sabotage maybe he doesn't want anyone to disturb the ruins?"

He shook his head. "I'm sure that his reasons have nothing

to do with morality or history." In fact, he knew why Simon had wanted to stop this trip— not that he was willing to share that yet. Then it occurred to him; what if this was sabotage from Simon and had nothing to do with the storm. He'd have to look at every circuit board and system on the ship to be sure.

Leslie was looking down at the phone and still trying to get it to turn on. "I don't think it's going to work." She looked back up at him. "We don't have any communication?"

He shook his head. "Not yet. I'm going to see if I can get something to work. I'll let you know. You might want to take some things and head to the lounge. That's where we're encouraging everyone to go. Once the storm passes, there will be moonlight. Do me a favor and try to stay awake for an hour. Let's just make sure it's not a concussion."

"Well, in that case, let me come with you. At least if we're talking, it will keep me awake."

"All right. Come on. Maybe I can put you to work." He watched to make sure she could walk steady. He wasn't a religious person, but he sent a prayer to the universe that somehow he could get this ship moving again.

32

BLUE FLAME

Leslie sat down in her cabin. Glad to relax after helping John for over an hour; searching through connections and circuits.

She was exhausted and so hot from the lack of air movement. She dug in her gear to find a flashlight. She flipped the switch. Nothing happened. Well, she had to try.

She grabbed her notebook, pen, and a pillow. In the hallway, a blue light was coming from the cracked door of AJ's cabin.

"AJ?" she called as she approached.

"Come on in," AJ answered, the blue glow dimming a little at the same time. AJ was sitting on the floor with various items spread around her. The blue light was coming from the lit candle sitting next to her.

Leslie smiled, "Thanks. What a crazy evening it's been."

"I'd agree. You spoke the other day of the strange light in the cave. I've had my own strange occurrence."

Leslie sat down opposite AJ. "Really? What was it?"

"Put your hand above the flame of the candle."

Leslie placed her hand well above the flame, not sure what to expect. She didn't feel any heat. She moved her hand down until she was almost touching the flame. "There's no heat."

AJ nodded. "That's not the only thing weird about it." AJ raised her palm up, and a blue flame grew from her hand. "That flame came from me. I didn't have any matches, and I wanted to light the candle, and then this flame happened."

Leslie took a step back. "Are you sure it's safe?"

"Yes. I've been experimenting with it." Among the items on the floor were a pair of reading glasses. She pointed at them. "I can't leave the flame on anything plastic, but it will stay on anything of wood and paper. And it won't move from one thing to another. It has to come from me. So there's no chance of this spreading."

"Amazing!" Leslie said. This weird circumstance made her nervous, but it seemed harmless enough. "It doesn't hurt?"

"No. My fingers are tingling, though." She wrapped her hands together, and the blue flame disappeared.

"Are you going to say this is something else we shouldn't question?" Leslie asked sincerely.

AJ sighed, her eyes gazing at the candle. "I would say that if I can still do that when I go home, I would question it. Right now, in this dark ship, I'm happy to be able to have a light."

"Okay. A little weird. But then I've never had a friend who could light a candle with their hands before."

AJ smiled and nodded. "Friend. I like that."

"Well, my friend, I was thinking of heading to the lounge, staying in there until they have things fixed. Care to join me?"

AJ stood up from the floor and carefully picked up the candle. "Okay. Leslie, I don't want anyone else to know about this."

"I understand." Although, Leslie wondered that if John could magically produce a blue dress, and AJ could produce a flame, maybe the others had had interesting and magical things happen.

The two women emerged into the lounge. Someone had found more candles and set them about the room. The door to the outside was propped open, but someone had placed a netting around it to keep out the mosquitos. At least the storm had brought some cool air that was keeping the lounge from getting too warm. Samantha, Devan, and Frederick were playing poker. Miguel was snoring in the corner, lying on the floor.

Devan stood at their arrival. "I told the captain you were pretty tough, Leslie."

"Did you speak to the captain? What is he doing to get us working again?" Frederick asked Leslie.

"He's down in the engine room. He and Jessup are doing their best, I'm sure," Leslie replied.

Frederick tossed his cards on the table. "I fold. I'm going to go see what they're doing."

"Frederick, you'd have a hard time finding your way there. Besides, the captain and Jessup know how this ship works. It's best to let them figure this out," Samantha said.

"And how do we know they are doing their best?" He picked up a candle. "I'll take this with me."

Frederick walked out of the room, extinguishing the candle with his speed. "Damn it." He came back, lit it on the wick of another candle, and headed back out, slower this time.

Leslie sat near another candle, AJ taking the chair near her. Leslie was too wired to sleep yet, so she started mapping out her articles about the trip. She wondered how or if she would broach the subjects of magic powers and gold.

Cesario came in, wiping his face on a towel, and walked to the dumbwaiter. "I don't have room in the refrigerator for this, and it's going to melt in this heat. If anyone wants chocolate ice cream cake, it's all yours. I also have decaf coffee."

"Hot coffee?" Leslie perked up, even if it was decaf.

"Yes. Nothing goes better with this cake."

Jessup came in, walked behind the bar, and ran some water into the sink, washing his face. "Whew, that was hot down there."

John plopped down on the couch and stared at the floor.

"Where's Frederick?" Asked Samantha.

Even in the dim light, Leslie could see John roll his eyes. "He's still down there. For some reason, he thinks he knows more than we do about engines and batteries."

"I guess no luck so far?" Devan asked.

"No." John's words were clipped and hard. "There's no juice in the batteries for the ship. Without it, we can't do anything."

"So what do we do?" Leslie asked.

He looked up at her. "For tonight, enjoy Cesario's coffee, play cards, and relax as much as we can in this heat. In the morning, we'll take another look. Maybe the daylight will shine a new light on the problem."

Jessup turned toward John, both of his hands were resting on the top of his head. He shook his head and arms. "John, nothing is going to work. Why don't you face that?"

"Because the alternatives are not looking very pretty right now."

Sun poked his head into the lounge. "Nice candle." He pointed to the candle with the blue flame. "I'll see you all in the morning. I'm sleeping in my room."

"What are the alternatives?" asked Devan.

John shook his head. "I'd rather leave those for the morning."

Everyone got quiet, chowing down on cake and coffee. After

they were done, they all seemed to silently agree it was time for bed.

Devan was considering the deck. "I wonder if I should sleep out there."

"The mosquitos would eat you alive," Leslie said.

He nodded and plopped down in a chair.

Jessup meandered to the stairs. "This body is too old to sleep on hard surfaces. I'll see you all in the morning."

Samantha claimed the couch as hers and then walked up to AJ's blue candle, wet her fingertips and reached out to snuff it.

"Wait!" Both Leslie and AJ called too late, the candle extinguished.

Luckily, the blue flame didn't seem to be dangerous.

"What?" Samantha pouted like she had been scolded. "I like the sound candles make when I put them out. That sizzle." She walked to another candle, looked defiantly at them and snuffed it out.

Frederick finally came in and found a spot on the floor. He had brought his own pillow too.

The moon shone brightly through the windows. Leslie wanted to close her eyes and go to sleep, but she was concerned about her nightmares. If she had one tonight, she would startle everyone awake.

From a chair next to her, John waved his hand and said softly, "Hey, you should go to sleep now. You might need a good rest before tomorrow. For tonight, don't worry."

Yeah right, easy for him to say. But then again, maybe it wasn't. She closed her eyes, turned on her side and drifted off to sleep.

33

RUDE AWAKENING

Leslie heard the sounds of the jungle and felt the softness of the bed under her. She was still at the resort. The ship hadn't even left yet. The breakdown had only been a dream. Except, when she opened her eyes she was lying on the thickly carpeted floor of the lounge, and the sounds were coming through the open door to the outside deck.

Soft snoring came from a few of the sleeping forms in the room. The morning sun was coming over the horizon, and a dense fog was wrapped around the trees. Even with the door open to the outside, the air was stale and felt too warm. Soon, the inside of the ship would be baking.

She grabbed her things and headed to her cabin. The small windows in the cruiser threw a little light to see by. She changed into some clean clothes, brushed her teeth, and headed back to the lounge.

Now, there was a flurry of activity. Everyone was helping Cesario move portable grills and food out onto the beach.

Soon, Cesario was serving up ice cream, grilled steaks, and a pot of coffee.

When John emerged from the ship, all attention moved to him.

"What are we going to do, John?" came the query from Jessup. "I know everyone here needs some answers."

John looked at the expectant faces around him. He sat and leaned his chin on his hand. The lines and dark circles under his eyes belied a hard morning. "Jessup is right. You all need answers. I can't say that I have any real ones. But I can say that we need to make plans to move out of here by this evening and get as far toward civilization as we can before nightfall. Whatever is wrong with this ship can't be fixed with what I have."

Samantha jumped up from her chair, her food dropping to the sand. "Can't be fixed? You mean we could be stuck here? I just, I just assumed we'd, well, that you'd be able to fix it." Her voice became more high pitched with each word.

Cesario dashed up to Samantha and put his arm around her and glared at John. "You've got to be kidding me! Walk, through this?" He pointed at the thick jungle. "I'm a cook. I don't hike."

John nodded and replied calmly. "This is the worst possible scenario. The one that was never supposed to happen. I know this is not right and that I promised you all something better, but this is the situation, and we just have to find a way to deal with it."

"So our options are either stay here or go through the jungle?" AJ asked. "How long would we have to be here before we could expect help?"

John shook his head. "Staying here isn't an option. No boat can make it this far upriver. There are no locals here to come to our rescue. There are some local tribes, but they have no way of getting us out of the jungle other than on foot. No one is going to realize that something is wrong for at least six days. Then there would be several more days before anyone would do anything about us being late. There's not enough food to last that long, especially without refrigeration."

"This is unacceptable." Frederick glared at John.

Leslie remembered saying just the other night, "I don't do jungle hikes." Sounded like she was going to eat those words. She looked over at Devan. Could he have fixed this? Forced them to make the trip? But certainly, he wouldn't do that. As if on cue, he spoke.

"Hike back through this?" Devan waved his hands toward the jungle.

Leslie rolled her eyes. Sure, he wouldn't want to hike through the jungle either.

Then Devan took a deep breath. "It does sound scary, but we need to all stay calm. I'm sure the captain knows what he's talking about. I'm no fan of hiking through all this either, but we need to stay together on this."

Cesario shook his head. His face was turning bright red. "So, we're supposed to just walk into the jungle and out the other side!" He stalked back to the ship and dashed up the gangplank.

John watched him go. "I'll talk to him in a minute."

AJ was quietly listening, her brows low. Leslie went up to her and whispered, "Don't worry, AJ. We'll get home."

AJ nodded.

Jessup spoke up. "Miguel, you and your brother have made the trip a few times. What are our chances of getting out of here to somewhere safe?"

Miguel took a slow sip of coffee. "My brother and I survive because we're cautious. If we can all keep our heads about us, we'll make it out of here."

"What do we do now?" Devan asked.

John stood up. "Right now, eat. I'll have Miguel and Leslie organize this move. And Sun, if he ever comes out of his cabin. Miguel, Leslie, I need to speak with you for a moment."

John turned to them as soon as they were inside the ship. "I want everyone to get a good breakfast, but then we need to get out of here."

"Why the rush?" asked Miguel

"Yesterday, I went across the river on an adventure of my own. I was curious about the lack of trees. Turns out it's a cocaine farm."

"This far out?" Miguel's voice reflected surprise.

John nodded. "And there could be more going on. I spotted several armed guards and a few Jeeps. Whoever's farm is out this far is doing one hell of a job trying to hide it. They're certainly not going to take kindly to anyone bringing news of it with them. I want to get out of here before they discover us."

Miguel nodded and headed back out the door.

Leslie decided to broach her concern. "John, I'm worried about AJ. Her feet are blistered with open sores. We're going to have to take special care getting her out of the jungle."

He reached out and touched her arm. "I'm sorry. I didn't realize she was injured. I'll make sure we have all the medical supplies that she might need. What about you? Are you okay?"

"I'm a little freaked out, but we have to do this. So, I'll calmly get all of these people ready to take a hike, and they'll never know that I'm worried or maybe a little scared."

He put a reassuring hand on her shoulder, and she knew she had an ally. Then he pulled her into him. She fell into the hug then felt a shock go through her when she kissed him softly.

He nodded. "I guess I'm going to have a problem with you."

Leslie took a deep breath to steady herself. "You're the one who started it."

"Yes." He finished off with a bear hug and then turned to go.

"Is it okay if that happens again?"

As he stepped down the hallway, he said, "Yes."

She'd look forward to that.

34

TRIBAL ANGER

Leslie headed toward the galley to see if there was anything else that needed to be taken outside. The sound of voices waved through the halls. She could easily recognize John's baritone and Cesario's anger. Without the air on, the ship was too quiet, and even whispers seemed to carry a long distance. By the time she got back outside, the discussion was continuing, and John had talked Cesario into joining in.

Jessup was addressing Frederick, loud enough so everyone could hear. "Let's say in six days; someone realizes we're overdue. They could send out a helicopter, but it would take at least another day for one to be brought into Nauta, then another day or two of searching before they found us. That's at least eight days."

"And what's wrong with that?" Frederick had stopped pacing, his eyes scowling. "We could wait here eight days."

Cesario shook his head and crossed his arms. "I don't think so. We only have food for only about three days. A lot less actually since the refrigerator is out. That food in there is going to spoil fast in this heat."

Leslie asked, "Cesario, if you figured in the nonperishable items, how many days of food do you think we have?"

Cesario thought a moment. "So, I'd say about two days, maybe two and a half. I guess we could stretch it to three if we forage a little."

Miguel stepped up. "I'd like to see everything we have Cesario. We may be able to stretch things out with a little with rationing."

Leslie turned to Miguel. "How many days do you think it will take us to get back to civilization?"

"There's a village, about three days hike from here."

"Three days, in the heat and jungle." Leslie decided to not address Frederick's interest in staying. "Let me tell you, everyone is going to need to pack as lightly as possible. Plus, we'll need to have room for everyone to carry food and water."

"What do you suggest?" Devan asked.

"We have a packing party," Leslie replied. "We lay out everything we plan to take. Throw out those things we don't need. Have Cesario with Miguel's input prep meals for the next three days, and portion it out for everyone. It's just like prepping for any other backpacking trip. The things we pack could save our lives, the things we don't need would just slow us down."

Miguel nodded. "Agreed. Everyone, once you're done with breakfast, grab the things you'll need. Bring them out here, and we'll go through the packs."

Cesario approached Miguel and Leslie and said in a whisper, "Miguel, there aren't headhunters out here, are there?"

Miguel nodded. "You mean cannibals known for taking the heads of their enemies and shrinking them? Yes, the Jivaro tribe lives in Peru and Ecuador Amazon. They're quite famous for their head-shrinking skills."

Leslie saw the panic in Cesario's eyes and quickly added, "But, even though we're a long distance away from a village, this isn't far enough in for them. Don't worry, Cesario; I don't think we'll get head-hunted."

Miguel nodded "Right." And Cesario's eyes lost some of their fear.

He walked away.

"Miguel, are you trying to frighten Cesario?"

Miguel looked down at his feet. "Well. I." He sighed and looked back up. "That was mean of me, but he's been pretty rude to me since I've been onboard. Then yesterday he cornered me and wanted to be all nice and asked me about gold. Samantha had told him about what we had found at the ruins. I have a feeling he's trying to figure out a way to get back here to the gold. If he stops being an ass, I promise I'll be nicer to him."

In the seconds it took her to nod at Miguel, she spotted a man standing in the jungle— and then he was gone. She whispered, "Miguel." She pointed in the direction of the man. "There was a native there. He was standing with a spear. Colorful headband."

"Sounds like a member of the Yora tribe. Sun and I have met them before. I'll be back." Miguel moved in that direction and disappeared into the jungle.

She watched as the last of the group, Samantha and Cesario moved into the ship, but her heart was pounding as Miguel disappeared behind the thick foliage. She practically held her breath until he came back through the jungle. However, the worry in his face was not comforting.

She walked out to meet him. "What happened?"

"It's the Yora tribe alright. But they're mad at us. He said that we must have done something terrible for Viracocha to strike us down."

"Viracocha?"

He nodded. "One of their ancient gods. I didn't even know they still believed in him. But he thinks Viracocha struck down our boat. I don't like this, Leslie. Contact with these tribes is tricky. They are superstitious and distrustful. Him thinking we're in disfavor with one of their gods puts us at odds with them. I tried to explain to him that it's just a problem with an engine, but he didn't seem to believe me."

"Will they harm us?" Leslie asked.

Miguel shook his head. "I don't think so. I think they expect their god to do more and are watching to see what it is."

"Where do they live?"

"The Yora are nomadic. They move throughout the remote areas of the jungle."

"Any more indigenous peoples we should worry about?"

He shook his head. "There's a tiny village, in between us and Nauta, but they are generally helpful. I hope that we don't have another freak storm or the Yora might take it as a sign. They might think that their god is asking them to take matters into their own hands."

"Great. This day just keeps getting better."

35

———

PACKING LIGHT

Leslie walked through the equipment that everyone had assembled. Boots, backpacks, lighters, candles, and other useful items were lined up. The smell of hamburgers and chicken barbecuing almost made it feel like a picnic.

She reluctantly walked over to the side where purple, pink, and blue were the predominant colors.

"Samantha, you can't take four pairs of shoes and matching hats." Samantha looked stricken.

"But these are all my good boots."

Leslie picked up the tan hiking boots with a four-inch heel. "I can't even believe they make something like this. But this pair is out." She picked up the matching tan hat. "If you wore these shoes you'd never get anywhere."

"I was going to wear those when we arrived in town. You know, make an impression."

"After several days in the jungle, I'm sure we'll all make an impression," AJ said as she re-wrapped her feet in duct tape.

Leslie set the high-heeled boots off to the side where other rejected items were piled up, like the bag of useless batteries found in Frederick's backpack. "These are out, Samantha. Now please, narrow this stuff down. One pair of boots to wear, and one hat to wear. You don't want to be carrying all of this, and we need room for everyone to carry food."

"Lunch is going to taste good after all the sweating and work we've done so far today," said AJ.

Leslie nodded and walked over to the grill, glancing at Samantha, who was holding her blue cowboy hat and her pink baseball cap. "Cesario, do we have a packable grill?"

He shook his head. "We're almost out of gas anyway. I will take the grill cover so I can use that over a fire to cook."

"And how's the food prep going?"

"Jessup's working on what I started. Everything's nonperishable, plus we have some fruit and vegetables that should make it at least for a day or two. I have some dry cheese and other items. He's digging through all of it now."

"Great, thanks."

John walked out of the cruiser carrying his gear to the pack pile.

"Are you sure we're going?" Frederick asked him.

John glanced over at Leslie. "Positive."

Earlier, the realization that everyone had to leave had somehow made Frederick less frantic. He had stopped pacing and had put his whole self into helping everyone pull out their equipment and search the ship for useful items. Leslie had been surprised to see him heft one of the grills outside earlier. For a writer, he was surprisingly strong.

Things seemed under control, so Leslie reluctantly headed inside the hot ship to her cabin. She needed to finish pulling together everything. She emptied out her purse and pulled out her wallet from the pile. She grabbed her makeup bag; the top was open and items spilled onto the bed. She stuffed everything back in. Did she need to take makeup? In a pile was her compact that she had nearly lost in Simon's car. It felt like meeting Simon had been months ago.

"Good job, getting this group in order," Devan said from the doorway.

Leslie tossed the makeup bag into the leave-behind pile. "Thanks. It kind of feels like that time I did the trek in Sweden. We did a repack the night before. Except then, no one was packing high-heeled hiking boots."

Devan let out his soft laugh. "I'm glad you're still talking to me."

"Well, I figure I have to put up with you for three more days, and then I can ignore you all I want."

"Ha, ha." He leaned against the door frame. "I'm betting you are going to thank me after all this."

Leslie stood and smiled, grabbing the door and closed it on him. "Not likely."

36

THE CHASE

John looked over the bridge for the last time with reluctance. The Toy was his life's work, and here it sat like a useless rock. At least his backup plan should be working, but it didn't help him and his guests right now. He wondered if there was a way to salvage her parts. Movement in the corner of his eye drew him away from the instruments to the windows. Across the river, he spotted three men in dark jungle gear and clothes pointing toward the boat and talking, their arms waving and their guns bouncing on their hips.

"Shit." He dashed down and out of the ship. He was relieved to see the gear was ready, lined up in perfect piles. Everyone was chowing down on the food that Cesario had cooked.

"No more time to eat," John boomed and immediately felt bad to see Samantha jump in her chair. "Sorry to be abrupt, but everyone drop what you have, and let's go."

"Why the rush, John?" asked Jessup as everyone looked at their food, Frederick ate faster. Leslie was the only one who got up, eating a drumstick while she walked to her pack.

"There's a group of men with guns, probably coming across the river soon. They are not friendlies."

"Are you sure? They could help get us out of here," said Samantha.

Frederick stood and shook his head. "No. Not out here. It has to be drug runners or drug growers. Let's go, everyone. A good reason to get out of here."

With Frederick's unexpected support, everyone else stood and went to get their gear.

John walked up to Leslie and Miguel.

Leslie began, "We were planning on walking along the beach of the river. It extends a few miles, then we could try and cross the river when we find a shallow area. Now, we'll have to start in the jungle."

John nodded, and Miguel moved toward the jungle. "Everyone, as soon as you have your gear, follow me in. Try to disturb the plants as little as possible."

Shit, John thought, how were they going to get through this jungle without leaving a trail? He'd have to take up the back with his gun close at hand, in case the men chose to follow them.

Everyone followed Miguel into the jungle, fighting back the plants. John waited, but Sun approached and rested his hand on his shoulder. "John, I'm sure you want to be in the back, but I have some techniques that should help mask our trail. Move on; I'll take up the back."

John felt strangely calmed by Sun's reassurance. "All right, but just yell if you need me."

Sun nodded.

John followed the rest of the group into the jungle. Frederick was just ahead of him.

"Frederick, did you bring your weapon?"

Frederick spoke over his shoulder while he pushed aside a

three-inch wide vine hanging in the way. "It's in my bag. You suspected that they were nearby all the time, didn't you? That's why you were insisting we leave."

"Yes."

"You could have told me." Frederick's voice was deep and serious.

"It's not like you could have phoned back to the DEA and told them anything. Besides, I've been wanting to keep everyone as calm and collected as possible. Until now."

John didn't want to talk anymore. He had to focus on pulling his feet out of the mud every step and getting past the plants without causing too much damage. It always seemed strange to him that many of the plants in the Amazon resembled houseplants. Here, in their overabundance, they were like piranhas, preying on other plants, and choking out the sun.

Perhaps their inhospitable nature would be enough to keep the armed men from following them.

37

SUN

Sun followed the group for a slow mile. When he felt it was far enough, he waited until they were out of sight and turned to the forest behind them. Even without trying to leave a trail, it was obvious they had come this way. There were broken branches everywhere and unmistakable deep boot prints in the mud.

He willed the trees and plants to regrow. He also willed the mud to boil, sending pockets of mud up to disguise the footprints. Then, he called to the wrath that was still within his power to command and set it moving through the jungle between them and the men with weapons.

If Simon's bandits came across the invisible wrath, they would think that the heat and humidity was sapping their strength. It wouldn't be until they were lying on their backs in exhaustion that they would realize they were dying. Too bad it wasn't night yet; the wrath would sap their strength within minutes.

Even more so than before, he could feel all of the energy

coming against this group of travelers. He would ensure that at least one would get out alive; the others, he wouldn't worry about. But first, he had to pick the one.

Soon.

38

THE JUNGLE

Leslie picked her foot up high to get over a vine, then bent her head a little to get under a limb. The line had started with a sense of urgency, but now that they had a couple of miles under their belt, everyone was moving more carefully and methodically and were tired.

Up ahead, Samantha's pink bedazzled boots sparkled. It happened whenever a ray of sunlight found rhinestones. She wondered how long before they would be covered in mud.

Every once and a while, a breeze would find its way into the trees. Unfortunately, all it would do was accentuate the feeling of wearing clothes that were damp with sweat.

"Ouch," AJ said, hitting her head on a limb. With a taller frame than anyone, AJ was having a hard time with some of the maneuvers. "This is like a human trying to fit into a hobbit house."

Leslie laughed, "Well when you're about six foot, I guess so."

"Maybe we should take a break? Jessup's fallen a bit behind."

Leslie stepped over a line of leaf-cutter ants and yelled toward Samantha, "Hey, ask Miguel if we can take a break."

When she and AJ caught up with the rest of the group, Miguel and Cesario were clearing out a small space for everyone to sit. Leslie sat down on the ground near a tree with bark that was covered in long, sharp thorns. Some of the thorns were as long as ten inches.

Jessup finally came through to the clearing, and not far behind him were Devan, Fred, John, and Sun. Jessup had fashioned a walking stick and was leaning on it.

Sun came over to the deadly looking tree. "See these thorns? These have been used by tribes in the jungle for centuries as darts." He pulled a six-inch spine off of the tree. "Gather some poison from frogs, and they had the perfect weapon." He pulled a large leaf off of a bush and rolled it up, and took a deep breath and blew. The dart flew across the small area and embedded itself in another tree. Cesario went to pull it out, but it didn't budge.

Leslie carefully pushed on a spine. She tried breaking one in half but succeeded only in it coming off the tree whole. "This is amazing. It would make a great fence too, to keep out predators or enemies."

Sun nodded, moving to pull out his canteen. "Exactly. Some of them were used for just that. Or grown so that enemies were forced to walk through them to their death. There are over twenty species of tree and bamboo in this jungle that have these spines. Some are more sharp and deadly than others."

"It sounds like your ancestors used the jungle wisely," said AJ.

Sun took a long drink from his canteen, then pointed at AJ. "Yes. Just think how they took a jungle and made it into a home. Using nature as a way to mold and guide their development. Much as your ancestors did."

"Such a strong civilization, and yet it didn't last," said Frederick.

Sun shrugged. "Nothing lasts forever."

Samantha shook her head. "This place is so much crazier than I thought. Caiman, piranha, trees; they all have teeth. What else in this jungle is deadly?"

Leslie couldn't help but think of other things with teeth, like snakes and jaguars.

"Take a seat, Jessup." AJ waived at the ground. He was the only one still standing.

He shook his head. "If I sit on the ground, it will take a crane to get me up. I'll just stand here, thanks. That's a good enough break for me right now."

Leslie walked over to Jessup, who was leaning heavily on his walking stick. She asked him quietly, "Jessup, are you doing okay? I know you wrestled an alligator the other day, but you're looking a bit thin."

"I'm doing just dandy. I'm getting a might thin, but I still have some muscle left on these old bones."

"Okay, just let me know if you need me to carry anything."

Jessup shook his head. "John offered too, and I'll tell you what I told him. The day I can't carry my own weight is the day that I give up on this world."

"Well, we don't want that to happen," Leslie said and squeezed his arm.

Movement behind Jessup caught her eye. She smiled and nodded at the scene behind him so he would turn and watch. Tiny, pint-sized, black monkeys were moving through the jungle, dropping out of a tree, making their way across the jungle floor, and then climbing out of sight again.

"I guess not everything here is deadly," Leslie said.

"Alright everyone, let's get going." John was putting his backpack on, and the rest of the group followed.

Devan fell in behind Leslie this time. "How are you doing, Leslie?"

"Well, I have a bruised shin, I feel like I've sweat buckets in the last hour, and I have a bug bite on my arm that won't stop itching. Still think I'm going to thank you when all this is over?"

"Yes. And I also think you'll agree to come to my wedding in June."

"Not likely. Devan. I'm curious. What do you get out of this bargain you have with John?"

"You being here, of course."

Leslie stopped and looked at him, deciding to take a stab at something she was suspecting. "And what about Cesario? What is it you're blackmailing him for?"

He wiped his forehead on his sleeve, then smiled. "Leslie. Blackmail is a terrible word to use in any company. I'm simply arranging for his help on something." He moved around Leslie and followed AJ on the trail.

Jessup wasn't far behind. Leslie waited until he caught up with her and then started slowly to keep pace with him. She wondered if she would find out what they were up to.

39

AN ANGRY GOD

The group made its way into an open area created by a few fallen trees. Above, clouds were forming for the evening's rain shower. Miguel was waiting for everyone. When John came up from behind, Miguel asked, "Should we take a break? We've been going for over an hour."

"Not yet. I'd like to cross the river first," John said.

"What the hell!" Cesario waved his fist at John. "I'm tired, damn it. We shouldn't have to keep going just because you screwed this up."

"Cece, that's rude," Samantha admonished.

Cesario was glaring at John. Leslie could practically see the wheels turning. Coming up with another insult, perhaps.

Leslie figured it was time to step in and throw her own punch. "So Cesario, I'm curious. How are you planning to come out to the pyramids? Hot-air balloon, or are you going to hike your way through the jungle?"

"What are you talking about? Why would I want to come back out here?"

"Cesario, don't play the fool with me. I saw you searching

for coordinates. Why? So you can come back, find the pyramids, and plunder them for what they have?"

The group was now watching the two of them. Sun had stopped hacking at the trail.

Cesario glanced around at everyone, then pointed at Leslie. "You're a liar."

Miguel shook his head. "She's not a liar, and I guess this is a good time to tell everyone that you were certainly asking me a lot of questions about the gold."

Cesario looked livid at Miguel and pointed a finger at him, opening his mouth, but Leslie wasn't done with him yet.

"Let's not get away from the point, Cesario. What is it you plan to do with those coordinates?"

Cesario was yelling now and glaring at everyone. "Like any of you care. You all have money to burn. Besides, the dead don't need gold. I do. And those pots that Samantha described could net me a pretty penny." Cesario came close to Leslie, pointing a finger in her face.

She was ready to spar again verbally but stopped when the silence enveloped the jungle. The only sound she could hear was her own breathing. The unnaturalness of it made her nervous; the memory of the last time it happened made her look around carefully.

Sun walked up to the group, glaring at Cesario. "This is true?"

From several feet away, Leslie could feel an intense heat coming from Sun.

"Look, don't worry about it. No one's going to miss that stuff." Cesario didn't even look at Sun, just waved at him as he continued to glare at Leslie.

Sun closed his eyes for a second. Leslie glanced around; no one seemed to realize that trouble was imminent; they all looked curious, not worried.

"And you!" Sun pointed a finger at Samantha. "You took something from the pyramid." His voice was growing in volume as if it was coming from giant speakers all around them.

"It was just a small thing." Samantha said meekly, her eyes wide. She pulled something from her pocket and held it out. A gold image of a frog sat on her hand.

It flew from her hand into Suns.

"You stupid humans." The voice came out deep and rumbling. Sun's body was expanding, filling up the small space.

Leslie stepped back, Cesario dashed a couple of steps back.

"I share my people's life with you. I share their mysteries, I give you a chance at greatness, and this is what you do? That it's all just so much gold and trinkets?"

Leslie stepped back, tripped and fell, landing on her side and her pack flying open. Everyone else was backing up too. AJ leaned forward to help her up, but the heat coming from Sun's expanding body made her throw her arm up in defense.

Leslie crawled backward, feeling something under her as she moved. She noticed that the sweat on her skin was steaming up into the air.

Sun looked down at Leslie, his eyes filled with contempt, and her heart thumped against her ribs. I'm about to die.

Then something sparkled in the heat, the squat statue of the woman, the one given to her for luck. The heat had hardened the eyes that now sparkled. Sun saw it too. He grabbed the statue with his platter-sized hand and cradled it. The heat from his expanding body stopped, and he began to shrink down to a normal size.

When he was down to normal size, he looked up at everyone. Tears were forming in his eyes but were turning to steam on his cheeks.

He pointed at Cesario. "You of all will pay. The rest of you. Death? I don't know if you deserve it, but I know none of you deserve the power." In the blink of an eye, he was gone, leaving scorched earth where he had been standing. Some of the branches overhead were smoldering.

Samantha dropped to her knees and started crying, "I didn't mean it." Frederick ran to her side and held her.

Leslie was still shaking; her skin was raw like sunburn. AJ and John crouched next to her.

"Are you okay?" Asked AJ.

"I don't know. I'm just trying to get my heart to stop pounding," Leslie said.

"Here." Jessup handed Leslie a canteen.

She sipped at the liquid. "So I guess we know who Viracocha is," Leslie said.

"Viracocha?" Jessup asked.

"Miguel says that some of the locals think we were struck down by their god, Viracocha." She nodded toward Miguel, who was staring at the spot from where Sun had disappeared.

"There's a problem with all of this," Jessup started. "Okay, there are quite a few problems. But he's been our friend for a long time. This explains why he's been a little different, but what happened to the real Sun?"

"Who cares!" Cesario screamed and pointed at Leslie. "This is all her fault." He had pulled a machete out of his pack. He stepped in her direction. "If she hadn't said anything, nothing would have happened."

Devan moved to stand in front of Leslie. John pulled out his own machete.

"Don't be ridiculous. I'm pretty sure it was your greed that did it," Devan said.

Cesario raised the machete, looking at Devan. "And you, you bastard." He swung at Devan and John parried it.

Devan kicked Cesario in the stomach, knocking him back a few steps.

Cesario moved forward again.

Frederick separated himself from Samantha and was holding a gun. "Stop where you are, Cesario. Put the machete down and step back."

Cesario stepped back and lowered the machete. He kept stepping back until he was on the edge of the clearing. Then he turned and ran. They heard the sound of him tripping, cursing and getting up to run again. A peel of thunder in the distance coincided with a blood-curdling scream from the direction Cesario had just gone.

40

RIVER CROSSING

The silence from the surrounding jungle ended. Birds and other creatures were singing again. The stunned silence within the group lasted a bit longer.

John stepped forward. "I'm going to go see if Cesario is all right."

"I'll come with you," Leslie said.

John nodded and helped her up. "Everyone else, just stay here. We'll be right back." He stopped to clap a hand on Miguel's shoulder. "Miguel, I'm sorry. Hopefully, we'll figure out what happened to your brother."

Miguel just shook his head.

Leslie and John made their way through the tangle of vines and limbs that Cesario had gone through. Up ahead, they spotted a wall of thick bamboo plants.

"Cesario?" John called.

She could see that John was talking to the figure of a man, standing among the bamboo.

"Oh my god!" Leslie exclaimed.

Cesario had made it only a few feet into the stand of plants.

It looked like he had stumbled headfirst onto the thorns that extended out of the bamboo. Several thorns were sticking out the back of his head, blood dripping down them and onto his pack.

John walked up and checked his pulse, although Leslie imagined there was no way he was still alive. "There's nothing." He pulled out his knife and carefully cut the straps of Cesario's backpack, lifting it off his back and stepping away. "We'll need the food he's carrying."

The movement was enough to loosen the spikes holding him up. Cesario's body slipped back and fell with a thunk.

Leslie jumped back from the body. Cesario's face was etched with a wild-eyed look and punctuated by holes in his forehead. John grabbed Leslie's hand and pulled her away from the body.

They walked back to the group. Jessup was inspecting the spot where Sun had burned a hole in the ground.

"Can you imagine how hot he must have been in order to do that?" Jessup said, fascinated.

"Cece?" Samantha asked as she saw them appear. Then looked horrified when she spotted his bag in John's hands.

"He's dead," said Leslie.

Overhead, the thunder peeled again.

John opened up his bag. "Get your rain gear on. I don't want us to stay here tonight." The downpour began as they threw on their gear.

John led the group with Jessup, both in a quiet conversation. Samantha cried, holding onto Frederick. AJ was keeping an eye on Miguel, who was still silent. Devan and Leslie brought up the rear. Leslie glanced back at the burned mass of plants, glad that she had survived the anger of a god.

It wasn't long before they reached the edge of the river. John led the way along the beach for a little while, then stopped.

"I know this is not going to be fun to do this while it's raining, but we need to get across the river. This looks like as good a spot as any."

A sandbar reached out across most of the river, leaving only a short stretch of water where they would have to get in the water. At least everything in their packs was wrapped in airtight bags, courtesy of the kitchen supplies. It occurred to Leslie that Cesario had been so helpful to get them all packed, and now he was lost to the jungle.

The river was uninviting. Leslie stuck her hand in the water. She couldn't see it. Too muddy.

"I'll go first," John said.

"Wait!" Samantha called. "What about caiman, or piranhas?"

John shook his head. "This part of the river is fairly shallow. Besides, don't believe the hype about piranha. These are small yellow fish that will not attack humans. The caiman, well, we'll have to keep an eye out. The water here is shallow enough for us to see them."

John walked carefully on the sandbar then stopped at the end. There were three feet between him and the other side of the river.

Leslie mentally crossed her fingers while he stepped out. He sunk down to his knees but made his way quickly to the other side. He turned and waved the others across.

One by one, they made it across. It was Leslie's turn. She hated the fact that it was raining. It created ripples in the water, making it impossible to see any movement in the water. Could caiman hide in three feet of water? Possibly.

She took a deep breath and stepped out into the water. It came up above her knees. She moved as quickly as she could through the sand. John reached out for her hand. She grabbed it, slipping a little, but one last struggle, and she made it up to the beach.

She sat down but looked around for any caiman. Luckily, they hadn't seen any yet. They just had to get Jessup and Miguel across.

She gasped when Jessup slipped on his way across and dipped into the water, but he swam across and made it fine.

Miguel, still looking stunned, but seemed to wake a little when he stepped into the water. His eyes looked more alive, and he was aware enough to grab John's hand.

Leslie realized she had been holding herself tense, worried about the crossing. Now she could relax a little. One obstacle down, yet how much more would they encounter?

41

RELEASING THE ENEMY

Sun held tightly to the idol. It was the only thing that kept him from killing all of the Toy's passengers. But that didn't mean he wasn't going to let loose the other gathering forces against the group. He felt like a jaguar, slowly dragging its prey into the trees before devouring it.

He moved through the ether the short distance to the house on the cocaine farm. He walked up to the house. A man sat on the steps, rolling a cigarette. He wore jungle gear and was carrying a rifle on his hip.

"Tell Simon that Sun is here to see him. I have some important information to share."

The guard gave him a quizzical look but picked up his radio. A second later, "Sir, Sun is here to see you. He says he has important information. Yes, sir."

Sun looked behind him at the vast cocaine fields that Simon had hidden here, deep in the forest. He wondered what it would be like to take the drug. His own people had their powerful narcotic, but as a god, he had never cared to use it. Maybe he'd find out before the end.

The guard led him up the wooden stairs and into the house. The house reminded him of the resort but on a smaller scale. Round buildings made from rough wood, tightly secured palm fronds for a roof, and several interconnected rooms to create a larger building.

Curious, Sun looked back through the layers of time. Simon had brought men here and made them work hard to cut down the forest. The house was built in a traditional style to make use of the materials at hand. Sun could see that several of the builder's bodies were buried in the middle of the field. If he wanted to give his powers to someone ruthless and cunning, he could certainly consider Simon.

Simon approached him with an outstretched hand. "Sun, good to see you again. Although I have to say I'm surprised. No one should be able to just walk up to this building without being stopped at the outskirts of the farm or shot, for that matter. How did you know of this place?"

Sun sat in the wicker chair. "John knows about it. We could all see it from the ship when it was in flight." He added the small lie to fan the flame of Simon's concern and anger. He could see the heat rising in his face. "John hasn't told anyone that it's you behind this, but he has figured out that you sabotaged him because you were worried about him finding this place. I know where the rest of the group from the Toy is located. I can give you their location. You should be able to reach them in the middle of the night if you would like."

Simon tapped his hand on his desk in rapid succession. "What would you like in return?"

Sun had to think about that. Was there anything that this man had that he wanted? His quick inventory revealed only things he could take for himself or things he would never want. Then he looked into the heart of Simon and saw lust and greed. He also saw something that surprised him. One of the old wraths of the deep jungle had touched this man and left a bit of madness behind. Eventually, Simon would succumb to the madness. "Nothing."

Simon's hand kept tapping, his gold ring clanging on the desk. "I happen to know your brother should be one of the passengers. You know what we'll do with them when we catch them, right?"

Sun nodded. "I'm under no illusions, Simon. Your cocaine fields have been known to me for a while. I have no interest in them. My brother . . ." —the mind he inhabited pulled up images of the past. Two young men exploring the world together, from bikes to canoes. He pushed those thoughts aside, Miguel was just another greedy human. "My brother and I are not on good terms. I'm fully aware of what will happen to him."

Simon stood and walked to a wall-size map of the Amazon, then turned back to Sun. "Too many deaths would cause a lot of questions. I don't suppose you know of a way to safely separate Leslie from the group? I'd like to take her separately, if possible."

Sun nodded. "That can be arranged."

42

NIGHTTIME

The group stumbled into an open space created by a tree that was far wider than any they had seen. The circumference was the size of a house. The roots reminded Leslie of the fins of a rocket, coming out from the tree up high and angling out to the ground. They continued to spread from the tree until they finally disappeared under brush and leaves.

John threw off his pack to the ground. "This looks like a good place to camp. Help me put up the tarp."

John, AJ, and Frederick worked on securing the top of the tarp to the tree. At the bottom edge, Leslie grabbed a rock and wrapped a corner of the tarp around it, then wrapped the rope around the bulge, securing it to a bush. The setup created the perfect cover with the fins of roots making tiny "rooms." The tarp didn't cover much space though; not everyone would fit under it.

Miguel watched but didn't venture to help or volunteer any information, so Leslie double-checked. "Miguel, this is safe, right? No ants or special animals are going to attack us here?"

"No. We're as safe here as anywhere. This is a strangler fig tree. No fire ants." His answer was remote and disinterested.

"Strangler?" Jessup asked. "What exactly does it strangle?"

Miguel shook his head. "Just plants. It starts off growing in the canopy, and its roots come down to the ground, growing around the host tree. Eventually, it takes all of the sunshine from the host, so the host dies, and the fig tree continues to grow."

Devan handed Leslie a pack of matches. "I'm thinking you're the best person to make us a fire."

Leslie glanced at Miguel. He had the most experience, but he wasn't able to handle anything right now. She looked around at the jungle, glistening with rain. "I'll see what I can do."

She looked for anything hanging from the trees that was still dry, collecting what she could. By the time she finished, the group was huddled under the tarp, waiting. The shock was still in play. The temperature was warm, but everyone needed the light of a fire before the sunshine disappeared and they were left in this dark, scary place.

Leslie piled up the driest pieces under the tarp. "John, I need the fire starter from Cesario's bag."

John pulled out the small, round tabs. "There are only two."

Leslie nodded. "We'll do what we can to keep this fire going all night. Then we use the last one tomorrow night if we haven't made the village yet."

John handed one to her. She picked a spot several feet away from the tarp and tree so that smoke wouldn't collect under it. She carefully piled up the tinder on and around it, leaving a little space for air. "Everyone. How about going around and gathering some wood. Find the driest you can," she said as they began to scatter.

At least she didn't have to worry about wind. It whistled through the tops of the trees, but in the rainforest, little if any reached the ground. She lit the match and set the tab on fire. The wood she had found started to smoke, but flames seemed to be beyond their ability. They were too wet.

She added her secret weapon that she had collected before leaving the ship. Paper soaked in wax was her go-to for rainy, wet wood. At least it hadn't failed yet. The flame on the tab was beginning to die, and the sun was quickly disappearing. She blew on the pile, giving the heat some more oxygen and was rewarded with a small flame.

By the time everyone had returned with their collections, she had the fire going. The smell of the smoke was comforting.

"Okay. Lets put some of these branches near the fire, so they dry a little before we put them on." Leslie moved some of the wood under the tarp and sat back. It was tough having people's morale in your hands.

"Jessup, you helped pack the food. Do you have an idea what we can do for dinner?" John asked.

Jessup nodded. "Spanish chorizo sausage with canned tomatoes and onions with some manchego cheese sprinkled on top." He waved at Frederick. "That's in Fred's pack."

Frederick bristled slightly at the shortened use of his name but moved to get the items.

Jessup went through the motions of cooking; Leslie was glad he assumed cooking duties. It didn't look like anyone else had the energy to do it. Surprisingly, Jessup pulled out a wine bottle from his pack. "I've been carrying this, and I think some of us could use a little wine after today." He uncorked it and handed plastic cups around.

It felt decadent, drinking red wine while sweaty and hot, during their mid-jungle escape. The vintage tasted of raspberries. It was slightly cool.

"Jessup, did you have ice in your pack with this?"

His sheepish look while he fussed over a pot answered

loudly. What else had anyone slipped into their packs when she hadn't been looking? All the energy expended to add extra pounds to his bag worried her, but she couldn't yell at him about it, especially as she sipped and enjoyed the fruits of his labors.

When Jessup handed out paper plates of food, she didn't feel hungry, but one bite of the sausage, and she couldn't stop eating.

Miguel spoke as he handed a plate of food to AJ, then picked up his own. "John, you knew those men by the river were up to no good. How did you know?"

"If you mean, did I know they are part of a drug cartel then yes. I went on my own hike yesterday and found a cocaine farm."

"This far out?" Miguel's eyebrows shot up. "That's a lot of resources someone had to use to get this far out into the jungle."

John nodded. "Not to mention they're on protected lands."

"Are we sure we want a fire?" Samantha asked. "Won't it help them find us?"

Miguel shook his head. "They'd have to be right on us to see our fire. Besides, I think they gave up. If they had been following, they would have caught up with us at the river crossing."

"If they reached the ship and realized we went into the forest, they probably don't think we'll survive, anyway," Frederick replied.

"Well, isn't that a positive thought?" Leslie answered.

"I don't mean it that way." Frederick rolled his eyes.

"What does this mean for us?" asked Devan.

"It means that someone could be following us, to make sure we don't know their secret. Maybe. But then if they were, you would think that they would have caught us by now."

John shook his head. "I don't think they'd be able to follow us." He explained about Sun's promise to mask their trail.

"Sounds like Sun was helping to cover our tracks. He must have known about the danger, maybe?" offered AJ.

"Well, he is a god," said Devan, shaking his head. "The man is a god."

Frederick took a big bite of dinner and swallowed it down with more wine. "We'll have to do shifts tonight, to keep an eye out for Sun or any intruders."

Jessup laughed, "and, exactly what are we supposed to do if a god comes calling?"

"Sun was our friend," AJ said. "Maybe he's not Miguel's brother or the same person you knew, Jessup, but the person I've gotten to know, although a bit quirky, was my friend. If he comes back, I say we just try to talk to him."

Jessup agreed to take the first watch, then everyone moved into the different sections created by the massive tree roots. Leslie laid out her blanket a few spaces away from where everyone was still gathered. She lay on her blanket and listened to the sounds of everyone moving around. The rain had stopped, but drips from the tree were plopping onto the tarp. She didn't say anything as John spread his blanket next to hers and stretched out. She rolled so her head was resting on his outstretched arm and she took his hand in hers.

"Sleep well," he said.

She didn't think she could but felt herself drifting off.

43
___

KIDNAP

Leslie awoke to the dark of night, the steady sound of rain on the tarp and the feeling of something small moving slowly up her back. She gasped and turned onto her back to squash the bug before it could crawl any further.

The pain that quickly spread in a line told her this was no easy bug to kill. She reached under her shirt and peeled the centipede off of her back. She tossed it in the direction of the fire. Standing up, Leslie turned on her flashlight and carefully looked around. There were no other centipedes close by, at least for the moment.

It didn't take long for the sting to become an itch. She could use some ointment from the first aid kit and maybe some painkillers.

Quietly, so as not to wake John, she dug into her bag. She grabbed her kit and her one item that she had felt guilty bringing, at first.

She walked to the end of the tarp where Devan was keeping watch over the fire.

She whispered, "Devan, can I get a little help? I need some cream on my back from a sting." She sat down in front of him.

"Ouch. I can see what you mean. That is a nasty red welt. Leslie, will you forgive me?" he asked as he applied the cream.

"Devan, I don't hold you responsible for, well most of this."

"That may be, but I'll hold myself responsible." Done, he tossed the cream into her kit and pulled her T-shirt carefully down.

It was a positive change to see Devan being a bit more down-to-earth.

He pointed at the book in her hand. "What's that?"

"It's a journal from Spafford. John loaned it to me. Spafford talks about his experiences in the jungle and his research on the local god, just before he disappeared. I'm hoping it might give me some insight into Sun." As Devan moved to sit back down Leslie waved him toward his bed. "Hey, go on to sleep. I'll keep watch for now."

He didn't argue but nodded and wearily walked away to his bed.

Leslie threw a log on the fire to brighten things up a little and moved so the light reflected onto the journal's pages. It was getting harder to read the words in the journal because Spafford's hands had started to shake toward the end.

THE DAYS here are long and hot. I can feel that every moment, every second the mettle of the man is being tested and stretched. My son seems to be holding his own here, better yet than many of my men.

The jungle is indeed testing me, I am sure, so I am hesitant to mention the strange things that have happened here lately. For the future reader might think that I've gone mad, and yet my men will vouch for the activities. In fact, some of the locals who carried our equipment have abandoned us.

First, it was the statue head of a snake that spooked them. Some spoke of a mad god on the trail of vengeance, although the translation could also be a god on the trail of the future. However, that, most certainly, wasn't the strangest incident.

Late last night, as I was drifting to sleep, an eerie silence enveloped the camp. I moved out from my tent. There came a sound-

LESLIE JUMPED at a shadow that crossed in front of her. Samantha was walking by, toilet paper in her hand, and clutching the gold purse to her chest. Maybe this wasn't the best time to read about scary incidents in the jungle, but it was too interesting not to continue.

THERE WAS a sound of screaming in the jungle. I had once heard a pig scream like that, as it was being skinned and came awake, the fool who had captured it had failed to kill it entirely before starting the skinning process. But that scream, it was the scream of something dying a horrible death. I couldn't tell if it was man or beast.

All of my men were out of their tents by then. I sent two men into the jungle to find the origin of the call. Those men never returned.

I prayed that it was indeed a beast, being hunted by a jaguar, perhaps. But the next day, several of the men were gone. Three more of the locals, and two of my men. Killed, or scared away? I couldn't say for sure. This leaves me with barely enough workers. Luckily we won't have much to carry back with us unless we find the treasure. We keep working, cleaning up the ruins to get a better look, and searching for a way into the pyramid. Meanwhile, I've persuaded one of the men to talk to me about this god they fear...

.   .   .

THE SHADOW of Samantha moved close by. Leslie wasn't sure how much time had passed since Samantha had walked away.

"Samantha, what is up with the purse? I know we agreed you wouldn't bring it, that it was just sentimental."

Samantha held it closer. "It's not my fault. I didn't bring it."

Leslie felt her eyebrow rise.

Samantha continued, "You know those powers you guys talked about, that Sun must have given us?"

Leslie nodded.

"I think it was that. I was so upset that my makeup wasn't holding up to this weather. Then when I looked in my backpack when we got here, not only did I have the purse, but it was filled with Armani and Dior makeup. There's even a Zadro mirror with a light."

Leslie noticed, in the dim light from the fire, that Samantha was in full makeup, carefully drawn eyebrows down to penciled-in lipstick. "Samantha, you realize no one here cares whether or not you wear makeup? You probably even look great without it. We're in the middle of the jungle."

She nodded, her brows knitted. "I know. And I almost was okay with that. But I haven't been in public without makeup since I was ten. It makes me feel stronger, if that makes sense."

"I get it," Leslie responded. "I'd probably feel the same way if I wore makeup starting at such a young age."

Samantha looked relieved. She went back to her bed, not far from the fire.

Jessup approached Leslie, favoring his right leg. "Interesting about those powers." He nodded toward Samantha.

"Have you had anything appear?"

He shook his head. "No. Maybe if I think real hard, I can get us rescued."

"I wish it would be that easy. But feel free to try."

"I'll take watch. I can't sleep right now anyway."

"How's the leg?"

"Hurts. I'm definitely too old for this."

Leslie nodded. She grabbed the book and kit. As she moved toward her bed, a fog suddenly enveloped her. She couldn't see what direction anything was. She knew she was moving the right direction for her sleeping space, so she slowly moved forward.

Stay calm, she thought, everyone is right here; I just need to find them again. She sighed in relief when her foot found the soft surface of her blanket. She knelt down, found her bag, and dropped her things in.

She still couldn't see anything around her, so she reached out to touch John, just to know she wasn't alone. All she found was the floor of the jungle. She moved out a little farther, just in case he had rolled out. Still nothing.

"John," she whispered, and the sound seemed to bounce back at her, like she was in a tiny room, all alone.

"Leslie," a man's whisper answered her, and she let out the breath she was holding.

She whispered back, "John, I'm so glad to hear your voice. This fog is insane."

A flashlight suddenly blinded her. "Hey," she was still whispering. Then she spoke up, "Hey! Get that flashlight out of my eyes."

The light came closer and lowered. "Leslie." came the man's voice again, "you must be quiet."

Leslie's heart beat faster as she realized it was Simon. Was this even real, or could they be getting rescued?

"We may be surrounded by villagers. We got word that you were out here and that the villagers think you all are American prospectors and they are bent on killing all of you to prevent them losing their village." Simon continued, "My men are here too. We're trying to get you out safely before the villagers can find you. Come with me."

"But what about everyone else?" Leslie replied, trying to peer through the fog.

Simon reached out for her hand. Leslie nodded at him. "I'll be right behind you."

"My men are taking care of them. Don't worry. But if we make any noise, we are sure to attract the villagers' attention."

Simon moved forward, the light from his flashlight doing nothing but bouncing back. She didn't know how he could walk so fast, not seeing exactly where he was going. Leslie glanced behind her, but all she could see was fog and the dim glow of the fire.

If Simon was right, they were surrounded by angry villagers. She couldn't risk yelling and putting her friends in danger. Or maybe, Jessup's wish for them all to be rescued was real. She focused on following Simon closely.

44

———

SUN'S DEBAUCHERY

Sun sat in the Jeep, directing Simon and the other vehicles that followed them to a location that would work for the attack. His anger at John and his group was beginning to wane, though. They were humans after all, given to weakness and errors.

Was his entire plan misguided? Did this world ever deserve his benevolence and help? He had given his own people two hundred years of good life. Perhaps that was all that was meant to be.

"Stop here," he said.

The Jeep came to a halt. Simon turned to him. "Which direction are they?"

"We're a couple of miles away."

"A couple of miles!"

The heat was rising in Sun's veins. The look he gave Simon quickly made the human step out of the Jeep to back away.

"Yes. A couple of miles. I won't tell you how, but Leslie will be brought closer, and you can walk her out safely. Afterwards, your men can move in and take care of the rest."

"Thank you," Simon said, slightly cowed, which satisfied Sun.

"Take the flashlight and head in that direction." He pointed into the jungle. "You will find her. Don't hesitate."

"I usually don't." Simon grabbed the flashlight and stalked away into the jungle.

Sun pulled a fog from the air into the camp and the surrounding miles of jungle. Then he warped the space around Leslie so that Simon could find her. He waited until he could see that Simon had indeed found her. Sun was satisfied that it had worked as planned.

It had been a slight challenge to come up with this use of his powers, but now he was bored. This really didn't interest him, and he didn't care what might happen now.

A memory of his beloved wife passed through his mind. He missed her, and his heart ached for her. Perhaps it was time for him to leave this world and forget his quest to find a worthy successor. However, he also wanted to explore more of the feelings, emotions, and sensations that this human body afforded him. If his wife were still alive, he would gladly make this a night to remember with her. He guiltily moved those thoughts to the side and focused on an ending that befitted a god. He knew he didn't belong but for a little longer in this new world.

HE PUSHED himself through the ether, back to Simon's farm, to the room with stacks of yellow wrapped bricks. He picked one up, its weight was heavy in his human hand. He took it with him into the ether to his next destination.

He reappeared at the restaurant's doorstep. The restaurant was dark, no light coming from the windows. Around him, the streets were quiet this early in the morning. Where would the women be at this time? He reached out and focused on Tabatha's and Terry's energies. He could feel that they weren't far away. He followed their energies to a decrepit looking building. The sign said Highway House Motel.

The door to their room was open, the light on. Tabatha's curvy figure was shadowy in the doorway. Sun felt the warmth in his body as he thought of the things they would do to each other before the light of day.

"Hey, Terry, it's Sun. Sun, what are you doing here at such an early hour?" Tabatha backed away from the door and waved him inside. She was wearing tight jeans and tight button-up shirt. Terry was sitting on the bed naked, Sun drunk in the beauty of her thin figure, and firm breasts.

He tossed the bag of cocaine on the bed,

Terry immediately grabbed it up. "Whoa!"

Tabatha shut the door. "Sun, I've wanted to get my hands on you the minute we met." Her smile wide, she wrapped her arms around his waist and tried to push him back toward the bed. He used his power to toss her carefully onto the bed instead.

She laughed. It was a light, happy laugh, and it made him like her even more.

Terry was still staring at the package. Sun pointed at it. "Let's get this started."

Terry leaped off of the bed with the package carefully in her hands.

Sun was curious about the process and went to follow Terry, but Tabatha kissed him. The sensation was one he hadn't felt in a long time. He closed his eyes and let her mouth softly envelop his. He kissed her back, and her mouth opened.

Tabatha jumped back. "Sun! I see where you get the name. Dude, you're hot. And I don't just mean in a sexy sense."

Sun brought his temperature down, then grabbed Tabatha's hand. He gave her enough power that her body could withstand his tendency to heat up. Terry grabbed his other hand and led him to the table with lines of white powder. He used that moment to infuse her with the energy and protection, too.

Terry snorted a line of powder into her nose. Tabatha followed suit. Sun raised a line of coke in the air and brought it to his nose, breathing it in.

"Whoa!" Terry said, looking at him.

"I'm mystical," he said.

Tabatha laughed and tried to push him toward the bed. She moved against the wall and pushed at him again. "Why won't you let me move you, mystical man?"

He shook his head. He was not one to be moved. He brushed his hands over her breasts. Then he was hit with a rush. A rush of knowing that he was a powerful god, that he could do anything he desired.

He split time into fragments so that each moment was farther apart. He wanted this pleasure to last as long as possible for all of them. Looking deep inside Tabatha's body, he increased her sensitivity to sensations. He could sense that Terry was more interested in watching, so he gave her a heightened sensitivity to the cocaine.

Terry laughed; it was the first time he had heard her laugh. She was genuinely happy. Sun was momentarily jarred at the sight of her as she floated by them, "I've never felt so light!"

He hadn't realized until now that they were floating. He obviously couldn't control everything in this state, but as long as the women were safe, that was all that mattered. He and Tabatha were still in a standing position only a few inches off the floor.

Tabatha's eyes were closed, her hands moving up her body. She started to unbutton her shirt, and Sun stopped her hands.

"No," he said, kissing her softly on the lips. "Let me do that."

As he reached for the top button, his hand brushed over her

breasts again. Her moan rolled through the room as the seconds stretched into what felt like minutes. He kissed her pale skin at each reveal, sending ribbons of sensation through Tabatha.

He could see Terry watching them and running her hands over her own body, moaning in the pleasure she found in watching them and in the drug.

At the last button, he let his tongue and lips explore the texture of the skin of her navel, her ribs, then found the soft, supple skin of a breast and a tight, hard nipple. A guttural growl released from his throat as he gently reached for the other breast, feeling the perfect softness of it in his hand, and used his thumb to caress her nipple.

"Oh!" Tabatha rolled her head back, causing them to spin slowly in midair. Wrapping his arms around her, he pulled her to him, kissing her softly on the mouth, exploring with his tongue when she opened up to him. She sucked on his tongue then backed away, then came back and ran the tip of her tongue along the top of his teeth. Capturing her tongue lightly with his lips, he leaned into her and kissed her hard. The growl came from deep in his chest. His heat was moving to his cock.

She reached for his belt, but he stopped her hands, again. "Not yet," he whispered.

Her frustrated sigh only made his heat rise. It took him a second to peel her shirt off. It floated away.

He stretched out his arm and let her drift away from him a little, their eyes locking in hunger. He turned her in the air and pulled her to him. Breathing in deeply at the back of her neck, he could smell a hint of perfume. He kissed the skin on her neck. Her perfume evaporated into steam. Now he could smell Tabatha's scent. Warm and floral. His breath quickened.

She wrapped her hands around his wrists and brushed his open hands up her body to her breasts. He thumbed her nipples until they peaked and she was moaning uncontrollably. Reaching down, he ran his hand over the zipper of her jeans down to where her heat was rising. Her jeans were tight, so he unzipped the threads woven together on the sides. The sudden freedom from the restrictive material, Tabatha caught her breath and shook for a long, fractured moment.

Sun could feel her release. He could also feel that she ached for him to be inside her. His cock was straining against the fabric of his jeans. He turned her toward him. His clothes were already singed in places; he raised his heat and let them burn the rest of the way off. The brief flames echoed in Tabatha's eyes. He loved that look in her eyes.

He pushed her gently to the wall. She wrapped her legs around him and with surprising strength pulled him to her. He plunged inside her deep, wet walls.

Her moans of ecstasy encouraged him to continue, starting with a slow, methodic rhythm.

"Faster. Please!" Tabatha screamed. He felt the heat rise all around them, and the bed below burst into flames.

He could feel her need, which matched his own. Soon they were shaking the walls in a staccato rhythm; their moans grew louder and louder until Tabatha came in a breathless, intense, wet orgasm. His release was immediate. The world exploded. The burst of the euphoria was more than he could handle.

HE AWOKE LYING on the floor in the smoldering remains of the bed. He felt everything. The guilt from losing his people and his wife, to guilt for leaving his new friends in the jungle at the hands of Simon. He felt white hot anger at Cesario and glee that he was dead. His body was squeezed of all its pleasure; a vibration that hummed inside of him. Terry was softly snoring next to him, her hands wrapped around the rest of the cocaine package. Tabatha was in a chair, watching him. The smoke from her cigarette was circling in front of scorched walls.

"Not tired enough to sleep?" she asked him. He shook his head.

"Anyone with that much blow has to have lots of money. Are you someone famous?"

He shook his head again. "I am not famous anymore." He remembered thinking earlier that he could be again, but that sounded too exhausting.

"Tell me about it."

And he did, he told Tabatha everything. About his rise to power, losing his wife to the Spanish, down to the idol that had fallen out of Leslie's bag and how it represented his lost love. The idol had fallen to the floor when his clothes had burned. He used his mind to bring it to him and held it gently.

"What's so special about this idol?" She came closer and looked at it as he cleaned soot from its facade.

His brow wrinkled at her question.

She waved her hand at him. "Okay. I know, it represents your wife, but why did you have such a reaction to seeing it?"

"Her likeness hasn't been seen in five hundred years."

"She didn't look like that, did she? A face of an owl?"

He shook his head. "It's a visual representation of her as a goddess. She was very much in touch with nature. Most animals, bugs, and other forms of nature bowed to her, just as she lifted up nature. It's very strange that this Leslie had it in her bag."

"Where did this Leslie get it?"

"I don't know."

"Dude!"

Her surprise made Sun stop twirling the idol.

She continued, "Something like that, you have to find out. Don't you?"

He considered her question. She could be right. But, what could it possibly mean? However, it might be an entertaining diversion.

His stomach rumbled. "Let's go get some food."

45

———————

FROM THE FRYING PAN

Simon led Leslie to a well-used Jeep parked on a rough, muddy pockmarked road.

"Get down in the back in case we run into anyone. I'm going to take us to a house. We'll be safe there. My men have orders to gather your friends and meet us there."

She got down but peeked out the back. She listened carefully to the jungle sounds but couldn't hear any people. Once the Jeep engine started, that was all she could hear. It was frustrating that she still couldn't see anything beyond the fog.

While Simon maneuvered through the mud and over ruts, Leslie thought of John. She hoped he had been rescued earlier and that's why she couldn't find him. "I didn't realize we were so close to a village."

"It's a small one, but the villagers are very wary of outsiders. At best, they would have chased you out by beating you, without much care to whether you made it out alive."

She thought about that as the trees passed by. This must have been the village Miguel had been getting them to. But

Miguel had passed through before; maybe if they recognized Miguel, the group would be okay.

The Jeep came to a stop. Simon cut off the engine and the lights. He led her to a small building, much like other local buildings: a circle of sturdy branches and a roof of palm fronds.

He took her inside. "Leslie, I'm so glad you're safe."

"Thank you, Simon. So much has happened in the last few days, it feels like I haven't seen you in forever."

He led her to a set of wicker chairs, then lit two candles sitting on a small table. She could see the place was sparse. On the other side of the room was only a small stove.

"I don't understand how you found us," Leslie said.

"Sun came to see me. He was worried about all of you and told us where you might be."

"Sun?" she asked. The image of his angry face flashed through her mind. "When was the last time you saw him?"

"Yesterday. I haven't seen him since then."

"That was nice of him to send us some help." She smiled up into Simon's face, but she knew Sun wouldn't do them a favor. Her heart was beating fast.

"So, did you find anything interesting out there?" he asked.

"Not really. A temple with a lot of dust. Although, their irrigation techniques were interesting."

"Nothing else?"

Did he know about the gold?

"Well?" He leaned in.

Or was he digging for information about the coca field? "I'm not sure what else to tell you. You had to be there. The ruins were intense."

He smiled and nodded, "Good. Good. I'm going to use the radio in the Jeep, check on my men, and see what's going on. Just stay right here, I'll be right back."

She nodded but leaped up when she heard a scraping at the

door. She pushed on it but it wouldn't budge. "Simon, what's wrong with this door?"

His voice moved quickly as his footsteps shuffled away. "Don't worry. It's just there for your protection. I'll be right back!"

There were no other doors and no windows. She wanted to kick herself for going inside. Instead, she kicked at the walls. The tall, thick branches were tightly packed and refused to budge. She peeked through a crack in the door. She could see that the sky was no longer an inky black, but was a deep blue. She couldn't spy Simon or the Jeep from this angle.

She might have a chance of getting through the roof, but there was no way to reach it. She could cut footholds into the walls, but that would take a lot of time. Probably much more time than she had before Simon walked back through the door. At least she felt Simon didn't mean her any harm. Right now. But what about the rest of the group?

She sat down. "What have I gotten myself into?"

46

TRIBAL RETURN

John ignored the poke he felt in his side, then finally decided it was important when he heard AJ call his name. Through the thick leaves above he could see a periwinkle sky, but from the north, a curl of towering clouds was coming.

"We have a problem," AJ said. "No one knows where Leslie is."

"What do you mean?" He sat up and looked next to him. Leslie's bed was gone, her bag, everything. He stood up, nearly knocking AJ over in his haste. "Sorry," he said. He glanced over at the fire. Jessup was hunched over the fire, stirring a pot.

"How long since anyone saw her?" John asked, hoping maybe she had gone off by herself at some point, although that didn't seem like something she would have done in the dark jungle.

"It's been a half an hour since I've been awake," AJ responded. "I noticed her bed wasn't next to you. I've walked around, and her things aren't anywhere nearby."

Frederick rolled up his blanket. "I've been awake for about an hour. I haven't seen her."

John threw on his rain jacket and grimaced at the tight muscles in his back. He looked again at the empty space next to his bedding and pictured her lying there. He had remembered her at the fire the last time he had drifted off to sleep.

"Who did guard duty after Leslie?" John asked.

Jessup stood up from his spot near the fire and raised his hand as if he were in a classroom. "I did. I took over for her. A crazy fog moved in about the same time. Maybe she got lost?"

John felt more panic rising and tried to suppress it. This meant that she had been gone since late last night.

John circled the campsite, trying to find a way that someone would have left. He passed their trail into the campsite and ignored it. Leslie had no reason to go back that way.

"Over here," Miguel said from the other side of the camp.

John ran over; AJ walked over to look as well.

"These branches are broken, and it looks like further on that there's a trail of sorts."

John followed it, and Devan and AJ were close behind. "You two don't need to come."

Devan answered, "John, I know you care about Leslie, but so do we. We want to help, so please let us help."

John turned without answering and let them continue. They hadn't gone far when he spotted two sets of prints in a deep pocket of mud. John backed away so Devan and AJ could see them.

"These are Leslie's," Devan said, pointing at the prints on the right. "I've followed her enough on this trip to recognize the imprint of her hiking boots."

John nodded. "The other prints look like wellies, too smooth to be hiking boots. None of us are wearing wellies."

"Leslie wouldn't have left the campsite on her own. Not without us," Devan said.

"I agree," John answered.

"But she was walking. She wasn't dragged. They must have held a gun to her for her to go with anyone," Devan said, his voice sounding more grave.

John shook his head. "We don't know that for sure. Stay calm, Devan."

Devan's brow wrinkled. "There's something else I didn't mention. I thought you'd all think I was insane. After the fog rolled in, I could have sworn I heard men talking, whispering. But it all stopped when the fog suddenly disappeared."

That didn't bode well for finding Leslie. They followed the trail, but it suddenly ended. There was no hint at another direction.

"What are we going to do?" AJ asked.

John hated to say it. "The only thing we can do right now. Go back and eat breakfast. Then figure out a way to get ourselves to safety, then find Leslie. We can't save her until we're safe."

As John made his way back to the campsite, he wondered if perhaps Leslie had been in cahoots with Simon. But that didn't make sense either. Then, he thought back to the way Simon had looked at her. He had met Simon at a party once, a beautiful, streamlined woman on his arm. He had looked at her like a prized ship. When he had found Simon and Leslie at the send-off party, Simon had looked at Leslie like something else altogether. But then, how else could anyone have found them unless Leslie had communicated with them? Once again, nothing made sense.

They walked into the campsite and were warned too late. Samantha, Frederick, Jessup, and Miguel were facing away from them, their arms in the air. A dark-skinned man in a ragged T-shirt, shorts, and bare feet was pointing a shotgun at Miguel.

The man holding the gun was talking excitedly in a language John didn't recognize. He had to assume it was Quechua, a local language. When he saw John, the man waved the gun at him, then back at Miguel.

John walked over, and kept his hands up.

Miguel was talking too, soothing sounds in the unknown language. He pointed at Samantha.

Miguel switched to English. "Samantha, do you have any autographed photos? I'm trying to convince him that we're a film crew. He's seen a TV set in Nauta once. I'm hoping we can convince him you're an actress."

Samantha stood up a little taller. "Well, of course, I'm an actress. I've got a photo right in here." She pointed at her gold purse.

The man pointed the gun at the purse. Samantha reached in and pulled out a glossy, publicity photo of herself. From his vantage point, John could see she was photographed in a black dress. The background was a poster for her first and last movie, Night of the Lepus.

Thunder peeled overhead. From seemingly out of nowhere, a Yora tribesman appeared in a bright headdress, thin loincloth and sandals walked up without a sound to the back of the villager, then smacked him hard in the head with the butt of his spear. The villager crumpled to the ground, the gun falling from his hands.

The tribesman shook his head, pointed at the collapsed man, and spoke to Miguel. Miguel put his hands down. Everyone else followed suit. The tribesman pointed to the sky, then walked away, disappearing into the jungle.

"What the hell just happened?" asked Frederick.

Miguel turned, a sheen of sweat clinging to his face and

neck. "The villager," he pointed at the man on the ground, "is convinced that we're here to steal land, kick him and his family out of here. I had almost convinced him we were a TV crew. Luckily, he's actually seen a TV once."

"Nartu, the Yaru tribesman—" he pointed in the direction the tribesman had gone, "says that their god isn't done with us yet, and this villager is interrupting the god's plan." Miguel walked to the fire and sat on the ground, wiping the sweat from his face on his sleeve. "I could use a drink."

Jessup handed Miguel a flask.

John pulled some rope out of his bag. "If one villager found us, more can't be far behind. We need to get packed and moving now. Everyone, let's get packed up."

"What about Leslie?" Devan asked.

John tied up the villager's hands, then tethered him to a tree. "I said it before. We've got to take care of ourselves."

"Oh," Miguel said and pointed east, "and Nartu said there's a road, not far that way. Made by the 'banana man,' whoever that is."

"So I'm guessing going to the village is out of our grand plan?" asked Devan.

Miguel nodded, then knocked back a drink.

John looked around while everyone scrambled to get things packed. He wished Leslie were here.

47

A CALCULATED FLIGHT

Leslie had no weapons, no way to fight her way out, and although Simon was being kind, she had a feeling he wasn't going to just let her go. He had given her his arm just a few days ago, and she had felt powerful muscles hiding under his shirt. She'd have to play it out until she could find a way out and make her way back to her friends.

There was a peel of thunder; then she heard the rhythm of footsteps in the mud outside. There was the scraping sound, then the door opened.

"Really? You had to lock me inside?" she said.

Sun walked in.

Leslie stood and stepped back. She held back her panic, taking deep breaths. She almost would have preferred it be Simon.

Sun seemed not to care though. He walked up close, grabbed one of the wicker chairs, and whipped it around to face her. Sitting down with a substantial weight.

Leslie gagged at the stench of locker room sweat that

permeated his being. She pulled her chair a little farther away until she could breathe untainted air.

Sun leaned back in his chair. From his pocket, he pulled out the statue. He rubbed it between his hands and let it go. It floated on the air over to Leslie. When it stopped rotating, its eyes stared at her.

She reached up and turned the eyes away.

"Tell me where you found this."

Leslie thought back to what felt like a year ago. "It was before we took off on the Toy. An old woman approached me. She gave me the statue and another package."

Suddenly, Leslie was transported to the beginning of the trip. The sun was shining, and she was out in the open. The boathouse was nearby, and she heard the old woman's voice.

"You. You come here."

Leslie walked over to the woman, but this time Sun was standing there, watching as the two of them talked and as the woman handed her the first package. Sun studied the woman's face up close.

Leslie wanted to step back, not to take the packages, but she seemed to be on remote. She couldn't turn away or change what had happened. She remembered the weird jump the woman had done, but it still made her jump this time too.

"I almost forgot." She produced a small brown package. "You'll need this, as well." She placed the package on top of the statue in Leslie's hand.

Then suddenly they were back at the hut, the sound of rain pouring down outside. Leslie felt a chill.

"What did you do with the other package?" Sun asked.

She pulled open her bag and dug through until she found it and handed it over.

Sun repeated the words on the cheap tourist trinket, "Nauta." And then he was gone.

Leslie glanced around the room, waiting to see if he'd reappear. He had left the door partially open when he had come in. It stood open now like a beacon. The last thing she needed was Simon to come back now. She closed up her bag and jumped up to the door. The rain was coming down in torrents.

The Jeep was facing away from the building, but she could see a form sitting in the driver's seat. It had to be Simon talking on the radio. She could run for it, but in this rain, she wouldn't make it very far.

She wanted that Jeep, but how to get it away from Simon without having to put up a physical fight?

Then the idea came to her. She stepped out into the rain. Closing the door behind her, she found a crossbar secured to the outside wall. She lowered it down, scraping the outside of the door as it dropped into place.

She backed around the building until she could see just a corner of the Jeep but enough to still see that someone was in it. She considered pulling her raincoat out of her pack, but she was already soaked.

Finally, the door to the Jeep opened. Leslie slid back so she couldn't be seen. She waited until she heard the scrape of the crossbar and quickly approached the door as Simon moved into the building. She shoved the door inward, slamming it shut, and pushing Simon hard, then slammed the crossbar down.

"Leslie!" Simon called. "What are you doing?"

She didn't answer. She ran to the Jeep, grateful to get out of the rain. There was a man's jacket on the seat next to her. She used it to wipe the rain off of her face. Underneath the jacket was a man's baseball cap. She wrapped her hair up around her head and put on the cap— it felt good to get the long, wet strands off of her neck.

Relief calmed her a little. It was an old military Jeep with a switch starter. No need to fight for keys or to walk in the jungle.

She quickly started it up, and the radio came to life. It didn't take her long to turn the Jeep around and hear that Simon's men had yet to find the rest of her group. They were still searching.

"How am I going to find them? I don't even know where I am." She tried to remember how long the trip had taken with Simon. It was challenging to guesstimate without a timepiece. She figured roughly an hour.

"Here I come, gang." She shifted into lower gear to traverse a muddy hill and checked the rearview mirror. She hoped the crossbar would keep Simon out of commission for a while.

48

RENDEZVOUS

The rain was coming down in sheets that cascaded down the Jeep's windshield. Unfortunately, the windshield wipers weren't able to keep up with the torrent. In frustration, Leslie cranked down the window so she could at least see and follow the edge of the road. She downshifted again as the Jeep climbed another muddy hill. At least with the sun rising, she didn't have to rely on the headlights, one of which kept blinking every time she hit a bump.

It felt like she had traveled for an hour. She was trying to think back to last night. Had there been anything on the road to mark their location? She didn't think so.

Up ahead, she saw something in the road. She couldn't tell what it was or whether she'd be able to drive the Jeep over it, so she came to a stop.

She climbed out and saw that was the form of a man, standing tall, with a gun pointed at the Jeep.

"My God! I almost ran over you. What the hell are you doing?" she yelled at the top of her lungs over the sound of the rain.

He stood staring at her, a gun in his hand pointed at her now. John obviously couldn't tell it was her. She removed the hat, and her hair spilled out.

He immediately pointed the gun down, walked up and hugged her. "Leslie. My God, we were worried. I was about to hijack the first vehicle I saw. I'm so glad it was yours."

Then shadows of people began to stand out against the surrounding forest, and she realized the rest of the group was emerging.

"You survived the village attack?" she asked.

"There was no attack, although we did have to hold off a single angry villager. That was after we went looking for you. We woke up this morning, and you were gone," John said

The relief at seeing everyone alive had sunk in, but Leslie wanted to keep it that way. "John, we've got to get everyone on the Jeep and get out of here, before Simon finds us."

"So it was Simon?"

Leslie nodded. "He said Sun had told him where to find us. He insinuated that the rest of you might be in great danger. I have a feeling that he means us harm."

"More than likely, that's his cocaine farm we spotted. I don't imagine he would want any of us to live to tell about it," John said as the troupe moved to the Jeep.

Leslie took a moment to help each person into the vehicle. Devan gave her a hard hug before he jumped in the back with Samantha and Frederick. AJ jumped in the back and sat on Frederick's lap.

Jessup took the front seat, squeezing Leslie's hand as she reached for the starter button.

"Glad to see you're okay, Leslie."

Even in the dim morning light, she could see he was looking pale and wane. She hoped this Jeep would get them all the way to Nauta, and soon.

Miguel stood on the outside of the Jeep on the passenger side, and John stood on the step outside the driver's side, holding on through the open window.

"Just don't move too far to the left or the right, or you'll rub one of us off of the Jeep," John said, winking at her as she started the engine back up.

She put it in gear. The wheels moved forward, and a bit of a cheer went up from the whole group.

Leslie got the Jeep moving as fast as she felt comfortable with, maneuvering through sharp turns and around and through deep ruts and mud. She crossed her fingers in the hopes that they wouldn't get stuck in the mud. Driving in these conditions was nerve-wracking, but every minute they drove, she could feel them getting so much closer to the way out. Coming around one sharp turn, she had a hard time seeing what was ahead through the rain. It appeared that the road was a wall of mud.

"Stop!" John called.

Leslie complied and jumped out of the Jeep, following John to see what it was. A tree had fallen down from a cliff next to the road.

"Damn it." There was no way out with the Jeep. They were stuck once again.

"Damn it, is right," replied John.

The group was climbing out and appraising the situation.

"Sorry, everyone," John called through the rain. "We're back on our feet. Let's just get around this tree and get on the road on the other side."

AJ was leaning on Frederick a bit, and Jessup was dragging his feet.

Leslie went back and dove into the front seat to retrieve her bag. She opened the glove compartment. Yes, a flashlight that worked. She added that to her bag. She heard John call her name but took time to check under the papers to see if there was anything else helpful. She stuffed the leather work gloves and the car charger in her bag.

She had the straps of her bag in her hands when she felt someone tugging at her, lifting her up.

"Ouch!" Her head hit the top of the Jeep on the way out.

John threw her over his shoulder and was running. She looked up and realized why. The cliff above the Jeep was giving way. It was moving down, like an avalanche of snow, but instead in a thick soup of mud speeding downwards.

A rumbling sound erupted from the cliff, and the mud was moving like a wave toward them. "Faster," she called to John. She wasn't sure he could hear her.

Leslie watched as trees cracked, pulled from the ground and breaking from the weight of the mud as it washed through the jungle. It soon covered the Jeep, and she watched in horror as it crossed the road and crashed into John's legs.

He stumbled and fell.

Leslie lay still at first. She did a mental inventory and figured that she was in one piece. She was lying a short distance away from John, on a bed of branches. She moved toward John and saw that he was trying to pull his feet out of the muck. The flow had stopped at the edge of the road.

"Damn it," he said. His feet had come out of the mud without his boots.

"Damn it, is right," Leslie replied.

One boot was entirely covered under several feet of mud, the other they fought to dig out.

John put on the one boot.

"What about the other one?" Leslie asked.

"Forget it; it'd take too long to dig it out."

They looked back at the Jeep. It had ended up on its side, and all they could see of it was a corner of the fabric top.

"Let's go," John said.

The rest of the group had come back at the sound.

"Where's Jessup?" Samantha asked, looking beyond John toward the Jeep.

They heard him call out. Leslie ran to the sound, and her heart hit the ground. He had been caught in the wave of mud. He was covered up to his chest, and a piece of a huge, cracked tree was lying across his legs.

Leslie didn't know how to react when she reached him. Jessup was laughing.

Jessup saw her and shook his head, still laughing. Then he took some deep breaths. "I knew this was going to be my last trip, and I figured I wasn't going to make it out. I just didn't think it was going to be like this."

Samantha gasped as she approached the site. "Oh, no."

John leaped down and began to dig at the mud with his hands.

Jessup shook his head again and put his hand on John's arm to stop him. "John," he said softly.

John stopped.

"It's no good. Even if you could get me out from under this mud and the godforsaken tree, I'm broken. Truth be told, I'm surprised I'm still breathing. You got to go. It's no good for you here."

Leslie had never seen a man so stricken with grief. John's eyes were welling. "We will not leave you here, alone," John said and glared at everyone as if anyone would challenge him.

Jessup responded even softer now. "I think I know how to solve that. I haven't used my power that Sun gave us yet. I tried to use it to save us, but that didn't work, so I'll use it to move on, quickly."

John shook his head.

Jessup tapped his hand. "Listen, John. You've been a great

friend to me. But it's time. I've lived a long life, much longer than I probably should have." He closed his eyes. His breath lasted for a moment more, and then Leslie knew he was gone.

Leslie moved to John and put her hand on his shoulder. She couldn't believe Jessup was dead.

Devan quietly pointed toward the direction they needed to head. One-by-one they each started to move off. John rested his hand on Leslie's for a moment, squeezed Jessup's hand, then moved to join the group on the move.

It was almost as hard walking on the muddy road as it was in the jungle. Leslie would take several solid steps and then slip in the slick muck. She finally tried walking on the furthest edge of the road, having to move around broken branches and vines, but it kept her from falling. The rest of the group eventually joined her in a line.

Samantha was the first one to fall by tripping on a branch; next it was Devan. Everyone was exhausted. Everything was taking its toll.

49

A DARK PLACE

Leslie stumbled, and a step later, Samantha fell for the third time.

Leslie tugged on John's jacket. "John, we're going to have to take a break soon."

He nodded. "We need to get off the road anyway. I'm worried Simon might send his men after us again. It would be too easy for them to find us here." To their left, the jungle terrain was steep. "Let's cross the road and go into the jungle that way." He pointed to his right.

A scream escaped from Samantha. She was pointing at a snake coming across the road. It was winding its way toward her. She backed up to the edge of the steep slope.

"Samantha, watch . . ."

Too late. Samantha slid and rolled down the hill, disappearing from view. Frederick moved, too late to try and catch her, the mud under his feet giving way. He tumbled too.

AJ, Devan, John, Miguel, and Leslie made their way down as quickly as they could and found Samantha and Frederick at the bottom of the hill. Samantha was crying. She had lost her hat, and the rain was running mud down her face in rivulets. Frederick was trying to stand, but he was a bit disoriented. Devan helped him up.

"Are you okay, Samantha?" Leslie asked.

"No!" She lifted her arms, and mud fell off of her in oozy piles. "I'm covered in mud, and this is not a spa."

A sharp intake of breath from AJ and Leslie saw what had startled her. A tarantula came up over Samantha's mud-covered hair and paused as if surveying the crowd. Its legs were so long that a millimeter more and they would have touched Samantha's eyes.

Their attention made Samantha suspicious. "What? Is there something else?"

Leslie smiled at Samantha. "Nothing to worry about."

She reached down, grasped the tarantula from the back, and tossed it behind Samantha, farther down the hill. AJ made another quick intake of breath.

"Just a branch in your hair," Leslie said.

"Oh, thanks."

Miguel helped Samantha up.

Frederick, also covered with mud, placed his hands on his back and straightened up. "What I wouldn't give for a massage and a nice soft bed."

John pointed in the direction that Samantha's fall had taken them. "Since we're here, let's keep going this way." He led the way. After a few steps, he said to Leslie over his shoulder, "I can't believe you just picked that up."

Leslie smiled and shrugged. "I guess after facing a god, nothing seems quite as dangerous."

"Did you notice the hairs on it? That was a red tarantula. One of the most aggressive of them all."

"Oh." That was good to know for the future. Maybe she should be a bit more cautious.

They were approaching thick foliage, and John pulled out his machete, then stopped. "We need to make it difficult for anyone to find us. We're going to have to get through without the use of the machete."

They moved slowly through the brush, being careful. Leslie spotted bullet ants on a nearby tree, climbing up toward the canopy. She reached into her backpack and pulled out an empty baggie. Starting at the bottom of the tree and, using the edge of the bag, she scooped up as many as ants she could reach, then zipped it shut, double-checking that it was closed. She carefully dropped it into a side pocket of her backpack.

The sound of a man's voice yelling from above caught them all by surprise. "It looks like they went this way."

Someone was just above them, near the road.

John waived at everyone to follow him. He moved through a heavily branched area, but it would give them the most cover, once they were through. Leslie glanced back. Frederick helped AJ maneuver through the complex tangle, Samantha cried silently, and Devan nodded at her grimly. Miguel determinedly pushed aside branches.

Leslie slowed down and waited for everyone to pass her. As they moved, she could see that they were still leaving a trail; boot prints were in the mud and broken branches everywhere. She grabbed a branch and rubbed at the boot prints, but it wasn't any use. She was relieved to see that up ahead was a stream and John turned to his right to follow it.

"No, let's go left," said Frederick.

"Why?" John asked.

"Because they won't expect it. They'll expect us to go right and head back toward the road."

It sounded logical. They turned to the left. Just as they were moving around a bend, Leslie looked back and thought she saw movement up in the trees.

She hoped no one had seen them. At least the rain was loud enough to cover the sound of their splashes.

Around another bend, John took them away from the stream and into the jungle again, moving to their right and up.

They went down another hill, and a clearing appeared, created by solid rock covering the ground. Up ahead it opened up into the dark mouth of a cave. Stone pillars stood on either side of the tall entrance. John moved toward it but slowed down so that the group could hear.

"What do you think? Do we take the cave?"

Frederick nodded. "If they figure out which direction we went, it won't be long before they catch up. It would be better if we take a defensive position. We can't keep moving like this; we're all exhausted." They moved into the cave. Inside, the roof sloped downward, making the cave much smaller inside than it had looked from the outside.

Frederick and John stood near the entrance, watching.

Leslie was at least happy to be out of the rain. Plus, the cool air from the cave was welcome after the heat of the jungle.

Samantha sat down and ran her hands through her mucky hair.

Leslie pulled the flashlight out of her bag. "I'm going to go and see where this cave goes." Her stomach growled.

"Have you eaten anything recently?" John asked.

"A granola bar about four hours ago."

He dug out a granola bar from his bag. "Take this. We had breakfast this morning."

Leslie took it, then thought about the fact that it was the last thing they had on them. If they got out of this, they'd have to do some foraging. And if she ever made it home, she was going to have a barbecue steak and a baked potato with all the toppings, and a tall, dark beer. Her stomach grumbled again, and she chomped into the bar.

As she walked into the back of the cave, it began to narrow. She didn't think it would go very far. She reached the back wall and stopped. There were no exits this way. She turned, and her flashlight revealed a drawing on the walls.

It looked like men in kilts fighting men in loincloths. The next picture showed the loin-clothed men carrying the heads of the kilted men. They were holding the heads high in the air.

Evenly spaced shadows drew her attention higher up on the wall. Above her head was a series of rocks extruding from the wall, like a series of floating steps. Above them was a small opening.

She was examining the way up when a gunshot echoed through the cave.

50

CAVE STANDOFF

John, Devan, and Frederick stared out from the cave's entrance into the surrounding jungle. John was pointing his gun outside. Everyone else was hanging back. As Leslie approached, Simon called from the jungle.

"John, I think we got off on the wrong foot. My men and I are here to help you. We have Jeeps on the road. We can get you and your passengers to Nauta within the hour. So please, come on out, and we can all go home."

"Oh, thank goodness!" Samantha stood up and grabbed her bag.

"Hold on," John said, turning to address everyone. "This is not a rescue. I'm certain that the cocaine farm we spotted belongs to Simon. The last thing he'd want is for us to get out and spread the word."

Frederick shook his head. "You say you're certain but are you a hundred percent? This man could be our salvation out of here."

"I agree with Frederick," Devan chimed in. "Sure, the

villagers are dangerous, but why would this guy mean us any harm?"

After glancing out at the jungle, John responded, "It makes sense because he was sabotaging my business. He knew that if we made it far enough out on the river, that there was a chance we'd spot the farm. Simon's tried a lot of things to get me to change the route, or move it altogether."

Frederick turned to AJ, who was quietly rewrapping her feet with more duct tape. "What does your gut tell you, AJ?"

"I glimpsed one of his men in the jungle from the river. If they're here to save us, then why the high-powered weapons? No," she shook her head, "they aren't here to help us, and I don't need my gut to tell me that."

"So what do we do now?" asked Samantha.

Leslie pointed to the back of the cave. "I found some steps that go up to what looks like a tunnel."

Holding his gun toward the jungle, Miguel waved his other hand toward them. "If we have another way out of here, that may be the only way we'll stay alive. I'll stay here and cover you."

"We've already lost two people, three if you include Sun. No one stays behind." Sadness passed over John's eyes, before determination set back in.

As soon as AJ had her shoes back on, everyone grabbed their things and gathered around Leslie. John nodded toward the back. "Let's go."

Leslie led the way with their only flashlight. The group followed Leslie as she scrambled over the cave floor. In the dark, AJ set her blue flame going; there were surprised murmurs from Samantha, but no one else seemed to care that AJ could produce her own light.

Leslie reached up to the bottom step of rock sticking out of the wall and tugged. It held firm. "Someone give me a boost."

Frederick offered. She stood on his hands, reached up for the step, and pulled herself up and then onto it. She reached down to help the next person up.

"Keep going, Leslie," Devan said. "We'll get up. Just go see if this thing goes anywhere."

She stepped onto the next floating stone, and it was solid, as were the next three.

Entering the tunnel, it was a tight fit. She had to crawl for a short distance and then as it aimed downwards, she had to be careful not to slide on the wet rock. Up ahead, her flashlight illuminated a larger tunnel that ascended a little.

"It keeps going," Leslie yelled, hearing the scrambling of them following her.

She waited just where the tunnel widened for everyone to pass her.

"What are you doing?" John asked, grasping her arm.

"Just leaving a little present for them, if they try to follow us."

She took the plastic bag of angry bullet ants, some of them were biting at the plastic, their large mandibles beginning to tear through. She opened the bag and dropped it carefully at the narrow part of the tunnel.

She took off running. They were moving around another corner when the sound of men's screams echoed behind them. Two gunshots rang out, and the screams stopped.

She caught up with the group. They were making their way through a zig-zag pattern of stone shelves that were floating out of the sides of the tunnel like the stone steps, only much larger. As they raced around each one, Leslie noticed that menacing faces had been carved on the fronts. Devan asked over his shoulder as they moved, "Do you think these are a trap, like in Indiana Jones? Pull on one and a big rock chases the bad guys?"

Leslie had read where the Inca had created ways to thwart their enemies, but this didn't seem like one. "I don't think so."

When they reached the end, Devan turned around and pushed on the closest stone.

"Devan! What if that sets up a trap or something?"

He shrugged. "It's not budging. Wait, there are handholds here."

He pulled on the stone. The sound of rock moving on rock told her it was shifting.

"Be careful." She kept watch down the hall of stones but didn't see any light coming yet.

The loud thunk that accompanied the stone falling from the wall reverberated through the cavern. Leslie looked around, and Devan was poised for something to happen.

Inside the shelf, behind where the stone had been embedded was a skeleton in a fetal position, with a crown of gold on its head.

"It's a burial chamber," Leslie said. "Come on, Devan." She grabbed his arm. "They can't be long behind us."

As he ran next to Leslie, he said breathlessly "Well, at least it put the stone in their way. They'll have to climb over it."

The tunnel had widened and now became a tall cavern. The group was up ahead, making their way around the elbow, turning the corner into the next, narrow tunnel.

"Leslie!" The yell came from behind her. She pushed Devan in front of her and glanced back. Simon was crawling over the stone face, from behind him, she could see several flashlights coming.

She took off, scrambling past three skeletons, one of which seemed to be holding a pith helmet in its hands and there were broken pots all around. It registered with her that it was more than likely the resting place of Spafford, but she couldn't stop to look.

"Hurry, everyone. They're coming," Leslie called as she approached the group. The way was rougher with several inches of water running along the floor and coming down the sides of the tunnel. Leslie recognized hand-carved irrigation channels running from the top of the open cavern and down the wall in front of them. "I think we might be under the river."

The tunnel turned to the left. Leslie could feel they were climbing, her legs pushing to ascend.

The tunnel began to level out, and up ahead, the stone facade of an entrance way appeared.

Leslie yelled over the sound of water, "My god, we're back in the pyramid."

51

A RISING TIDE

"What did you say?" John asked.

Leslie pointed at the doorway. "When we were exploring the pyramid with Sun, Devan and I went into the cave attached to it. We found this doorframe. It's the same one. The water from the runoff is being directed to these four stones."

"Shit," John said. "Just what we need, to have to start over."

She followed everyone through but hesitated on the other side. This setup had all the makings of a trap. If she could figure out how to spring it, it might be their last hope of survival.

The rough rock and thick mortar doorframe were built all the way up to the cave ceiling. There were fragments of the ceiling that should have fallen long ago but were being held up by the stonework.

"Leslie. What are you doing?" John called.

"I have an idea." She held the flashlight up high and moved around the rocks. If she were right, the trigger would have to be on this side of the doorframe.

There was no handle though. Nothing that might trigger something. The image of Sun grabbing a rock and pulling to open the pyramid doors inspired her to run her hands over the stones.

"Leslie," John whispered. A flash of light and sounds of running feet were getting closer.

She felt along the jagged rocks and found a loose one. "Stand back," she said and then tugged. Nothing happened; it was just a loose rock.

John grabbed her hand. "Come on." He started to pull; she pulled back and grabbed one more loose rock.

The rock offered resistance. She used the increased power of John's strength to yank hard. The sound of scraping rock made her think she might have succeeded. Before they turned the next corner, in the light of the oncoming flashlights, she could see that the four large stones at the top had come apart. They were redirecting all of the water, in a fast rush, onto the doorframe. The weak mortar in the door frame would soon give way under the pressure of the water, and with it would go the rocks piled on top.

There was a deep rumble as they ran and she could feel a vibration in the floor. Then the sound of crashing rock and water rushed through the cave. There were screams from men. Then suddenly the sound of falling rock and men's cries were silent.

They ran hard until they came upon the group again.

"I think we can slow down," Leslie said between heavy breaths. "That trap back there collapsed the ceiling. I don't think they'll be following us."

AJ slowed down, leaning on the wall of the cave while her hand continued to carry the strange blue flame that was helping everyone make their way through the cave. "If I make it through this, I'm going to stay in shape."

Samantha replied, "No problem. I'll put you in touch with my personal trainer."

AJ laughed. "I'll follow up as soon as I've had two weeks of eating all my favorite foods."

"Are we sure there aren't any more of them behind us?" asked Devan.

"I'll keep watch." John waved ahead. "All of you should see about finding a way out of the pyramid."

Leslie handed him her flashlight. "I'll stick with AJ for light; you'll need this."

John went back, his light quickly melting into the darkness.

Miguel, Samantha, Frederick, AJ, Devan, and Leslie walked down to the pyramid entrance. The outlines of the doors were easy to spot, but nothing stuck out as a way to open them.

Devan pushed on them with a grunt. He slammed his hand against the stone. "Damn, thing doesn't even budge."

"There has to be a lever, a stone, something that will open it up from the inside," Miguel said, feeling around the rocks.

The thick stone facade didn't appear to have anything obvious that she could see. But Leslie went to work knocking and checking sections of the surrounding wall.

The flashlight coming toward them scared Leslie for a moment. John flashed it onto his face so they could see it was him.

"I didn't see anyone, but we have another problem." John pointed behind him with the flashlight. Water was pooling, and they could see it was getting higher. "I think we've let the river in. Soon this place is going to be underwater."

"Oh my god!" Samantha backed up and leaned against the wall.

"Don't panic." Miguel patted her shoulder. "Let's keep looking for the way out of here."

Leslie pointed back at the cave. "I'm going back and double-check that the tunnel is impassable. If it opened up to the river, maybe there's some daylight and a way to climb out."

"I'll come with you." John waved at everyone. "We'll be right back."

What a difference, of how she had felt so inquisitive the last time they were here. Now, she felt panic. As they walked toward the collapse, murky water grew deeper, and the sound of pounding water grew louder.

"Great idea, figuring out that trick," John said from behind her.

"Yeah, great. I just might have drowned us all."

He grabbed her hand and turned her around. "Leslie, you gave us time. Maybe the time that we need to find our way out of here. Otherwise, we'd be dead by now."

Leslie grimaced and nodded. "Alright. But I'll feel better about that trick once we do find a way out of here."

The loud waterfall was coming from the top of the cave. John shined the flashlight over the rock pile. There was no way through to the other side of the cave.

"I'm just going to turn off the light for a second," John yelled over the sound of the waterfall, darkness surrounding them. "I want to see if we can see any daylight through the ceiling. It might take a moment for our eyes to adjust."

They stood there quietly for a moment.

"Do you see anything, John?"

She felt the hand and arm encircle her too late. She struck back with her elbow, but the person grasping her wouldn't relinquish the hold. She stopped when she felt the cold edge of a knife on her throat.

A flashlight came on. She gasped. John was lying on a pile of rubble, his eyes closed, blood dripping from a head wound.

Simon whispered into her ear, "I lost my flashlight back there. Thank you for being so kind as to bring me one." He moved forward, pushing her with him, through what was now a foot of water.

Did he have John's gun? She didn't see it in his hands.

He switched off the light as soon as he spotted the others, scrambling around the doors. "What are your friends doing?"

"They're looking for a way to open the doors."

"You mean, there isn't a way out?"

Leslie wasn't going to let him hurt anyone else. She didn't like the idea of what she would have to do, but she remembered where to find the ceremonial knives. "There's another exit."

"If there is another exit, why aren't they taking it?" He moved the knife back to her throat.

"I haven't had a chance to tell them. We only just realized we were in the pyramid. I found it when we were here before."

"So take me to it. Now, move."

It was slow going, moving through the deepening water and keeping in the shadows, all the while shuffling with her reduced freedom.

"Where are we going?" Simon asked

"There are stairs on the other side. We need to get to those. The exit is upstairs."

"Fine. Keep moving."

"Leslie!" The sound of John yelling her name from the adjoining cave gave her some relief. Then she could hear him retch.

"Damn it. I didn't hit him hard enough," Simon said as they started up the steps. "I was hoping he'd be out for a little longer, or even better, dead. But at least I know he'll have to face drowning."

From her peripheral vision, she could see the others rushing to help John.

"Leslie!" John called again.

As soon as the light from AJ disappeared into the distance,

Simon switched on the flashlight. He pushed Leslie quickly up the rest of the stairs.

When they came upon the door to the storage room, Simon pushed her against the wall. He put his hand around her throat while he opened the doors with the other hand.

"That's not it," she struggled to say.

"Yes, well, I'm not exactly trusting you right now." He moved his flashlight around the room, viewing the various pots.

She hoped they wouldn't end up underwater, along with her. "Leslie!" The loud cries down below told her they were worried, but she hoped they were still searching for a way to open the doors.

"Alright, where's this exit?" He swept his flashlight toward the dead end. She pointed at that end.

"I found a lever that opens a door."

He pushed her in front of him. She barely kept her footing, just managing to catch herself from falling.

"I'll make you a deal, Leslie. Find me that lever, and I'll let you live."

She croaked out a laugh while she steadied herself against the wall. "You can't let me live. I'd give away all your secrets."

"No, you don't understand." He turned her to face him. "It's my destiny to rescue you."

"Rescue me? This is a rescue?" She pointed at the knife.

"You obviously don't know what you're doing. You ran from me twice now. I have to protect you from yourself and from John. It's his fault you are on this dangerous journey. Besides, I'll tell you something I've never told anyone."

He looked side to side, as if someone might overhear him. His eyes were wide, and Leslie wondered if he was on something. A man with a knife was bad enough; a crazed man with a knife made her even more nervous.

"I consulted a wise-woman from Nauta once. She told me

that a green-eyed woman would be my salvation. But obviously, she meant for me to save you first. Now, let's get out of here, my dear."

She paused, to give him the idea that she was contemplating his words. Then she walked up to the dead end and reached into the crevice. "The lever is here somewhere. Hold on." She carefully found the gold sacrificial knife. She felt tears well in her eyes. Killing someone like this wasn't going to be easy, but more than anything, she wanted to survive, and she wanted her friends to survive.

Simon was looking at the wall with anticipation, expecting a door to open. When he saw her standing there, facing him, his eyes bulged wide. "Why isn't it opening?" he yelled. He didn't see the glint of gold in her hand but threw himself at the wall, as if to push open the nonexistent doors.

Leslie backed away, toward the stairs. After a second of his hysteria, he stopped and turned.

"Where do you think you're going, Leslie?" he yelled and came running at her, the knife poised in his right hand to strike.

She dodged to his left and folded her body out of the way of the knife, raised the warm gold in her hands in between his arms, toward his neck, and jerked her wrist.

Simon crumbled to the ground.

She dropped the knife onto his body and gingerly pulled the flashlight from his hand.

"Leslie?" John was coming up the stairs. "Thank goodness."

She held John close for a moment, but the splashing of water and Samantha's high-pitched worried voice reminded her there was still work to be done.

52

ONE WAY OUT

The group was collected at the bottom of the stairs still searching the wall. AJ was swimming up through chest-high water. If they didn't find a way out soon, they'd all drown in this cave.

"Thank goodness you're okay, Leslie," Devan said as they came down the stairs. "The water's gotten too deep. We're taking turns diving in and searching the walls around the doors."

AJ nodded as she sat on a step, still in the water. "We don't know what else to do. We've pulled on every rock down there." Her normally spiky hair was plastered to her head.

Leslie looked up the stairs. "Sun had said they used this for storage. The rocks around the exit are too low to reach if you're carrying anything with you. What about something along the stairs? Something at hand height or easy to find."

John moved down into the water and inspected the wall next to the stairs. "Everyone spread out on these stairs, and study those walls, pull on anything that might shift."

Leslie walked into the water and dove down to take a look at the area around the bottom steps. She felt along the wall, feeling the rocks. She had to go up for breath. The rest of the group was scanning the walls with their hands and whatever light they had.

Leslie took another deep breath and dove. She kept her eyes closed while she felt along the rocks. She thought she felt a divot in the wall, but had to go up for air again. The water had risen another couple of steps already; the group was running out of room.

"I think I might have found something," Leslie said. "One more dive." She climbed up another step to get some momentum, took a breath, and dove. It took more strokes to get down to the bottom steps. She reached into the divot, her fingers curving into what felt like a handle.

She tugged at it in different directions, her lungs begging her to return to the surface.

The curved hole in the rock suddenly gave way, and she flew back. She started fighting her way back up. Then she found herself being pulled down. She swam harder. Her lungs were burning.

A hand grabbed her flailing arm, and she was being pulled up, toward the light.

She gulped air. John, AJ, Samantha, Frederick, and Devan, had locked arms and pulled her up. It was taking all of their combined strength to pull opposite the power of the water rushing out the open doors of the pyramid. Leslie could still feel herself being pulled backward, but the group quickly worked together, and Leslie helped pull herself out of the water.

She lay there a moment, her head resting on the cold, wet steps. She raised it up so she could watch as the water receded.

A whirlpool formed just above the exit, swirling dirt, debris, and a shine of metal whipped around like a tornado. Then a loud sucking noise and the water poured through the exit like a rushing river. Sunlight reached in.

"Yeah!" they all cheered.

"Let's get out of this black hole," said John. He held out his hand for Leslie and helped her up.

They all walked out to the stairs and slowly made their way down to the ground.

Exhausted, Leslie collapsed onto the first open patch of grass she could find, looking up at the midday sky, and smiled.

"Now what?" Devan asked.

"Yeah, we're back where we started," Samantha said.

John was sitting next to Leslie, still holding her hand. "I say we head back to the ship. We can at least have some shelter for the night. Figure out what to do tomorrow morning. Maybe I can even scare us up a fish or two before nightfall."

Frederick smiled. "To hell with shelter. Just think of those nice, comfy beds waiting for us."

"Yeah, hot, and steamy beds. But you're right. Comfy." Samantha said.

"Plus we have safe drinking water in the ship system." responded John.

Leslie's stomach growled. She stood. "I say we get going now. Get to that clean water, and maybe get some fishing done or scavenge for what we can for dinner."

"Leslie, where do you get the energy? I'm not moving at least for an hour," AJ said.

Leslie shook her head. "If I lay down for a good amount of time, I want it to be for a nice eight-hour nap. I couldn't stay in one place right now."

"I'll stay here with AJ. We'll head back soon," Frederick said.

Samantha stood. "I'll go. I can't stand the thought of being covered in filth any longer."

As they approached the ship, John put his hand out. "Hold on. The lights are on, looks like something is going on. Everyone, wait here. I'll go take a look."

John stepped forward. Leslie had no intention of staying behind, and she was surprised to see Samantha following along with her. Miguel and Devan kept up with them, as well. John looked back, sighed, shook his head, and kept moving.

They approached from the back of the boat. The gangplank was down, but no one was in sight.

John held the gun out at the ready as he entered the boat, glancing both directions in the hall. He moved toward the center of the cruiser.

Leslie grabbed a hatchet from the pile of discarded items they had left near the door and followed John. Samantha grabbed a frying pan.

"I'm going to check the lobby," whispered Samantha.

"Do you want me to come with you?"

"No. I'll be fine." Her eyes had a steely gaze.

"Okay." Leslie followed John. He was heading to the bridge. They walked around and didn't find anyone. John was looking over the instruments.

"Levanta las manos!"

They moved their hands up as they turned. The man pointed his weapon at Leslie and John. They could see a frying pan raised in the air behind him. The sound of it hitting his head echoed through the bridge.

He collapsed, a look of surprise on his face. Samantha turned and walked away.

"Samantha, that was pretty impressive," Leslie said.

She disappeared down the ladder. "I just want to go take a

bath without someone trying to kill me. I'll be in my room if anyone needs me."

John grabbed rope from a storage drawer. "Let's tie this guy up. Then we can check the engine room. See what they've done and if there are any more of them."

Leslie picked up the frying pan, just in case they needed the extra firepower.

53

BACK FROM THE BEGINNING

Leslie opened the gangway as AJ and Frederick approached. When AJ felt the air conditioning, she leaned on Frederick and let out a long stream of words, Navajo, by the sound of them.

"Do we have power?" Frederick asked incredulously.

"Not enough," said John as he approached the group. "We've had some visitors. They were trying to use a car battery to run the ship's systems. That was like bringing a double A to run a car. However, it's enough power to run the radio, the AC, and the water heater."

"Radio? Were you able to call for help?" AJ asked expectantly.

A grin spread across John's face. "Yes. There was already a helicopter just outside Nauta- apparently, some friends of Leslie's started to worry when they didn't get any word from her. The helicopter should be here tomorrow morning."

They let out whoops of joy.

Samantha walked into the hall, wrapped in a pink robe and

her hair in a towel. "Do you mind? You're letting all the cool air out."

John hit the switch, and the door shifted closed. "On a more serious note, after everyone is done relaxing, and we sit down for dinner, assuming I can catch us some fish, we need to discuss our stories."

"Stories?" asked Devan.

John nodded. "What we're going to tell the world about what happened here."

"What about the truth?" Samantha said, walking closer so that the light from the hallway glared off of her green slathered face.

John just shook his head and walked away.

AJ shook her head too. "Do you think anyone is going to believe that a god smote Cesario and left us stranded?"

Samantha turned toward her cabin as Frederick led AJ that direction. "I just think it would just be so much more amazing if people would believe us."

Leslie nodded and headed toward the deck to try her hand at fishing.

54

LESLIE

Leslie set the magazine down on the table. She had looked at the cover a few times. John, Samantha, AJ, Frederick, Devan, and her, holding glasses of rum and Coke, the best thing the bartender could put together that day, besides a banana daiquiri. Miguel had not wanted to be included in the photo. 'Intrepid explorers raise a toast to Jessup Bostwick, their story on page 12.' It felt good to see her name in a byline again.

She had included a note, found in Jessup's cabin, in her article. "Dear friends, family, fans, and the world at large. I found my heart in Peru, and I have no interest in returning to the States. I will stay here, and as I have been invited to join the tribes that wander the Amazon basin, I will live simply and happily. Jessup Bostwick."

He must have had some idea that he wasn't going to make it out alive. But the note would certainly keep the legend of Jessup alive for a long time to come.

This left the Peruvian government none too happy, the

thought of an American roaming Peru without a visa—but they had no interest in chasing after him.

John walked into the hotel lobby. "It's here," he said and pointed outside.

The bus rambled up the dirt road, kicking up a little dust in its wake. Of course, it hadn't rained for a few days. The bus halted outside, and Leslie ran out to greet AJ.

Samantha yelled out, "AJ, get back on the bus. Give a minute for the dust to settle, we need to get a good shot." She moved back to the cameraman.

AJ and Leslie exchanged smiles; AJ climbed back on as instructed.

Samantha walked up to Leslie. "So, here's the plan. You shake hands with AJ when she disembarks and thank her for accompanying the new bus from the manufacturer. Then you'll present the bus to the school bus driver and the children."

Leslie was working with Samantha and a film crew to show the poverty level and to raise money for several buses for the children. Maybe later, a school of their own.

She planned to stay until tomorrow to see the bus off on its first trip, a load of children going to a middle school about an hour away. Then she would head back to the States for a while. She'd had enough of Peru and its insufferable heat. One crazy hike through the Amazon had been enough for her.

An iridescent butterfly landed on her arm.

55

SUN

Sun appeared in the middle of Nauta. He would wait here until he found the old woman. He would ask her about the statue, and then he would die in peace. More than likely, she was a priestess of the old ways.

He suddenly felt a pull at his powers. But all of the humans had used their one opportunity. He had even helped Jessup cross over quickly. This was different. It was familiar.

The old woman was walking up the street toward him. As she approached, her wrinkles and the cataracts in her eyes faded. Her crown of bugs revitalized to a halo of silver over her now flowing black hair. Her clothes turned into loose purple silk and rippled in the breeze.

He said her name out loud, "Quilla." It felt strange to be able to say it after so long. "You're alive! So many hundreds of years without you. I thought you were lost to me."

"The Spanish bastards might have had me abducted, but they weren't able to hold me. I escaped within a year."

"But then, why haven't you come to me?"

She shook her head, her eyes filled with the love he had for her. "I tried. I never had the same power you do to move through the ether. And the few times I tried to reach you, to get to our home in the jungle, the wraths pushed me back."

"The wraths?" Sun was surprised. That his creation would attack her was abominable.

"They can sense what power I have. They would attack and drain me until I turned away from their territory. I never had a chance to reach you. The only thing I could think of was to use the humans. I tried with the humans who went to the pyramid many years ago, but it didn't work. I sensed that these other humans would also cross your path."

Sun held her, his eyes welling with the tears he could never have cried as a full god.

Her voice was soft when she said, "You've been with another woman." She said it without accusation, but he felt the deep knife of regret.

"But I have only ever loved you."

She smiled at that. "This I know."

He looked into her eternal brown eyes. "I'm ready to leave this existence. Are you?"

She nodded. "I've been waiting a long time. I'm ready."

"One last look back." He took them both to the pyramid and conjured up the image of history. The natives were bustling, bringing honors to their gods. The land was cleared for miles, the buildings bright with care and use.

He made sure images of women and children, walking into the fields, were seen by Quilla. He set in motion the last few tasks he had to complete. Then he took her hand, and they disappeared. The images of people and the open land slowly dissipated.

EPILOGUE

Deep in the jungle, trees and vines, hearing the call of a god, began growing faster. Thorny bamboo sprouted in a mile-wide circle. Birds and animals ran from the site, frightened by the unnatural creaking, groaning, and slithering.

After two hours, the birds and animals began to return to the area. Everything was as dark, impenetrable, and secretive as the rest of the jungle.

Find out how AJ Bluehorse gets to know her new powers, inherited from an Inca god in *Gamble of the Gods*.

GAMBLE
OF THE
GODS
Idol
Makers
Book 2
SONJA
DEWING

GET A FREE BEST-SELLER, AND EXCLUSIVE IDOL MAKER MATERIAL

I love writing, but I also love connecting with my readers. I often ask for input on future story ideas and some of my fans have even named my new books. I occasionally send newsletters with details on new releases, special offers and other bits of news relating to my Idol Maker series and other new tidbits.

And, if you sign up to the mailing list you'll get two free short stories, including a free copy of the best-selling and award-winning short story, *The Glass Mountain*. Find out how Leslie Kicklighter got her start when she goes on a harrowing climb in Alaska.

You can get the short stories for free by signing up at http://eepurl.com/cAzV5v

ENJOY THIS BOOK? YOU CAN MAKE A BIG DIFFERENCE

Reviews are the most powerful tool in my arsenal when it comes to getting attention for my books. The more reviews, the better my books do on Amazon's algorithm. I wish I had the financial muscle of a New York publisher, but I can't take out full page ads in the newspaper or put posters on the subway (but wouldn't that be cool if I could!)

But I do have something much more powerful and it's something that those publishers would kill to get their hands on - A committed and loyal bunch of readers.

If you've enjoyed this book I would be very grateful if you could spend five minutes leaving an honest review (it can be as short as you like) on the book's Amazon page.

Thank you very much.

ABOUT THE AUTHOR

Sonja Dewing is an award-winning and best selling author of the fantasy novels in the Idol Maker series. You can find her online at www.sonjadewing.com and you can connect with her on Facebook at https://www.facebook.com/AuthorSonja Dewing or email her if you fancy a conversation at sonjadewing@gmail.com

ALSO BY SONJA DEWING

Time to do some more reading! Find all of these on Amazon or by going to my website. www.sonjadewing.com

In the Idol Maker Series - Find them on your favorite platform:

Book 2 - *Gamble of the Gods*

AJ Bluehorse, a software developer who's inherited powers from an Inca god, never counted on having to solve a murder on the Navajo reservation. If she doesn't find the malevolent skinwalker soon, she might be the next victim and the old gods will have to find someone else to save the world.

Book 3 - *Castoffs of the Gods*

John Holbrook has gone back into the Amazon and promptly disappeared with no word as to his whereabouts. Leslie Kicklighter and AJ Bluehorse team up to return to the Amazon and find their friend. They think their biggest problem is the jungle, but they'll find that a dark power is building its evil plan, and they may be the only thing standing between it and the end of the world.

Book 4 - *Relics of the Gods*

In the final book in the series, AJ Bluehorse and Leslie Kicklighter are facing down Demi-god Alex bent on world domination. They'll have to find the second staff of Viracocha before Alex does or he'll warp the world into his own vision.